FIDESSA

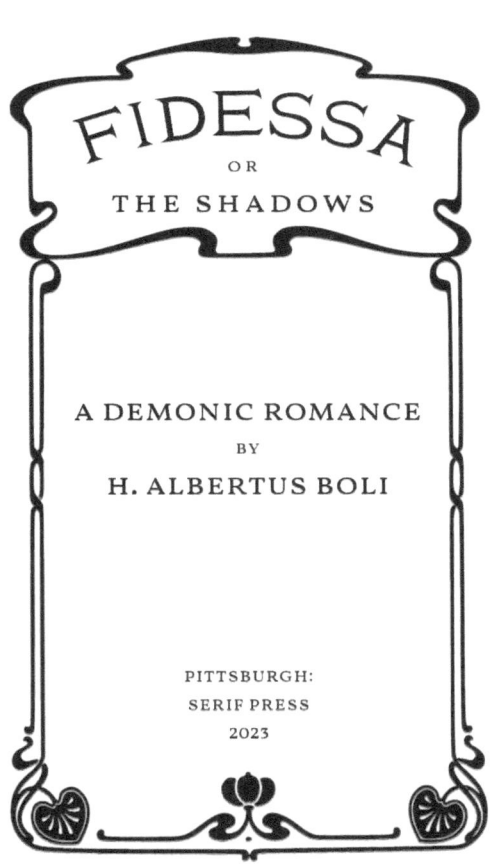

FIDESSA

OR

THE SHADOWS

A DEMONIC ROMANCE

BY

H. ALBERTUS BOLI

PITTSBURGH:

SERIF PRESS

2023

The frame on the cover and title page was designed
by Bauer & Co. of Stuttgart in 1900.

FOR TERESA
WHO DISPELS THE SHADOWS

BOOK I.

CHAPTER 1. HOPE.

THE first thing Adam noticed when he came in was that they were out of the Guatemalan. He didn't know how the morning could begin without the Guatemalan. There was something from Honduras, so he swallowed his pride and settled for that. But it wouldn't be the same at all. It was a bad start to what would doubtless prove to be a bad day. Could the sun rise on Honduran-coffee power? No, it could not: here it was the middle of May, with flowers blooming everywhere, and the morning sky was grey and flat and drizzly. Nothing could go right on a grey day with no Guatemalan. Well—almost nothing.

One thing was going right. His usual seat was ready for him. No matter how early he got there, no matter how crowded the Wild Beans was, the one friend he could rely on was always there already, sitting at a table for two with one empty chair. Did she stand outside the door and wait till the place opened in the morning? She was one of the unaccountable mysteries of the universe.

There she was, sitting against the wall, with her usual tea and coffee cake. Could it be proper to eat coffee cake with tea? That would give him his opening this morning, anyway.

"I'll never understand how you can drink tea with coffee cake," he said as he set down his own generous cup of the wrong coffee and then sat down behind it. "The very name of the thing cries out for coffee. It's tempting fate, that's what it is."

"I've found that fate can stand a lot of temptation," she responded, and she defiantly picked up the tea in her delicate hand and took a very deliberate sip.

"We're all doomed anyway. They're out of Guatemalan." He took a sip from his own cup and twisted his face into an expression of moderate disgust.

"You're too proud to drink a different kind of coffee?"

"I'm not proud. I'm exceptionally humble. You'd have to go a long way to find someone as humble as I am." He looked down into the coffee. "It's just a matter of having standards."

"Your standards..." She appeared to decide that it wasn't worth finishing that thought. She didn't need to finish it anyway: Adam had heard it before and knew how it ended. Instead of finishing it, she set down her tea and leaned forward on her elbows. "So tell me about last night. I'm guessing it didn't go well."

He leaned back in his chair. "What makes you say that?" It was true, but was it fair that she should guess before he told her?

"You came in grumpy and sarcastic. That's what happens when it goes badly. If it goes well, you come in with "Good morning, Miss Masaryk," and tell me what a beautiful day it is, even if it's beastly hideous weather. So—" (she leaned forward just a little more) "—all I really need is the details."

Adam picked up his coffee, took a sip, and made another disgusted face. This was actually the opening he had been looking for. "It was horrible, Hope. Worse than this coffee."

"But 'horrible' isn't a detail."

True. How to pick a detail that would convey the raw horror of it? He looked down into his coffee, and then briefly at Hope's coffee cake. Maybe he should have ordered some coffee cake to drown out the taste of the coffee. He looked up at Hope and at last decided on the illustrative detail: "Bra straps."

"What?"

"You know how I hate visible bra straps. She was wearing this sleeveless dress, and it was showing off her bra straps. Pink ones. Under a blue dress."

"You know, Adam, some men might think ahead to the point where the bra comes off and you don't have to look at the straps."

That was almost embarrassingly direct of her. She could do that sometimes, and he was never quite sure what reaction she was trying to provoke. "They were pink," he reiterated a bit helplessly.

"There's a human female under them. Are you telling me your date was 'horrible' because you could see her bra straps?"

"It wasn't the bra straps per se..."

"Oh, here we go with the 'per se.' Now you're going to quote Aristotle's treatise on lingerie and Hegel's Phenomenology of Bra Straps."

"It was what they represent."

"They represent a bra. Some women wear them. Even I do once in a while, on special occasions."

"But the machinery is supposed to be invisible." He picked up his coffee again, but he was still talking. "When a man admires a woman's—um, figure—he doesn't want to think about the block and tackle that makes the figure look like that."

"Block and tackle." She leaned back in her chair. "You're a real poet, Adam."

All right, so maybe his choice of words was not entirely appropriate. He abandoned his metaphor and approached the question from a different direction. "Showing off bra straps—it's a teenage-girl thing, right? It says, 'Look, I've hit puberty.' You should be over it by the time you're twenty-six, shouldn't you?"

"Were the bra straps really what made it a horrible evening? If you want sympathy, you're going to have to come up with something worse than that."

He took another sip of coffee, thinking hard enough that he forgot to make a face. "She says 'like.' "

" 'Like'?"

"Every third word out of her mouth is, like, 'like.' "

"And you, like, hate that."

"Don't make fun of me."

"Somebody's got to do it. I don't think you've been getting nearly enough of it."

He set down his coffee emphatically. "I don't think I could stand another evening of listening to it. I have—I have standards."

"The trouble with your standards is that they eliminate all the real women on the planet and leave only the ideal in your head." She smiled one of those sad little smiles that suggested pity with a tinge of moral superiority. "But you can't have a real relationship with an imaginary woman."

"All my best relationships have been with imaginary women." He sighed and picked up the coffee again, took another sip, and didn't bother to make the disgusted face. The point had been made already; no use belaboring it. "Anyway, it's not true that I eliminate all the real women. You don't say 'like' all the time, and I can't see your bra straps. I don't even know if you're wearing a bra."

"And you don't care." She leaned forward a little again. "Really, Adam, if I meet all your standards, why aren't you asking me out?"

This was a test, he thought to himself, and it threw him into a bit of a panic. Every once in a while she would hit him with a test like that, and he never knew exactly what to make of it. He was sure that bad things would happen if he suggested that he was attracted to her, but what response was she looking for? "Why ruin it? We already have a perfect relationship."

"Define 'perfect.'"

"I get everything I want out of it. What other definition is there?"

Hope leaned back and crossed her arms. "I can think of at least one other definition."

Something told him he had insulted her, but he didn't know exactly how to undo the damage. Turning it back on himself might work. "Anyway, you couldn't stand me. I wouldn't meet your standards."

The arms uncrossed themselves. "What do you think my standards are?"

"You want a man…" He looked at the egg-and-dart chair rail behind her, but the test answers weren't printed there. "You want a man who doesn't talk about 'standards' all the time."

"Well, that's more self-awareness than I gave you credit for." She leaned forward a little and spoke in a slightly lower tone. "But you'd be surprised what I can put up with."

"Even I can't put up with me sometimes." Was he passing the test or failing?

She smiled. "Well, that doesn't surprise me. Finish your coffee. We need to get to work."

Did the smile mean he'd passed the test? That was the other thing about her little tests: Adam was never quite sure what his score was at the end.

Hope picked up a big chunk of coffee cake, but held it up and gestured with it instead of biting into it. "Some day, Adam, a woman will come along who will yank you out of yourself and turn your life upside-down and inside out. And the question is: What will you do when it happens? Will you fight her and pull back into yourself? Or will you let her drag you where she wants to drag you? And will you even know which one you ought to do?"

He smiled. "I'm sure you'll give me good advice."

"Don't count on it." She shoved the whole chunk of coffee cake into her mouth at once.

CHAPTER 2. THE WOMAN IN RED.

THE pride of Brackenridge Avenue is its iron arch, an eruption of wrought-iron filigree that spans the street and sidewalks between the Metz Building on the south side of the street and the Schiel Building on the north side of the street. Wrought-iron letters spell out "Brackenridge Avenue Historic District," and the street well deserves its designation. It is certainly the best-preserved streetscape of its kind in the city, and very probably in the country. The architecture is German-American Victorian—heavy brick storefronts with occasional Romanesque or Baroque ornaments. These days the buildings are filled—often from the basement to the third floor—with trendy little one-off shops, bars, restaurants, and small nightclubs. But at twilight, when the details become a little indistinct, it is easy to imagine that the whole street inhabits an alternate world where progress stopped in 1890. Adam always felt as though it was passing through the arch that did it: the arch was the portal to that alternate world, and the rules of our universe ceased to apply the moment one passed through the iron gateway.

In spite of the drizzly morning and the wrong coffee, the day turned out to be sunny and warm, and the evening was perfectly delightful. Adam had dinner—alone—at a little Thai restaurant that spilled out onto the sidewalk not far from his office. By the time he had finished, the sun was setting, with just the right number of clouds to turn the sky into a work of art, a Turneresque composition in peach and gold. It was a perfect evening for a stroll. Adam went inside to pay at the register, leaving a generous tip to help defray the cost of the sunset; then he stepped out into the air again and headed for nowhere in particular.

The cafe was on a side street off Brackenridge—a side street whose modest shops faded into dignified rowhouses as it distanced itself from the main business district. Adam walked further into the res- idential section, leaving the noises of the main street behind him. The sidewalk was herringbone brick with occasional lumps where a root had buck- led it. Birds twittered spring songs, and the rich, bitter scent of boxwood hung low over the neigh- borhood. If he had money, Adam told himself, he would live in a neighborhood that was old enough and wealthy enough to smell like boxwood.

He passed a corner house where a violinist was playing Bach behind an open window while a small dog barked incessantly in the same room. Adam wondered whether the violinist was so caught up in the beauty of Bach that he didn't even hear the dog, or whether he was defiantly continuing his practice in spite of the dog, or whether Bach was a purely mechanical exercise to the violinist, the sounds being merely proof of skill. And what did the dog think? Did the dog say, "I could get some sublimely beautiful yapping done if it weren't for all that squawking"?

The colors in the sky were richer and darker now, deep reds and roses and violets. Adam turned the corner at the violin house into a side street—a short block flanked by the sides of two houses on each side and crossed by a narrow service alley between them. The violin still played, and the dog still barked, and as Adam left them behind and approached the next corner, the dog and the violin merged into the bird songs and the boxwood and the herringbone sidewalk and the pink light from the last of the sunset, and the dog was part of the beauty now, a beauty that would have been diminished and incomplete without the dog. And as he turned the corner, the dog and violin faded, and other noises took their place—dishes clattering in somebody's kitchen, a bicycle whizzing by on narrow tires whose rubbery swish was quieter than silence, a pair of shears snipping at a hedge, a mantel clock in someone's front parlor chiming the half-hour. Take one of them away, and the scene would be changed. Perhaps the beauty of it would simply pop like a soap bubble.

At last, under a purple sky that bathed the landscape in a soft unearthly light, Adam turned the corner at Brackenridge Avenue and walked under the iron arch. The street was lively, illuminated now equally by the purple of the sky and the artificial light of streetlights and shop windows; pedestrians were transformed altogether as they passed from one light to another; and suddenly the world was different because *she* stepped into it.

The effect was unaccountable. A woman in a bright red dress stepped out of a little store that sold handmade Peruvian clothing and doodads. Her hair was straight and black and fell to her waist; as she stopped briefly under a streetlight to rearrange her bags, Adam caught a glimpse of a pretty face with East Asian features that burned themselves into his memory at once. Then she turned and walked away from him, and he followed.

He had the excuse that he had been going in that direction anyway, but something had happened to him—something at least as much physical as mental. At his first glimpse of her, before his mind had a chance to tell him what he was seeing, a feeling came over him that was something like the bottom dropping out of his stomach. Actually, it felt more like the bottom dropping out of his soul, and he simply hadn't realized before that the soul was located about where he thought his stomach should be. Nothing could explain it. The woman was pretty, but he knew prettier women. He could argue that his friend Hope was prettier, given certain definitions of "pretty." But no one had ever given him that strange feeling, composed of equal parts heavenly choir and impending doom.

Now she crossed the street and walked into a narrow side street, and he would have to make a definite decision to follow her. He made it. He was just wandering aimlessly, after all, and he might as well stroll in that direction as in any other. He quickened his pace, and then thought maybe he ought to slow down, because after all one might argue that quickening his pace made the difference between aimless strolling and stalking. The sidewalk was too thick with pedestrians for him to quicken his pace much anyway. And it made no difference. When he got to that little side street, she was gone. She might have turned into the parking garage on the right, or she might have hopped in a car parked on the street and driven away, or she might have been completely imaginary. She might have vanished as soon as she left the purple twilight world of Brackenridge Avenue.

❧

"Nothing like it ever happened to me," Adam told Hope the next morning.

"You mean you've never been a stalker before?"

"It wasn't stalking." Adam said it cheerfully, not argumentatively: the Guatemalan had returned, and all was right with the world. "I don't know what it was. It was— It was—"

"We've all done things like that, Adam. I remember once, when I first started working, I saw this man across the room, and I felt fluttery. —Don't laugh. I didn't laugh at you. Something told me I had to get to know this guy. I couldn't explain it. It hit me like a shovel."

"Exactly!" He straightened up and pointed a finger at her as if she were the source of all enlightenment. "It's like something physical, some sort of... So what happened? With that man, I mean."

"Oh, it turned out it was only you."

"But this girl, Hope—I know I'll never see her again, but for a moment there it felt like being in love." He was looking down into his coffee now, because it was a little embarrassing to talk about it with her. With anybody, but especially with her. It was embarrassing to admit that his brain had made so much of it. He was displaying a weakness, and the Cro-Magnon in him hated to display a weakness in front of an attractive young woman, even Hope.

"Love at first sight," she said. "Don't worry—it's just hormones. They go away. Like hives."

"Is that true?"

"No." She picked up her tea, and there was silence for a little while. A conversation two tables over was getting louder: "So I said to her, I said, 'Listen, I'm sorry you feel that way, but you know what? I don't care.' She had her chance, you know what I mean? And now she's all like, 'Oh, you should have known.' Well, I didn't know, and you know why? 'Cause you didn't tell me. So anyway, she gets all mad, but I'm not changing my mind now..."

Adam leaned forward and asked in a low voice, "Do you suppose we sound like that?"

"No. We sound much more intellectual. We have the Oscar Wilde table over here."

"That's good to know. Except now I have to come up with an epigram."

In the pause that was not filled with an epigram, the other conversation—which was really more of a monologue—was still seeping over. "Because I need to think about me, right? So you know what I said to her? I said, 'If you want to leave, you can walk right out that door.' And what do you think she said? She said, 'Oh, you'd like that, wouldn't you?' Trying to put it all on me, see? But I wasn't going to fall for it. The problem is, is that she wasn't addressing the issue. So I said, 'It's not about what I like. You've been sitting there telling me "I don't like this" and "I don't like that." So why do you even want to keep up this relationship? I'll tell you why. It's because you...' "

Adam spoke quietly again: "How many conversations in the world right now are simply rehashing old conversations?"

"Most of them, probably," Hope answered.

"It's all some people talk about: 'I said'—'she said'—then 'I said' again. It's like they're compiling a book: *One Thousand One Times When I Was Right and They Were Wrong*."

"And what's the book you're compiling? *How I Got to Be Better Than You*?"

"You're making fun of me again."

"Just doing my job."

Adam sat back in his chair, holding his cup of Guatemalan in front of him but not drinking. "I wonder how often she comes to Brackenridge Avenue."

CHAPTER 3. THE WOMAN IN BLUE.

"GOOD morning, Miss Masaryk," Adam said with a bright smile as he set down his usual cup of coffee and installed himself in his usual place behind it. "Did you see the sunrise this morning? Breathtaking. Four stars. Could hardly be improved. Nature can be proud of herself today."

"Red in the morning, sailor's warning," Hope replied.

"I'm not going sailing. Anyway, who's responsible for these old saws? It's about time they were updated for the modern world. Like 'Red in the morning, golfer's warning,' or something like that. There should be a committee, and a referendum, and ice cream. There should always be ice cream."

"So it went well last night," she observed with a smile that was not exactly forced, but not exactly natural either. "Give me the details. And be graphic, not suggestive. Don't leave anything for my imagination to fill in."

"What, the date? Oh, it was horrible. Worse than the last one. On the list of top ten worst dates of all time. Well, twenty, anyway." He took a sip of coffee and considered raising the number to thirty, but she was already talking.

"But you came in here all full of 'Good morning, Miss Masaryk' and 'It's a beautiful day.' How can you do that after a horrible date? Just when I think I have you figured out."

"I don't know. It must have been the sunrise." Actually, now that he thought about it, he was pretty sure he did know, but he wasn't at all sure whether he was ready to tell her. He set down the coffee to give himself more freedom for gestures. "Anyway, I'm not sure I want you to have me figured out. I think I'd rather be a dark and intriguing mystery."

"I'm sure you'll be mysterious enough when you start to tell me what went wrong with your date."

Adam sighed dramatically. He hoped it was dramatic, anyway, "She talked philosophy."

"Philosophy?"

"The whole evening,"

Hope set down her tea with a clank and leaned back with a very dubious expression. "Adam, you talk philosophy all the time. Nothing will stop you once you get started. I say 'Look at the flowers!' or 'Strange weather we're having,' but you always bring it back to Hume or Descartes. You can't help it. It's a reflex. The doctor hits your knee with a hammer, and you say 'Thomas Aquinas.' Now you tell me your date was horrible because she talked philosophy. For you, that's like saying your date was horrible because she turned out to be heterosexual."

"I never got to the point of finding out whether she was heterosexual, because she talked philosophy the whole time."

Hope's head tilted a little to the right. "You don't actually ask your dates 'Are you heterosexual?,' do you? Because that might be one of your problems."

"No, of course not. Not usually. Unless I—"

"Don't give me the 'unless,' " she interrupted with a hand raised to block the rest of the sentence, "because I'm pretty sure it's not going to make me think any better of you. Just explain how her talking philosophy, which I know you like better than sex, made your date horrible."

Adam understood that she had a point, but he was sure she would see it his way once she knew the facts. "She's a deconstructionist."

"A deconstructionist?"

"Stuffed full of Derrida."

"Oh! I see." She smiled and picked up the tea again. "The problem wasn't that she talked philosophy. The problem was that she *disagreed* with you." She took what Adam thought was an unjustifiably triumphant sip of tea.

"Now, that's not fair," he told her.

"You mean it's not true?"

"No, it's not fair because it *is* true. How am I supposed to defend myself against the truth? Truth gives you an unfair advantage."

"And I'm not afraid to use it. So what have we learned here? That your ideal woman—no, your barely acceptable woman—has to agree with you or keep her mouth shut?"

"Of course not," he insisted—although part of his mind said that a woman who always agreed with him might be just the sort of woman he was looking for. "Look, it's not like she was a Platonist and I was an Aristotelian. We're talking about deconstructionism here. How can you have any conversation at all with someone who believes that all language is ultimately meaningless? It's like planning a gourmet dinner with a breatharian. You can deconstruct deconstructionism in five minutes or less, and then what's left to talk about? You're just spinning your wheels in the mud."

"And that's what you told Derrida-woman?"

"Of course not. What do you take me for?"

"I—"

"Don't answer that. No, I tried to debate for a while, but this woman was a conversational steamroller. She was like a mile-long freight train—once she got up to speed, she just kept rolling down the same track, and woe betide anything that got in her way."

" 'Woe betide,' " Hope repeated. "Do you commonly think of your dates in terms of heavy machinery? That might be another one of your problems."

"The worst part was that there were no awkward silences. Give this woman a silence, any length, and she can fill it. At least if there had been awkward silences, she might have got the idea that the date was going badly. Instead she probably thinks I was fascinated by her, because I just shut up and let her do all the talking."

Hope allowed a little silence to pass, probably because she was making some sort of point with it (Adam thought it quite within her power to use silence as irony). Then she asked, "So how did you leave things with her?"

"She said she'd call. She said a lot of other things in the same sentence, so there was no way to break in and say "Don't bother." Now I have to figure out what to do when she calls."

Hope set down the tea gently and assumed a very serious and thoughtful expression. "Here's what you do. You move to New Zealand and contract a very rare contagious disease. That way you have at least two good reasons why it's not convenient for her to see you again."

Adam thought of pointing out that she was making fun of him again, but it was pretty clear that she already knew she was making fun of him. Instead, he decided it was time to bring up the subject he had been a little afraid to bring up with her:

"I saw *her* again last night."

"You mean Derrida-woman?"

"No." She had missed it entirely, that special emphasis he gave to the pronoun. "The lady in red."

"The Asian chick you were stalking?"

"I wa—" No, he wouldn't let her bait him like that. "She was in blue this time. Blue jeans, blue or dark grey T-shirt. I'm positive it was the same woman."

"Positive? You only say 'positive' when you're not really sure."

"Ninety per cent positive. Eighty-five. In a way, she looked totally different."

"What, now she was blonde and Swedish?"

"No, still Asian. She was dressed differently, and that made a difference—jeans instead of a red dress. And there was something about the way she carried herself. But that could be the difference between jeans and a skirt."

"So you think it was the same woman because... she was Asian? There are a lot of Asians around here. Some of my best friends—"

"No, not that." It might be difficult to explain this

next part, but he would try. If he could explain it to Hope, maybe he could explain it to himself as well. "You know how I said it felt the first time I saw her? Like the bottom had dropped out of my stomach? It happened again—the same feeling the moment I saw her, before I even had a chance to realize what I'd seen. The very same." He looked down into his coffee. "It had to be the same woman."

Hope watched him sip a bit of coffee, half a smile half-illuminating her face. "So you're saying you recognized her by her effect on your digestion? Be sure to tell her that if you do get to speak to her. Women love that sort of romantic talk."

Adam looked a bit sheepish—he knew because he could feel the sheepishness stealing across his face. "You think I'm ridiculous."

Now there was a whole smile. "It's one of the things I like about you. It's endearing."

"Endearing," Adam repeated. "Isn't that the word for people who are too helpless to be annoying?"

"If you like. But tell me more. Did you stalk her again this time?"

"I wasn't stalking her!" She had succeeded in baiting him. "I just... walked in the same direction for a while."

She didn't say anything, but she was smiling, which was very provoking.

"Okay." Adam began, since he had decided to tell

the whole story. "I had just walked under the arch, right? And suddenly there was the feeling. The bottom-dropping-out-of-the-stomach feeling. And I saw her—the back of her, anyway. So I—"

"Hold on. You recognized her from the back?"

"The long hair, and of course the shape of her..." Hope was nodding. "Do I really have to sit here and prove to you what a pig I am?"

"No proof necessary. You gawk at mine sometimes when you think I don't notice. —Don't worry. I take it as a compliment."

That was so disconcerting that Adam momentarily lost his place in the story. "So—um—I had—okay, so I was sure it must be her—ninety per cent sure, at least—and I kept walking and kept my eye on her, and I did that for something like four blocks. No, it wasn't stalking, so don't give me that smirk. I was walking that way anyway, you know. And then she stopped in a doorway—halfway between the pretzel shop and that expensive hardware store—and opened the door with a key and went in."

Hope allowed a moment to pass before she asked the next question. And Adam knew what the next question was going to be, and he knew that she was waiting to see whether he would volunteer the information; but he did not.

Finally she gave up waiting and asked it: "So what

did you find out about the door?"

"Nothing. It doesn't have any sign on it. Just a number. Could be offices, could be upstairs apartments."

"In other words," Hope said rather gravely, because it apparently stuck her as a matter of some gravity, "you may have found out where she lives."

"That's a possibility," he agreed.

"And what are you going to do with that information?"

"Nothing," he answered immediately. "I'm not a stalker."

Hope's fixed glare told him she didn't think that was the whole truth. She was right, of course; and he knew that, one way or another, she wouldn't let him get by without admitting it.

"Well," he said at last, "I might take a lot more walks on Brackenridge Avenue."

CHAPTER 4. THE WOMAN IN BLACK.

THE day seemed intent on proving the veracity of the old saws. After that five-star sunrise, lines of thunderstorms began rumbling in—just spring showers at first, but graduating to "severe thunderstorms" by noon, with two or three apocalyptic ones in the late afternoon. But the storms had passed by the time Adam was ready to leave the office, and he stepped into a world scrubbed clean and created anew—which is the purpose of an apocalypse, after all. The air had a bracing chill, and the scent of wet pavement hovered over the whole neighborhood, mixing with the perfume of slightly battered lilacs. Everything glittered as the sun made one more late appearance, reflected and refracted in a countless multitude of drops and droplets. There was no rainbow, however. The rain had stopped well before the last of the clouds passed by. Adam felt a bit cheated: there ought to be a rainbow after a late-afternoon thunderstorm. It's supposed to be part of the package. Didn't old Noah get a written guarantee of rainbows? Someone should complain to the Manufacturer.

It was certainly not an evening for hurrying home to sit in front of the computer: it was an evening for a cheap dinner for one, and then another long aimless stroll—perhaps a stroll that would include a few blocks of Brackenridge Avenue, especially in the historic district.

He chose Cambodian this time, and ended up eating something he had picked from the menu almost at random, a sort of egg-crepe thing piled high with vegetables. He liked it and resolved to remember the name of it, and then as soon as he stepped out on the sidewalk again he realized that the name he had remembered was "ban shee," which he was almost positive was wrong. But at least he remembered that it was number 36. Or 38. Somewhere in the thirties, or possibly twenties.

At any rate, here he was on Brackenridge Avenue, and another tremendous sunset was in progress. Colors were crashing across the sky with such violence he could almost hear them. He was about to walk under the arch when he suddenly conceived the superstitious idea that it was the wrong time to enter that alternate world. He should enter it when the colors had faded from pink and orange to violet and indigo, when the effect, the unearthly magic of the place, would be at its most pronounced, and perhaps everything would work together to produce the vision he longed to see again.

So he turned down Frick Street instead, passing the half-block of side-street shops and wandering once again into the boxwood-and-lilac-scented residential section—a quiet sanctuary from the bustle of the main street, where an almost material sense of peace hung over the neighborhood, and he could be alone with his thoughts. So Adam was thinking when his phone rang.

It was Hope. He answered at once, because Hope never called him unless she had something exceptionally interesting to say.

"Are you stalking her right now?" was the first thing Hope said when he answered.

"I wasn't—" he began; then he changed his mind and just answered, "No."

"Good. I have someone I want you to meet."

"Meet?"

"A potential date, personally curated for you by me. If you won't take me, at least you deserve second-best."

This might be one of her tests. How should he respond? "Usually I pick my own dates," he said, carefully avoiding her reference to herself.

"And usually you whine to me the next morning that her feet were the wrong shape or you could smell her conditioner. Listen, this one's perfect for you. She doesn't talk philosophy all the time, but she's interested in learning more. I've never seen her bra straps. She has cute feet, and she hardly smells like anything, and her Facebook profile picture isn't a blurry selfie, and she doesn't say 'like' all the time, and I made sure to ask if she was heterosexual, and she said she was well qualified. Is there anything else you hate that I missed?"

Adam thought for a moment. "Any tattoos?"

"Not on the places that show. As for the rest, you can have fun finding out."

"Well…" Adam said.

"Don't give me 'well.' She really is perfect. She's smart, she's cute, she's never smoked, she doesn't have any of the things you hate, and she's willing to take a chance on you because I recommended you. Unless you've got some other prospect I don't know about, I suggest you call her. No, I demand you call her. I have a right to demand after all the work I've done for you. Will you do that for me? Will you please do that for me?"

For form's sake, Adam gave her a sigh of resignation. "What's her name?"

"Rose. Rose Middleswarth. See? Even the name! You love those old English names." (Adam was about to make a disparaging remark about flower names, but he realized it would not lead the conversation in a direction he would enjoy.) "I'll text you her number. Call her tonight. Don't just text. Let her hear your voice. And sound pleasant and enthusiastic. Let her discover your snarky and sarcastic side later. Or never."

"You like me for my snarky and sarcastic side."

"Are you going to call her or not?"

Adam sighed again. "I'm going to call her."

"You're going to call her tonight?"

It was just like her to suspect his good intentions when they actually deserved suspicion. "I'm going to call her tonight," he promised grudgingly.

"Call her as soon as you get the text. She said she'd be home any time after seven. Oh, and this is perfect: she's just getting over a bad breakup. Rebound! You can't miss."

"Who's a pig now?"

"You are if you don't call. And I'll be checking up on you, so no shirking."

That was all she had to say. Adam reiterated his promise to call, and ended the call feeling trapped. He did not look forward to making that call. It would have to be done, of course, and he would at least have to meet this woman, because Hope would hound him until he did. And it was not very likely that he would enjoy the meeting, because...because he had standards, and there seemed to be so very few women his age capable of meeting them, and if it didn't work out, what a lot of explaining he would have to do with Hope! And she would look at him like *that*, with her very-displeased look—or even worse like *that*, with her I-pity-you-for-having-to-be-you look.

And there was the text noise.

The message just gave her name and telephone number. He could look her up on Facebook to see what she looked like, but what good would it do? He had to meet her anyway. Hope would not accept "I didn't like her profile picture" as a good and sufficient reason for shirking. No, it would be best to call her at once and get the thing over with.

He dialed the number in the message and put the phone to his ear. Birds were twittering mockingly as he listened to the ringback tones. But maybe she wouldn't answer. Maybe it would go straight to voice mail, and he could just leave a perfunctory message: "This is Adam Mueller, leaving you a perfunctory message because Hope Masaryk runs my life. So if you'd—"

"Hullo?" said an English-sounding voice on the phone.

"Um," said Adam. And then quickly recovering: "Hello. This is Adam Mueller."

"Oh yes!" Definitely English. "Hope told me you might call."

"She's very eager for us to meet." That put the

blame on Hope, leaving this Rose person a good way out if she wanted out: she could politely blame Hope's enthusiasm without personally rejecting Adam. Adam liked to give women a way of rejecting him painlessly, because he really didn't like the painful rejections.

But in fact there was no rejection. "She's told me so much about you that she's made me a bit eager, too."

"It's all lies." That gave her one more chance, but she laughed—a pretty English-accented laugh, Adam thought. "But since she's put so much effort into fooling you, would you like to meet for coffee— or tea, or whatever you drink?"

"Tea would be lovely. Or coffee. I go both ways." The pretty laugh again.

"Well,—um, when would be good for you?"

"Actually," she said, "I'm not doing anything tonight."

It suited Adam to get it out of the way. Hope would at least applaud his initiative. The first meeting-place he thought of was the Wild Beans; she knew where that was, and she was only a few minutes away. He told her what he would be wearing and something about what he thought he looked like. She told him she'd have a bright red sweater on, which should be distinctive enough.

So—a successful call, apparently. Adam disconnected and asked himself what he was getting into. "Just what you keep hoping for," part of his mind answered. "A date, maybe a relationship." Another part of his mind answered, "Whatever Hope wants you to get into, because you're too much of a wimp to say no to her." He looked at the time on his phone: still a quarter-hour before he was supposed to meet Rose. He had time to stroll down Bracken-ridge Avenue and— But it would be wrong, wouldn't it? No, of course not. Only if he was planning on stalking her, and of course he wasn't, because he wasn't a stalker. But still, it felt wrong. He might see her if he walked under the arch, and he shouldn't see her right before he met Rose. So instead he wandered in the back streets for a few more minutes, and then headed for the Wild Beans by a route that didn't take him through the Historic District.

It was nearly dark by the time he got there, but the place was busy. Young people with tablets and laptops, university professors with stacks of papers, a couple of older regulars from the neighborhood, all kept up a low chatter that easily merged into one indistinct undertone. Adam ended up at the table he usually occupied in the morning, except that he took Hope's usual place against the wall so he could keep an eye out for red sweaters.

Meanwhile, his mind wandered to the question

of what this Rose would look like. Of course it was useless to speculate, since he would know the answer in a few minutes—but when has futility ever prevented a man from speculating? Hope said she was "cute," but Hope would say that, wouldn't she? Not drop-dead gorgeous, then, but presentable. The accent was middle-class suburban London, from what he knew of British English. And the name Rose Middleswarth—how much more typical-average-English-girl could you get? So: pale complexion, freckles, sandy hair, thin lips, a broad and smiling face—that was the Rose he pictured, his image of the typical average English girl. Adam was pleased with himself: he expected his predictions to prove themselves true with a fair degree of accuracy, and he confidently awaited the moment when he could revel in his tiny triumph. He made a little bet with himself: if she—

"Adam?" A woman in a red sweater was standing in front of him.

It took a longish moment for his mental transmission to engage. Then he jumped up, banging the table loudly, and extended his hand. "Rose—?"

"I'm very happy to meet you," the woman said, taking his hand.

"Sorry—I was lost in thought there," Adam said a bit sheepishly. "I do that sometimes."

She was thin with medium cocoa skin, black hair

cut short, a face longer than it was broad, with full lips and a nicely shaped nose. Absolutely different from the way he had imagined her—except that she was smiling. But the accent was definitely English middle class: "Oh, yes, I do that all the time. You get completely lost, don't you?"

"I do, anyway. Can I get you something? They have good tea here, Hope tells me. I don't know anything about tea, but she does."

Rose thought a cup of tea would be lovely, and one of those round chocolate things under the counter—Adam called them "hockey pucks"—would be lovelier still.

From here on, the conversation went surprisingly well. Adam tried to be witty and was conscious of failing, but Rose laughed easily, and that helped. He learned a little about her: her mother came from Jamaica, and her father's family had been in Rochester since time immemorial, whenever that was. She had come to America as a graduate student, and she was hoping to have her doctorate in theoretical physics in a year. Adam confessed that he was a little intimidated by scientists, and she laughed again. He gave her the abbreviated version of his autobiography, and halfway through it realized that he hadn't abbreviated it nearly enough—but she listened with a smile and made him feel as though she really did want to hear it.

Her smile was very pretty. In fact, there was no better description than Hope's: she was cute. Not
movie-star gorgeous, but definitely attractive. In
the upper 20% of women Adam had been out with.
He was a little ashamed of himself for having a rat-
ing system in his mind, but not ashamed enough to
stop using it.

An hour and a half passed that way, and at ten
o'clock Rose mentioned that it was getting late, but
she would very much like to get together again.

"Do you like Cambodian?" Adam asked.

They agreed on Cambodian for dinner the next
day, which made Adam feel as if he had triumphed
in a small way. All his resentment of Hope's inter-
ference had vanished. As they stood up to leave,
Rose asked if she could drive him anywhere, but
Adam answered her that he had just a little way to
walk.

Later, as he was walking, he wondered whether
that had been the right answer. Was "Can I drive
you anywhere?" some sort of dating code for—
something else? Rose didn't seem like the type to
sleep over after an hour and a half's acquaintance,
but on the other hand Hope was always accusing
him of being oblivious to these things. He thought
of the lingering touch of Rose's hand as they
parted. He was very much looking forward to dinner tomorrow. Rose was pretty, charming, and easy

to get along with. He would enjoy getting to know her better. He would enjoy imagining getting to know her much better. He was imagining very pleasant things when he happened to walk under the iron arch, and the bottom dropped out of his stomach.

She was walking toward him half a block away. At first it looked almost as though her disembodied face was floating toward him, but the illusion was dispelled as she passed through the pool of light from a store window, which revealed that she was dressed in tight black pants and turtleneck—like a cat burglar, Adam thought immediately. The sidewalk wasn't crowded at a quarter past ten; she would be walking right past him a few seconds from now. He kept walking; she kept walking. He tried not to stare as she came closer. Just before they passed, her eyes turned and locked on his, and she smiled.

She was past, but that face, and that strangely suggestive smile, were burned into his memory indelibly. He kept walking, and for the next few steps he didn't dare look back. But after five seconds or so, he couldn't help it. He turned his head to glance back at her.

She was still walking, but she had turned her head to look back at him. She was still smiling, and now, in the light of a streetlight, she winked. Then, just after she passed under the arch, she turned right on Frick Street and disappeared.

CHAPTER 5. THE WOMAN.

"A SECOND date," Hope said in her most impressed voice. "I'm proud of you. It calls for a celebration. You should get yourself a doughnut or something."

"I was going to celebrate by going on a second date." He was cheerful this morning, and even though he knew Hope was going to taunt him, he had decided he wasn't going to mind it.

"Good idea! When was the last time *that* happened?"

"February," Adam said, looking a little less cheerful.

"Oh, I remember that one. The only thing you told me the next morning was that you didn't want to talk about it. What really happened?"

"I don't want to talk about it. But Rose was really easy to get along with. I don't think I'll have night-mares about *her*. I'm actually looking forward to tonight."

"Well, you shouldn't sound so surprised. I put a

lot of work into the selection process. I made a list of all the things you hate and measured every candidate against it."

Adam's eyebrows rose. "How did you come up with this list?"

"Oh, please! You come in here after every date for a post mortem." Hope set down her tea and counted off on her fingers. "She says 'like' all the time. She smelled like cheap perfume. She had a kitten tattoo on her shoulder. She wore a T-shirt with a slogan on it. You could see her bra straps. She made a humming sound while she ate. Her feet were distorted by high heels. My list is numbered. The numbers go up to twenty-seven.'

"Have I really—"

"Yes."

"Hmm." He took a sip of coffee and decided not to pursue the question further.

Hope leaned forward and tapped the table with her index finger to emphasize each syllable: "Don't mess this up."

"How do you think I'd mess this up?"

"By being you! By prodding and digging until you find something—anything—that bugs you about her. By being too proud to adapt."

"I'm not too—"

"Yes you are!—Look, Adam, this is your best shot. Rose is smart, she's sweet, and she's almost as

good-looking as I am. You could keep looking for
years and never find anyone better for you. It actually costs me something to say this, but Rose is the
one for you."

"Isn't it a little early to jump to that conclusion?"

"Maybe. But..." She sighed and leaned back
against the wall. "I care about you. I want you to be
happy. I want you to be happy in spite of yourself.
If I could make you happy myself, I would, but
you— Well, I think you've been unhappy. You've
been looking for love and not finding it. I think—"
her voice was getting softer "—I think you could
love Rose." Then back to full strength: "But put
some effort into it!"

"I am!" He felt as though he had to defend himself. "I'm taking her out for ban shee."

"What?

"Well, whatever it's called. Cambodian food."

"Oh! Nice choice. What are you bringing her?"

"Bringing?"

"You're an idiot. Bring her flowers. No!" She
raised a finger in the air to mark a sudden inspiration. "Bring her a single rose. A perfect red one."

Adam looked dubious, or at least he tried to look
dubious and hoped he pulled it off. "Isn't that a
bit...trite?"

"Of course it's trite. Flowers are trite. 'I love you'
is trite. Weddings are trite, at least the ones that

aren't embarrassing. You know why all our romantic gestures are trite? Because that way no one can
possibly mistake what they mean."

"But making a pun on her name—I'm sure somebody has done it before. Something a little more
creative might—"

"Get her a freaking rose!" Hope almost shouted.
Then, glancing around to see how much of a spec-
tacle she'd made of herself, she resumed in a more
normal tone: "Take it from a woman: you can't go
wrong with a rose. If you'd brought me a rose the
day after we met, I'd have fallen into your arms that
day, and into your bed the day after that, and we'd
have four children by now."

"I've only known you two years."

"I'd have worked overtime! For the love of Mike,
Adam, can you just stop arguing and get her a
freaking rose?"

"I'll get her a freaking rose!"

A moment of silence, and then Hope smiled.
"You see? I don't ask for much. Just unconditional
surrender."

❧

The date went well. There was no better or more
succinct description for it. Rose talked freely; she
let Adam know that she was "recovering" from a

breakup and wanted to "go slowly" with any new relationship—but she had to admit that she was hoping this relationship with Adam might go somewhere. (She was absolutely delighted by the rose.) Adam found it very pleasant to talk to some-one who laughed when he was trying to be funny and (unlike Hope) didn't laugh when he was trying to be serious. And at the end of the evening, Adam walked Rose to her car, and she gave him a light kiss on the lips, which was really thrilling—Adam could definitely enjoy getting used to those lips.

"Clear out half your medicine cabinet," Hope ad-vised him the next morning, "and empty some drawers. And call in a cleaning service to give your apartment the deluxe treatment. She'll appreciate that."

"Aren't you jumping the gun?" Adam asked.

"She said she wants a relationship. She kissed you. You'll be living together in six months. I've seen your apartment, and that's how long it'll take you to get ready."

Adam was dubious about her prediction. But it wouldn't hurt to clean up his apartment a bit and make it more inviting for guests. He resolved to do that soon. Within the week. He had that long: his next date with Rose was a week away. In the mean time, she was going to Baltimore for a few days to visit an old friend who had somehow ended up there. By the time he saw her again, he resolved, the apartment would be ready for...anything. Not that he expected anything right away, but he could be ready for it just in case. It was very pleasant to imagine being on more intimate terms with Rose, and he decided it would be a very good thing if Hope turned out to be right.

But he had to do something with the week till he saw her. He was getting text messages from her now—they began with a very promising "Miss you already"—but he still needed to occupy himself with something in the evening. And since it was Friday night, and the museum was open till nine, he might as well look at some art.

It was his favorite retreat when he had nothing else to do on a Friday evening. Adam wasn't a connoisseur of art—in fact, he usually avoided talking about art for fear that he would pronounce most of the artists' names wrong. But he did like to look at some of the pictures, and he did have taste, even if it wasn't necessarily very good taste. Even better, the museum was nearly deserted on Friday evenings: he could have whole galleries to himself.

He wandered through the nineteenth-century section, where all his favorite unfashionable painters resided, enjoying the fantasy that he owned the whole gallery, thinking a couple of times that it would be good to bring Rose here. He could introduce her to John Singer Sargent, if they weren't already acquainted. "Mr. Sargent, Miss Middleswarth. Miss Middleswarth, Mr. Sargent." Here and there in the sterile and almost silent galleries he would stop in front of one of his favorites and imagine showing it to Rose, trying to think of intelligent things he might say to her about the composition—things more intelligent than "It's a woman, and she's pretty," or "I like boats."

At the end of the nineteenth-century section was his favorite gallery of all—a small room with burgundy walls, stuffed with nineteenth-century American artists, all hung close together, covering the walls in imitation of a Victorian picture gallery. Here he could easily spend half an hour or more just gawking at pictures: the great fire in Pittsburgh, 1849—coast of Maine, with appropriate rocks—interior of a foundry. And of course there was his very favorite part, nearly a dozen paintings by the great caricaturist and satirist David Gilmour Blythe. Adam could lose himself in those pictures, picking out details he had never noticed before. Here was a horse with an attitude problem furiously kicking the remains of a cart to pieces; every flying splinter was rendered in such perfect detail that you could plot its trajectory. Here was Honest Abe with his Emancipation Proclamation, surrounded by such a pile of symbolic details that

Adam had never succeeded in sorting them all out. Here was—

"You seem to be a fan of Mr. Blythe," said a melodious voice beside Adam, and the bottom dropped out of his stomach.

He turned, and there she was. How had he known her voice? She was smiling. "I didn't mean to startle you."

"Uh," he answered. "Uh—that's all right. Yes. Yes, I'm a fan of David Gilmour Blythe. I always make this room the—uh—the grand finale of my visit." He was trying not to gawk at her, because it wouldn't be polite, and worse it would make him look silly. But it was hard not to gawk. His brain told him that, objectively speaking, this was not the most beautiful woman he had ever seen in his life. But his heart, or at least a powerful feeling of constriction in his chest, was telling his brain to shut up. He had never seen her this close in a good light before, and here she was wearing a long dress that fitted her shape perfectly. The urge to gawk was strong.

"He is unique," the woman said. "I have tried to study him—to see how he combines his realism with—with—character is the right word, the word that describes it. I have never been able to duplicate it."

"Oh—are you an artist?" Adam realized at once

that he sounded too impressed, like a rube from the sticks on his first visit to the big city.

"I paint portraits," she answered.

"That's very interesting." Could he possibly make himself sound like more of a dunce?

"Sometimes it is," she said with a faint smile. "Sometimes it's a job, and nothing else."

"You mean that's how you make your living?" Well, apparently he *could* make himself sound like more of a dunce.

"A good living. There are many businessmen in this city who want portraits of themselves, or their wives, or their dogs. If you have the contacts, the reputation, there is work to be had."

There was something about the way she spoke— not with an accent, but precisely, as if she had learned English rather than grown up with it. Her expressive use of pitch variations, too, was not quite native. It was more musical, less monotone, than the way a born American would speak.

"That's very interesting," Adam said, and were there no duller words he could spew out of his mouth? "I've never met a working artist before," his mouth said before his brain could stop it.

"And I've never met another fan of David Gilmour Blythe before. Have you ever been to the Chatham Club?"

"Too rich for me. I've never even been to Sam's Club."

"You must go if you have a chance. There are paintings by Mr. Blythe there that are never seen outside the club."

"Really?" If he kept her talking, he had an excuse to keep looking at her.

"And of course it is the center of all power in the city, and it is always good for an artist to be at the center of all earthly power."

That smile of hers! Oh, it was a smile to die for. It started in her golden brown eyes, spread to her mouth, and lit up her cheeks with unexpected color.

"This one," she said, walking over to Blythe's famous portrait of a coalman—"this one is my favorite, and the one I would imitate if could. It's simply the most perfect character study I know."

And from there she continued to all the other paintings in the group. She had something to say about each one of them, and it was always something clever and interesting. And Adam did his best to keep up his end of the conversation, and he was very conscious of not being clever and interesting. But he still kept up the talking, because it was still giving him an excuse for looking at her. For her part, she charmed him by finding him interesting —nothing, after all, is more charming to a man than a woman who appears to find him interesting.

They had been talking for a while before it occurred to Adam that he didn't know her name—nor did she know his, for that matter.

"I'm Adam Mueller, by the way," he said, extending a hand.

"My name is Fidessa Hao," she responded, taking the hand in a soft and lingering grip.

"Fidessa—that's an unusual name."

"I had unusual parents."

She let go of his hand after a time that felt long enough to mean something, but short enough to leave some doubt.

"Um," Adam began—"I, um, think I saw you on Brackenridge Avenue last night."

"I don't think so," she said, seriously and definitely. "I think this is the first time you've seen me."

Then she smiled and winked at him.

If Adam had been able to see his own baffled expression, he might have reminded himself to close his mouth.

"But," Fidessa continued, pulling out her phone and poking at the screen, "it doesn't have to be the last. Do you have a phone with you?"

"Yes," he answered, pulling it out of his pocket.

She held up her phone for him to see: a number was displayed on the screen. "Here's my number. Text me yours."

She waited patiently while Adam fumbled with

his phone, until he had eventually succeeded in entering her number and sending her the text.

"Thanks," she said. "I'm sure you'll be seeing me again."

And with that she walked away, leaving him another over-the-shoulder smile and wink to remember her by.

Adam stood there with Blythe's caricatures smirking at him for a few minutes. Eventually he roused himself enough to walk out of the gallery and head for the museum exit.

It was nearly closing time, and the grand staircase was practically deserted. The whole building seemed silent and empty except for his own echoing footsteps. It had been inviting earlier, but now the silence seemed oppressive and a little frightening. Adam was happy to walk out into the fresh air and noise of the street.

On his way down the steps in front of the museum, he heard the text noise. Right on that step he stopped to yank out his phone and read the message.

It was from Rose. "Safe in Baltimore," she wrote. "Still thinking of you."

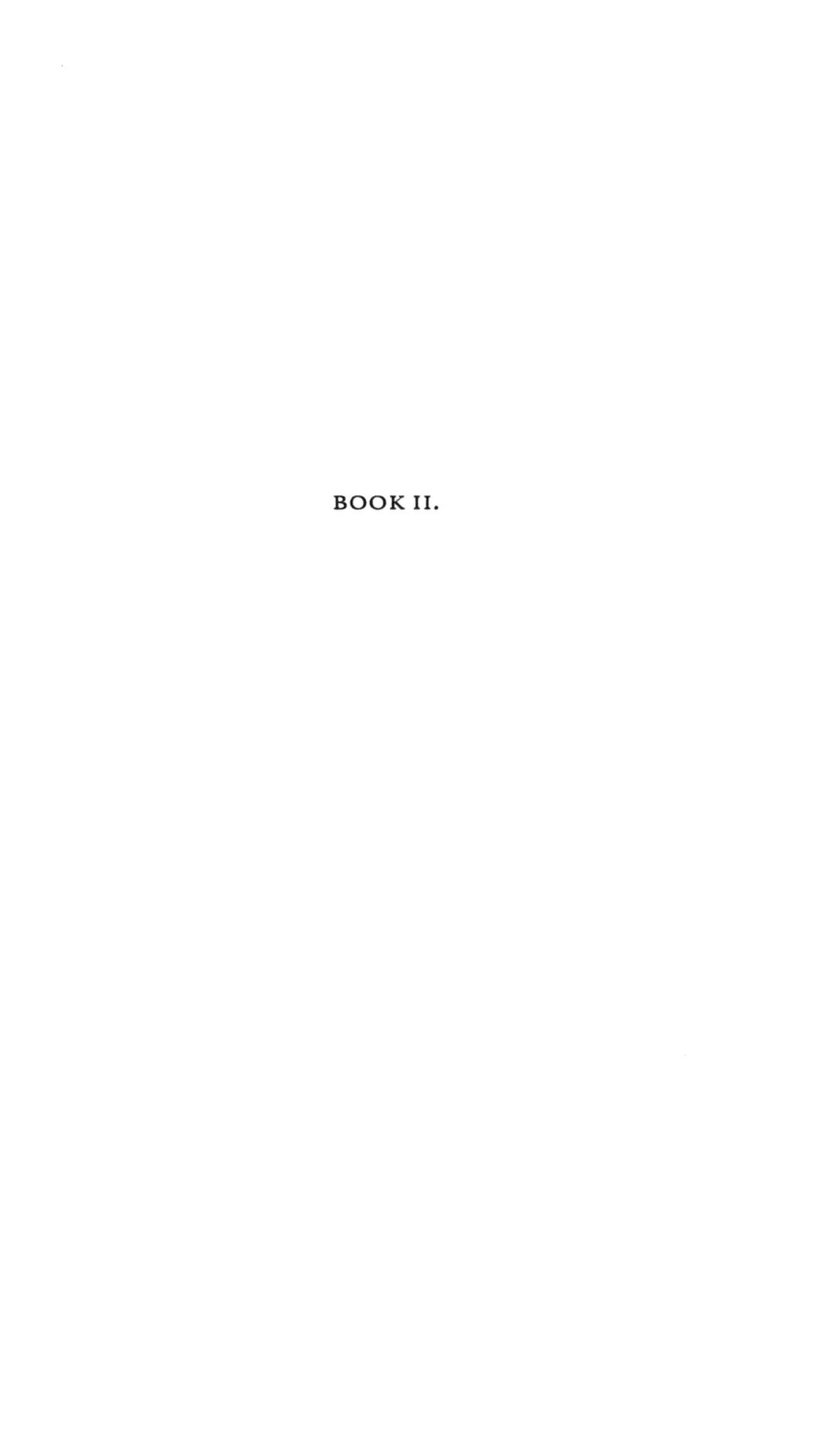

BOOK II.

CHAPTER 6. NOTHING HAPPENS.

ADAM woke Saturday morning to the sound of an arriving text. He reached for the phone without opening his eyes and ended up with his wallet instead. On the second try he did retrieve the phone, but only gradually came to understand that it did him no good without opening his eyes. The opening of his eyes would have to happen eventually. He couldn't curl up in bed all day like a sloth. Well, maybe he could, but he'd never know who sent that text. And he did want to know; the only question was whether he wanted to know badly enough to open his eyes.

He tried a partial opening. It was not a success. There was too much light in the room, even though the room had a southwestern exposure. His eyes objected strongly. They shut themselves and voted to stay shut. But Adam decided he would be the boss of them. He sat up with great labor and forced his eyes to open. The world was a blur, but he

worked on focusing. Then, having accomplished
that, he worked on finding the phone, which had
disappeared in the bed somewhere. Finally he
found something hard wrapped up in the blanket,
which he managed to extract after many unsuc-
cessful attempts to unwrap it. After all the effort of
retrieving the phone, Adam was pretty thoroughly
awake; so he was able to manipulate the thing well
enough to get to the message in a few seconds. It
was from Rose. It said "Good morning."

How should he respond? Anybody could text
"Good morning" back, and Adam hated to write
what just anybody could write. He sat for a minute,
and another minute, and five minutes, thinking
about what he might say. It wasn't like him. He
might not be the most organized person in the
world, and he might not have much luck with
women, and he might not be much more than competent at his job, but he had always thought of
himself as a man who had something to say for any
occasion.

He started thumbing "Good morning," and then
erased it letter by letter. "Have a—" wasn't going
anywhere but "have a nice day," and he wasn't going
to say that. At last he settled on "Big plans for today?" And then he sat back, leaning on his pillow,
and thought about Fidessa.

No, not Fidessa. Rose. Rose was—she was a bird

in the hand. No! What an ugly metaphor. Rose was someone he respected, someone he liked, someone who didn't deserve to be treated poorly. Rose was what he had been looking for all his life. What did Fidessa have to offer him? Just that punched-in-the-gut feeling. Was that even pleasant? And what caused it? Was it that perfect cascade of black hair? Those infinitely deep brown eyes? Was it the glowing smile? Was it the rear view in jeans or a tight red skirt? Nothing accounted for it. Fidessa was some sort of infection in his brain, making it do things he couldn't understand, making his whole body throb with longing whenever he saw her—

A text came in. It was from Rose: "Inner Harbor, something called Lexington Market," she replied. Replied to what? Oh, yes, there it was: "Big plans for today?"—that was the question he had asked. He replied:

"You'll love both. Wish I could be there."

It was true. He knew Baltimore. He could have enjoyed introducing Rose to the Lexington Market. He could enjoy introducing Rose to a lot of things closer to home, too. Did she know the Strip? Maybe this summer he could take her to Presque Isle and find out what she looked like in a bikini. And there were all his favorite strolling spots, like the Brackenridge Avenue Historic District. Yes, said a dark and poisonous spot in his mind, she could help you stalk Fidessa.

Another text: "Maybe next time we can go to-gether," and a smile. That was promising. She was already thinking of trips together. It suggested things to look forward to. What would he have to look forward to with Fidessa? Why was he even asking that question? Even Rose was perilously close to out of his league, but she had seen some-thing in him. A woman like Fidessa—well, what was a woman like Fidessa? Was she really so much more beautiful than Rose? Not by any reasonable measurement, if "measurement" was a word that even applied—or, for that matter, "reasonable." Reason was not the faculty to which Fidessa appealed.

But he ought to respond to Rose's text. What should he say? He got as far as "I'd like tha—" be-fore he erased it all and was back to a blank text. "Baltimore + you = heaven"—no, way too much way too soon. Erase. Some people could just send a smile or a wink. He envied them: he was constitu-tionally incapable of it himself. What about "Look-ing forward to it"? Maybe not. Too presumptuous. He erased about half of it, and then retyped what he had erased, and looked at it for a while, and then erased it all. At last he settled on "Anywhere with you," and then instantly regretted sending it. How could he be so...so bold so early in their acquaintance? Now he absolutely dreaded her next text. He had gone too far, too far. He might as well have typed "Will you be my wife?" into his phone. She would think he had been far too clingy so early in their relationship: he had assumed too much.

A text came in. Would he look at it?

Well, of course he would have to look at it. The alternative was to throw the phone into the river and move to another city so that he would never accidentally run across Rose again and get himself slapped. And obviously Baltimore was out, which was a pity because he liked Baltimore.

He unlocked the phone and looked at the text. It was a little red heart. That was all.

After only two dates! This relationship looked like it might be serious. Women are serious about hearts in texts, aren't they? He lay back in a warm haze of little red hearts and closed his eyes and saw Fidessa winking at him.

He woke up again an hour and a half later. It was the middle of the morning—very late by Adam's standards. He never slept in past 8:30. Coffee was obviously what he needed: coffee he would make himself, correctly, in an hourglass-shaped coffeemaker with water heated to just the right temperature, from beans he had just ground. He had time to do that on weekends. The ceremony of making coffee was something he more than enjoyed, something that almost took the place of prayer for him. If he did it just right, he was rewarded with perfect coffee, more perfect than what any commercial establishment could serve him. It took time. It couldn't be hurried. Hurry would kill the flavor: he might as well dip into the little jar of instant coffee he kept in the freezer for dire emergencies. But there was no need for hurry on a Saturday. This Saturday, especially, he had nothing to do: he had set aside the day for cleaning the apartment. And how long could that take?

That heavenly scent of fresh Ethiopian filled the tiny kitchen as Adam ground the beans to just the right coarseness. Then there was the water to heat to the point where there was just the right amount of steam. Then the filter was shaped into a cone in the top of the coffeemaker, and the grounds were lovingly placed in the cone; and then it was time to pour the water, bit by bit, over the grounds. The smell of the coffee and the precision of the brewing made Adam happy in a simple and primitive way. But nothing could equal the pleasure of that first perfect sip of perfect coffee.

With his cup, he sat down at his desk and woke up his computer. It might be fun, he thought, to look on the Web and see if he could find any paintings by Fidessa Hao. She might have her own site.

He could find out what sort of portraits she really painted.

But then he stopped himself. He should not be thinking of Fidessa. He should be thinking of Rose.

Why not find out more about Fidessa? It was only curiosity. He had never met a working portrait artist before. He was curious to see what kinds of portraits were in fashion these days, and what kind of painter his new acquaintance was. Acquaintance? Teetering on the brink of obsession. No, not an obsession: just an interesting character he had met, about whom he was naturally curious. —But he shouldn't be curious about a woman who made the bottom drop out of his stomach: he should be thinking about Rose. Try imagining Rose in a bikini again. Adam looked at his left shoulder, and then his right, and asked out loud, "Which one of you is the angel and which is the devil?"

In any event, he didn't look up Fidessa Hao on the Web. He read an academic philosopher's blog that he hadn't caught up on for several months, and that took some time, because there were several months' worth of posts to get through. Then it was past noon, and it was a beautiful day for a walk, so he walked half a block and caught a streetcar downtown, and then walked to the Point, and back through the theater district, and across to the Dia-mond; and then it was the middle of the afternoon, and if any apartment-cleaning was going to get done, he had better get back and do it.

When he stepped off the streetcar, he decided he ought to get a few things at the neighborhood market, which took him another three-quarters of an hour; then he had to put the groceries away, and he might as well make an early supper for himself while he was at it. And after that it was five o'clock, which gave him plenty of time to work on cleaning up. He would start by organizing the books in the little second bedroom he used as his office, so that more of them were on shelves and fewer in piles. At half past six, he realized that he had read more of Diogenes Lertius' *Lives of the Philosophers* than was strictly necessary for deciding what shelf to put it on. Then a text came in: it was from Rose, who said, "Inner Harbor beautiful. Lexington Market delicious." And then, before he could answer that one, another came in: "Miss you," with a little red heart.

He thought again about what he ought to say to her. It should be at just the right point on the spectrum between tentative and intimate. "Loafed all day and thought of you," he wrote. He didn't add "in a bikini."

"Dinner next," she replied. "Greek."

"I love pastitsio," he replied. Then he worried that she might not know what pastitsio was, in which case his message would sound like a weird non-sequitur, and she might doubt his sanity.

But her next message was a single word: "Spanakopita." So she did know what he meant, and she didn't think he had come unhinged. That was a good thing.

After that brief flurry of texts, Adam took a break to make coffee again. While he drank it he thought he might as well watch an old movie. He was in the mood for The Maltese Falcon. And after that it was nine o'clock, and there was really no point in any more apartment-cleaning this evening, so he sat for a while and read Diogenes Laertius; then he took the book to bed with him and read for a while more. At about half past ten there were a few more texts from Rose telling him how delicious dinner had been and naming some things she ate (galatoboureko earned a smiley face). She ended with a "Good night" and another heart.

It was not altogether a bad day, but Adam lay back in bed thinking that he had wasted the day in pure idleness. The one accomplishment, if he could call it that, was the text correspondence with Rose, which was very pleasant to contemplate. He lay in the dark contemplating it for a while, but the last image he was conscious of in his mind was the picture of Fidessa smiling and winking.

CHAPTER 7. TIME PASSES.

SUNDAY passed in utter idleness as well; so it seemed to Adam, at any rate, as he reviewed the day in his mind at the end of it. He was inclined to call it a rerun of Saturday. It began again with a light flurry of texts from Rose, followed by coffee, followed by the best apartment-cleaning intentions which somehow did not make the apartment any cleaner. Then more texting and more smiles and hearts, and an afternoon in Shadyside shopping for nothing in particular, and then an evening of seriously considering the possibility of cleaning the apartment. Then more texting, a "Good night" with not one but three hearts, and now here he was in bed thinking over a day when nothing had happened, and yet on the whole he had been happy. The one thing he was not happy about, at least not entirely happy about, was his private estimate that he had spent almost as much time thinking about Fidessa as thinking about Rose. That seemed

wrong. Not that he had made any promises to anybody—the most Rose could say was that he had
kissed her once (really she had kissed him) and that
he had suggested hopes of a closer relationship in
the future (but really she had been more suggestive
than he had). —But why was he even indulging in
these legalistic arguments? He had no intention of
using them. He would follow this relationship with
Rose as far as it would go. Perhaps it would go
nowhere, and then he had Fidessa's number. But he
wouldn't even think of that possibility until— That
is, he wouldn't even think of that possibility at all.
Unless it came up.

"Trust me, Adam," Hope told him Monday morning, "when a woman is lying in bed sending you a
text with three hearts, it means she wishes you
were there with her."

"She did mention maybe going to Baltimore together some day," Adam said. He was exceptionally
cheerful this morning because he was, for the first
time in a long while, basking in Hope's unmitigated
approval.

But now Hope was giving him her I-pity-you-for-
being-clueless look. "I didn't mean the city. I meant
the bed. She's lying in bed thinking of you and filling the ether with hearts, and if I have to draw you
a more explicit picture than that, you have no
imagination at all."

"Well, that's a...pleasant image." He was very conscious of temperature changes in his face.

"You've gone all pink."

"Sorry—I, um..."

"It's cute. I should embarrass you more often."

"I'm sure you'll find a way."

There was silence for a time while Adam sipped coffee and Hope stuffed a chunk of coffee cake into her mouth. At length Adam broke the silence with a simple question that was obviously meant to sound casual but came out sounding carefully rehearsed:

"You remember that woman on Brackenridge Avenue?"

"The chick you were stalking?"

"I wasn't stalking her!"

Hope's expression had quickly changed from pleased to wary. "What about her?"

Adam noticed the sudden wariness, so he poured an extra half-gallon of casualness over his next statement. "I met her Friday night."

"Met her?"

"Mmm-hmm," through a very casual sip of coffee.

Hope's eyebrows lowered. "Did you ambush her outside her door?"

"No! Why would I do that?"

Hope's face suggested that she could easily imagine him doing exactly that, but Adam continued:

"I met her in the Carnegie. We were both looking at the David Gilmour Blythe collection."

"And you talked to her?"

"She talked to me." The whole casual thing wasn't working out at all, and now Adam was feeling defensive. "I didn't even know she was there until she asked me if I liked Blythe, too."

"I see," Hope said, which (Adam was pretty sure) was her compact way of indicating "You have told me a half-truth, Adam Mueller, and if you know what's good for you you'll tell me the rest of the truth before I have to drag it out of you." But it wasn't a half-truth, was it? He hadn't told her about the bottom falling out of his stomach, but what business of hers was that?

"So I said yes, I liked Blythe. I don't know much about art, but I'm allowed to like Blythe."

"I see," Hope said again, a little more frostily.

Obviously he should not have brought the subject up. Why did he want to tell Hope about it anyway? But now that he had begun, there was no way to say "never mind." Hope would not allow that. He would have to continue, and he poured another quart of casualness over his next statement:

"Turns out she's an artist."

"What kind of artist? The kind who covers herself in horse manure and wails like a tropical bird?"

"No—not a performance artist. Very respectable. Paints portraits of rich people. Apparently she makes a good living at it."

"Hm," Hope responded, expressing a world of suspicion with a single grunt. "And what else happened?"

"Nothing, really. Her name's Fidessa, which I thought was unusual, but we didn't really talk much about that. Mostly we talked about Blythe—and really she did most of the talking—for about ten minutes. Then she left."

Now it was Hope's turn for studied casualness. "Did you get her phone number?"

"Um," Adam said while he frantically tried to decide what the proper answer to that question was, "yes."

Hope leaned forward, fixing him with those surprisingly piercing green eyes of hers. "Get rid of it."

"Why would I do that?"

"Because Rose!" She pounded the table with her index finger. "Rose, Rose, Rose!"

"Oh, come on, Hope! It's not like I—"

"Do you know how much it cost me, personally, emotionally, to set you up with her? Can't you see it's Rose you want, Rose you need? Just think of her lying there in bed at night filling your text stream with hearts. Think of what else she's doing. Get a vivid image of it in your mind. Hold on to it and think of it every time this Fidelia—"

"Fidessa."

"Whatever. Kick her out of your brain and fill your mind with Rose, Rose, Rose all the time, twenty-four hours a day."

"Trust me, I've been thinking of Rose."

"You'd better be." She leaned back and collected herself. "You know I can't make you do anything." (Adam thought that was a slightly disingenuous thing to say, coming from someone who had certainly made him call Rose in the first place.) "But if you'll take my advice, you'll get rid of that number. Never think of her again. It's Rose for you now. Maybe—just maybe—Rose for the rest of your life. Don't screw it up at the beginning."

"Why are you so worried about Fidessa?"

Hope looked down into her tea and didn't look up as she was speaking. "Because I know that love-at-first-sight thing," she said much more softly. "I know... how hard it is."

"Oh, I'm over that," Adam told her with a dismissive wave of the hand.

"No," Hope insisted, still not looking up. "No, you never get over it."

Adam got very little writing done at work that day. He didn't exactly waste time: he simply stared at the things on his screen and found himself unable to comprehend them. There was a very distracting conversation going on between his left shoulder and his right, and he concluded that the two invisible beings were not an angel and a devil, but rather some sort of spiritual representations of Rose and Fidessa.

More than once he picked up his phone and brought up the contacts, thinking that Hope was right. He ought to get rid of that phone number. But then he would look at it, and it seemed like such a prize—such an accomplishment to have the thing. Surely there was no logical reason to delete it. And what if he did want to call her for some rea-son? What if he, say, wanted to have Rose's portrait painted? Now, that would be a perfectly legitimate reason for calling the only portrait artist he per-sonally knew, wouldn't it?

And besides, who was Hope to tell him what he ought to do with his own contact list? Yes, she was his best friend, and he would grant that the intro-duction to Rose had been a much better thing than he expected. But did she really expect that he would run everything in his life according to her dictates? Was he going to give her absolute control over whom he associated with? Did she think she was responsible for every one of his relationships, just because she was admittedly responsible for a very promising one? No, he wouldn't let her get away with that. He was the master of his own destiny, or at least his own contact list.

And so stubborn pride conspired with indecision and indolence to spare the entry for Fidessa Hao in his contact list.

That evening there were a few pleasant texts from Rose, and he drifted off to sleep thinking of her. But in spite of Hope's admonitions, he had not succeeded in banishing Fidessa from his mind.

CHAPTER 8. ANOTHER DAY.

ADAM woke the next morning from a dream so pleasant that he fought desperately not to wake up. He lost that fight, but he lay in bed a good bit longer than usual remembering the dream and trying to fix the details in his mind. He did feel a little guilty that the woman in the dream had been Fidessa, but he hoped maybe Rose would soon be doing for him what Fidessa had done in the dream, and that was a pleasant enough prospect that he felt as if he was doing the right thing by Rose. He could have spent an idle day imagining things that way, but he did have to get to work that day, so staying in bed wasn't a real option.

By the time he reluctantly got going, it was later than usual, and Adam had just enough time to fling on his clothes and rush out the door.

"You're five minutes late," Hope announced as he sat down across from her. She showed him the time on her phone.

"Got a late start," he responded. He looked a bit abstracted.

"Punctuality is one of your few virtues. Don't take that away from me."

Adam smiled, aware that she had said something humorous and wanting to make sure she knew he appreciated it. He had spent a good bit of his walk over thinking about his dream, but now he was trying not to think about it and was not succeeding. He sipped a bit of coffee and tried to think of something to say, but his mind flatly refused to come up with anything clever, and he was not willing to say something dull.

"Heard from Rose?" Hope asked.

"Oh, yes," he answered. Here was something to talk about—something that actually interested him. "More hearts last night. I usually don't like hearts and smiles and things in texts, but from her they just seem... natural. Appropriate. I especially like the hearts."

Hope was smiling her smile of approval. "What's she been up to?"

"Seeing Baltimore, apparently. Yesterday her friends took her on an Edgar Allan Poe pilgrimage."

"Hm. And then she fills her texts with telltale hearts. But they tell a different tale."

Adam's turn to smile. He wasn't really sure that Hope was right about those hearts, but she was a woman after all. She would know better than he would.

Hope devoted the next minute or so to her coffee cake, and Adam had nothing more to say at the moment. After an audible intake of breath, Hope spoke again:

"Did you erase that number?"

It occurred to Adam to lie; and then it occurred to him to feign indifference and ask her what number she meant; but he knew perfectly well that she would see through those stunts. So he answered honestly and directly, after only a moment's pause to consider dishonesty: "No."

"Didn't think so." She didn't sound surprised or even disappointed, and Adam was provoked to ask,

"Why didn't you think so?"

"Oh, I probably couldn't have done it in your place." She sighed an old-movie sigh. "My advice is better than my example."

"I didn't call her," Adam added.

"I didn't expect you to—yet." Her smile was an encouraging sign: she wasn't angry at him. "It took me a week to get up the courage to call you, remember?"

"Yeah, and that was only for morning coffee between friends."

"Yeah." She looked down into her tea, and then decided to pick it up and drink some.

Another minute or so of silence, and then Hope asked, "So what are you going to do with it?"

"What, the number?" Adam honestly didn't know the answer to that question. "Maybe nothing. I don't know how much Rose is into art. Maybe she'd be interested in meeting a working artist."

"Right." By which, of course, she meant, "You're lying."

"Well, it might be fun to get the two of them together."

"Might be," Hope agreed, "but that sort of thing will have to wait until you know Rose a lot better."

"That's not what I meant."

"Go ahead. Tell me you're not thinking about it right now."

"Now that you've put the idea in my head?"

"If I had to put that idea in your head, you're not an American male." She picked up a chunk of coffee cake and shoved it into her mouth.

"Anyway," Adam said while her mouth was busy, "I don't have any plans that include Fidessa. I'm still looking forward to seeing Rose on Friday. I was thinking of suggesting Nepalese."

Hope swallowed. "But you still have the number. The idea of it is festering in your brain. And you're avoiding asking yourself the big question."

"What's the big question?"

"Which one of them do you really want? That's

the big question."

Adam leaned back. "Don't be ridiculous. Right now I'm dating Rose."

"Right now."

"You're doing that thing where you repeat what I say as if I meant something different by it."

"That thing?"

"Stop that!"

She laughed. "I can still annoy you. It's a good sign. It means you still care about me."

"Of course I care about you."

"I know." She picked up another chunk of coffee cake. "It makes me sad sometimes." And the chunk went into her mouth.

Sometimes Hope said the most unaccountable things.

Not much time ended up being spent on productive work that day. Adam worked, but it was not work he would call productive. In the morning he mostly sorted old writeups, so that they would be more readily available when he needed them, if that ever happened. You never knew. A client from years ago might call and say, "Remember that ad in the *Leader*?"—and then Adam could reach into the drawer and pull it right out, if all the old writeups were properly sorted. After lunch, he decided that the sorted things would stay sorted much better if they were stapled. By half past one he had spent an hour and a half stapling, and yet there was still a pile of sorted things that remained unstapled. Then the stapler jammed, and Adam put quite a bit of labor into getting the mangled staple out. His neighbor heard the banging noises and the mild swearing and stopped by to offer the use of a working stapler, but Adam argued that he would need to make the thing work sooner or later, and it would be an appalling waste to throw out a stapler, and he wasn't going to give the thing the satisfaction of defeating him. So his colleague shrugged and walked away, and Adam finally did clear the mutilated staple out of the stapler by fabricating a special tool for the purpose from a paper clip. Then it was a quarter to four, and there was just time enough to finish all the stapling by four-thirty, which was quitting time.

So it was not a day of great accomplishment, but on the other hand things were stapled, and that would make future work go faster, if he ever needed to find old writeups. So really he had been investing in the future.

Meanwhile, while he had been investing, he had been pondering two of the annoyingly unanswerable questions Hope had asked him. What was he going to do with that phone number? And which did he really want—Rose or Fidessa?

It was obviously a stupid question, that second

one. Of course the answer was Rose. He had spent hours, not to mention dozens of texts, getting to know Rose. With Fidessa he had had one short conversation, and it had mostly been about one artist, and furthermore she had done most of the talking. And Rose was...nice. She was as nice a girl as anyone could hope to meet. And hearts! Rows of hearts in his text stream. He had made that much of an impression on her. Surely he could learn to love Rose, and maybe soon he would have the same gut reaction to her that he had to Fidessa.

But then why was he keeping Fidessa's phone number? He told himself he had already solved that conundrum. She was an interesting character, and one he might enjoy getting to know a little better—but not much better, of course!—unless the thing with Rose didn't work out. And the thing with Rose would work out.

Then he was back to Hope's question: what was he going to do with that number? Nothing was a possibility. He could do nothing with it. But if he did nothing, if he intended to do nothing, then he might as well delete it after all. Maybe the thing to do was text her something neutral, or something art-related: "Enjoyed meeting you Friday. Any portraits of yours on the Web?"

Now, the trouble with that was that he had already let five days pass. Grass had grown under his feet. It would seem odd to her if he suddenly texted her about Friday and didn't have any more to say than that. He would have to think of some occasion, some reason for getting in touch with her. But in spite of his devoting much mental effort to the project as he walked home, he wasn't able to think of any suitably impressive reason for texting Fidessa. And perhaps it wasn't such a good idea anyway—not while Rose was away. Not that he had made any promises to Rose, but still—little red hearts!

Back home now, he didn't feel like making any elaborate preparations for dinner, so he ate something dreadful from a can. And then he thought about taking a walk, but he should really stay in and clean the apartment. So he did stay in.

At a little after eight his phone rang, and he saw, much to his consternation, that it was Derrida-woman calling. What should he do? Should he answer? Of course he should answer. But what should he say? He should tell her it hadn't worked out. He should make sure she knew right away that there wouldn't be any more dates. How do you say a thing like that? "Sorry, but I don't date deconstruction-ists." That sounds racist. "I hated talking to you" was a bit too blunt. How about "I only have six weeks to live, so I guess there's no point in getting to know me any better"? Not likely to be taken as intended.

He could say "I found somebody better than you," but that was not the sort of thing a gentleman would say, was it?

Then the problem solved itself: the phone stopped ringing, and a moment or two later it told him he had a new voice mail. Now he had only to solve the problem of the voice mail. He should answer it as soon as possible, of course, because he didn't want it hanging over his head.

But then a text came in from Rose: "Two days till I see you," and a heart. And of course that demanded a more immediate response from him than the voice mail from Derrida-woman. He had never felt closer to being in love with Rose than at that moment, when she had spared him from the droning philosopher. He replied, "I can hardly hold out till then," and she replied with an even more affectionate message, and soon the air was filled with little red hearts on both ends of the connection. "I feel so close to you already," Rose wrote toward the end of the text storm, and Adam replied, "Can't wait to be even closer," which earned him a smile and a heart from her.

With all this phone activity, Adam felt as though he'd had a very busy evening. But no apartment-cleaning got done.

CHAPTER 9. WAITING FOR ROSE.

SLOTH would not consume another day, Adam decided. He would get real work done, and he would make decisions instead of putting them off.

"I still don't know what to do about philosopher-girl, though," he told Hope. She had decided to try an apple pastry instead of the usual coffee cake, but she was consuming it by her usual method of breaking off bigger-than-bite-size chunks.

"Maybe you could be honest with her," she suggested, pointing at him with a hunk of pastry.

"You mean, 'Listening to you rattle on about the emptiness of all language made me want to blow my brains out'?"

"No!" Her mouth was full, so she chewed and swallowed before continuing: "You can actually be polite about it and still be honest."

"How about 'I'm very sorry to tell you, madam, that listening to you rattle on made me want to blow my brains out'? Polite enough?"

"Sure. Go ahead and tell her that." She was making her sarcastic face.

"I can't tell her that."

"Didn't think so."

"So what am I going to do?"

"Do you want my advice or my prediction? Because my prediction is that you're going to dither indefinitely until the situation is completely out of hand, and then come in here and ask me, 'How did I get myself into this mess?' And I'll say, 'Gee, Adam, I don't know,' but I'll be using my sarcastic voice."

"I don't like the sarcastic voice."

"Then call her! Just tell her things have changed, which they have, and she might be disappointed— or not—but she'll understand."

"It's the 'disappointed' part I hate. And what if she starts pleading with me?"

"You have a high opinion of yourself, don't you? How often do you have women pleading with you?"

"It could happen. Theoretically."

"Fine." It was the kind of "fine" that really meant "I'm tired of arguing with you, Adam." "Then do the cowardly thing and just text her."

"'What do I say?"

"Say 'Moved to New Zealand and caught a rare contagious disease.' "

"That *is* cowardly." He didn't say it disapprovingly.

She looked at him suspiciously. "You do realize I was being sarcastic, right?

"But it could solve the problem."

"So would jumping off the Liberty Bridge."

"But I'm afraid of heights."

There was a period of silence during which Adam sipped coffee and Hope chewed on an oversized chunk of pastry. When Hope had finished chewing, she asked, "Are you going to call philosopher-girl?"

"You don't have to nag me." He set down his coffee. "We're not married."

"We could be. Then I could nag you every day."

"You nag me every day anyway."

"Not on weekends." Another big chunk of the pastry went into her mouth.

"Nagging without benefit of marriage. Some people would be appalled by the immorality of it."

Hope spoke with her mouth full, but decorously blocking the view with her hand: "You love me for my loose morals."

Just the words "you love me," coming so soon after the mention of marriage, raised danger flags for Adam. Were they one of her tests? He couldn't think of anything properly deflective to say, so he said nothing.

Hope swallowed. "And you're an old sinner yourself, you know, if you put off calling philosopher-girl. Sloth or idleness—it's one of the big old deadlies."

"I'll call her," Adam insisted. But he didn't say when.

Adam got some real work done that morning. It was not great or important work, but he did write two pages of a white paper. Then he realized that one of his figures was off by an order of magnitude, which meant that the conclusions he had based on that premise were worthless, which meant that the two pages—nearly three hours of work—were worthless and would have to be redone. But it was time to go to lunch anyway.

The afternoon didn't go as well. Adam tried to summon up the courage to attack the white paper again, but the courage just sat there and refused to come when it was called. It thumbed its nose at him. He thought about Fidessa for a while, and then suddenly realized he was thinking the wrong thoughts and thought about Rose. Tomorrow night he would see her. Third date! He would have to ask Hope if there were any third-date traditions he was supposed to know about. It had been a while since he'd had a third date, and considerably longer since he'd had a fourth one, which suggested he ought to brush up on his third-date etiquette. He thought of looking up "third-date etiquette" on the Web, but he really ought to be using the computer to get his white paper done, not to advance his romantic prospects. Nevertheless, no more of the white paper got done.

In the evening Adam dawdled on the way home. He went into the drug store on the corner near his apartment, but he couldn't remember what he wanted to buy there, so he walked out empty-handed, which made him feel like a shoplifter, which of course was silly and ridiculous, because innocent people walked out of stores without buying anything all the time; but he nevertheless felt obliged to walk out slowly and casually, and to pause on the sidewalk in front, just to make it obvious that he wasn't trying to sneak something out. After that, he didn't quite feel ready to go home and stay in yet, so he took an aimless stroll around the neighborhood. He thought of directing his stroll through the Historic District, but he might see Fidessa there, which was of course the reason he had thought of taking a stroll through the Historic District, and he didn't want to have to explain why he hadn't made use of the number she'd given him, at least not until he had decided how he was going to make use of it. And besides—Rose. He thought about her, and the thoughts were very pleasant, until he started to ask himself again what she might expect of a third date. It began to seem like an insoluble problem. If he pushed too hard, she'd be put off. If he moved too slowly, she'd think he wasn't interested enough. How does a man convey the idea that he's looking forward to an intimate relationship, but he wants to respect the woman's own pace, but he is definitely attracted to her, but it won't kill him to wait if that's what she wants because he knows it will be worth it? What a minefield this dating thing is. It seemed to Adam that he had been rather lucky not to have many third dates so far. No, that couldn't possibly be the right way of looking at it, could it?

When Adam did get home, it occurred to him that the apartment still hadn't been cleaned. He spent ten minutes shoving things under other things, which made the place look a little more civilized. But if Rose did happen to ask "My place or yours?"—well, he knew which answer he would give.

At a little after nine, a text came in from Rose: "Made it back home. Looking forward to tomorrow."

"Welcome back," he replied. "Good trip?" That was neutral and friendly enough to give him time to think of what else he ought to say about her return from Baltimore in his next text.

Another text: "Fun. Would have been more fun with you." And a smile.

That was nice. How should he reply to let her

know he missed her, without pouring it on too thick? "Dull here. Wasted time thinking of you." As soon as he sent it, he decided it had been the stupidest possible thing to say. It implied that thinking of her was a waste of time, which wasn't what he meant at all.

Then the phone rang, and it was Rose. Well, either she was mortally offended or she wasn't. If she was, then at least he didn't have to worry about the third date stuff anymore. He answered.

Rose's "Hullo" was cheery and not at all offended-sounding. After the preliminary greetings, she continued, "I wanted to settle the details for tomorrow. When should I meet you? And where? That sort of thing."

"Well, I was thinking of a Nepalese place I know in Lawrenceville."

"Oh! I think I know the one you mean. I've been wanting to try it. Isn't it funny how we both had the same idea? Would you like me to pick you up? I think you're sort of on my way, aren't you?"

Adam agreed that it would work out fine that way, and she said she would pick him up at seven. They talked a little about Baltimore, but soon she said she was very tired and would have to "crash."

"Happy dreams, Adam," she said in a soft and very appealing tone.

"Maybe you'll be in some of them," Adam replied,

once again instantly wondering whether he had said too much.

Rose laughed lightly. "You'll have to tell me the details if I am."

A minute and a half after she hung up, the phone rang again. It was Derrida-woman. This was Adam's chance to do the right thing. He'd begin by saying "I meant to call you," or maybe "I was just reaching for the phone to call you," which was less a direct lie than a polite fiction, since he truly had been intending to call her soon. But perhaps it would be best just to leave it at "I meant to call you," and then go right on to "Look, um—" What was her name? Well of course it was right there on the phone. "Look, Julie, I don't think—"

The phone stopped ringing. He should call her right back. But she was probably leaving a voice mail right now, so he should let her finish that first. And then he should definitely listen to her voice mail, and also the one she left the night before, in case she had something to say that he needed to respond to. The more he thought about it, the more responding to philosopher-girl in an appropriate manner seemed like a major undertaking. And you don't begin a major undertaking at half past nine in the evening, It should be the product of fresh and mature judgment. Do the words "fresh" and "mature" really go together that way?

A chime from his phone indicated that she had left her voice mail. No, wait—two chimes. One of them must be a text, or a voice mail from someone else. He unlocked the phone, and indeed there were two message icons waiting for him: one a voice mail, doubtless from philosopher-girl, and one a text, which was probably from Rose. He opened the text.

It wasn't from Rose. It was marked as coming from Fidessa Hao: "Meet me at the Carnegie tomorrow night?"

The bottom dropped out of Adam's stomach. He immediately started thumbing a response: "What ti—"

He stopped. He had something else planned for tomorrow. It was something he was supposed to be looking forward to.

But Fidessa wanted to see him. For just an instant, that seemed more important than anything else. Then his rational mind clamped down and reminded him: Rose. Rose Rose Rose.

It seemed odd—didn't it?—that Rose resided in the rational part of his mind.

He erased what he had typed and started over: "Busy tomorrow, but want to see you. Saturday?"

It was a very reasonable response, he told himself. Then the rational part of the mind stepped in and reminded him that he was attempting to make a date with another woman for the day after his third date with Rose. —No, not a date, said the rationalizing part of his brain. Just a meeting. A getting together. It was just because he was sincerely interested in her as an artist. He would do exactly the same thing if she were a man instead of the most thrillingly heart-stoppingly gut-wrenchingly beautiful woman he had ever seen in his life.

A text came in: "10:30 AM in front of David Gilmour Blythe paintings."

Adam instantly responded, "I'll be there."

And she instantly responded, "See you in my dreams," and three hearts.

Oh—wait—that one was from Rose.

CHAPTER 10. AT HER OWN PACE.

"WHAT do women expect from a third date?" Adam asked Friday morning at the usual table, as if it were a matter of idle curiosity.

"Diamonds," Hope answered. She was back to coffee cake this morning, a big chunk of which went into her mouth.

"I don't believe you."

"Good." She was talking with her mouth full, once again blocking the view with her hand. "You're learning."

"But really, what's...expected? I mean, you know what you expect, right?"

"Rose and I are different. I know what I'd expect. I have a list. But Rose said she wanted to go slow, right? So you'll probably just make out a little."

"But what... First of all, did you say you have a list?"

"Date by date, what I do on each date. —Oh, don't look at me like that. It doesn't get really kinky until the sixth date."

"What's on the list for the third date?"

"If you want to find out what I do on the third date, you have to take me out three times. That's the rule."

"Is it on the list?"

"It's in the preamble. Look, Adam, it's not as hard as all that. She's into you, you know that. Hearts. So just follow her lead. Let her go at her own pace. When you're walking, let her be the one to take your hand. When you're kissing, let her be the one to start with the tongue. Just be enthusiastic when she does, and you'll be on the right track."

"Sounds simple."

"That's right." She broke off a chunk of coffee cake. "It's simple. Your life can be simple for once."

The chunk went into her mouth.

"Simple," he repeated. He decided not to mention his appointment with Fidessa or the fact that he hadn't called Derrida-woman back yet.

Rose picked him up at precisely seven, almost to the second. Adam was waiting in front of his door for her, since he was actually looking forward quite sincerely to seeing her, and since it was a splendid evening anyway. There was a space right in front of the duplex, and he recognized her as soon as she pulled up in her little Honda. He opened the door and hopped in. She was smiling, and after what looked like a moment's hesitation she leaned over for a kiss. He willingly gave it to her: just a light kiss, but Adam wouldn't have minded a thousand more like it.

"I missed you," they both said at once, and then they both laughed.

Rose was a very cautious driver—partly because, as she pointed out, "you drive on the wrong side over here." She took Adam's directions and made it to the restaurant in about fifteen minutes. Adam could have driven the same distance in ten, he thought, but Rose's caution was part of her charm.

Because of the caution, they didn't talk about much besides the route while she was driving, because Rose could answer only in cheerful monosyllables, devoting the rest of her attention to keeping the car from drifting over into the left lane.

So it wasn't until they were in the restaurant called Kathmandu, and had already ordered some unpronounceable things by the numbers, that any real conversation could begin. And like all such conversations, it began with a banal question:

"So how was Baltimore?"

"Lovely," Rose answered without hesitation. "I saw everything, didn't I? Edgar Allan Poe house, the Walters Art Gallery, the aquarium (which is brilliant), the Inner Harbor, the conservatory at Druid Hill (which isn't a patch on Phipps, by the way), Jones Falls, the shot tower (very phallic), and the Washington Monument. I didn't even know there was another Washington Monument, but it's right around the corner from Alice and Mark's house."

"So you got the royal treatment."

"I did, didn't I? And of course Alice had to ask me all about you."

"Me?" Adam asked with a smile.

"Oh, the first night I was there she had to know everything. You see, she spent hours on the phone with me when I—when Brad and I broke up,—and so the first thing she had to ask me was 'Do you have a new boyfriend? Do you have a new boyfriend?'"

"And what did you tell her?" Adam asked the question casually, with a carefree smile, but he couldn't help investing a lot of emotion in her answer.

"Well, I thought about you, and how much I enjoyed our times together..." She reached across the table and took his hand in hers, and the touch sent a small but warm electric surge through his body. "And I said yes." She was looking straight into his eyes, "Did I say too much?"

"Not as far as I'm concerned," Adam answered with a feeling of relief and general contentment; and then, to reinforce the point, he added,

"—girlfriend."

She smiled, lowered her eyes, and squeezed his hand. "I was afraid I'd gone too far too fast. But you were so sweet the next morning. 'Anywhere with you'—I thought that was the most romantic thing, anyone had ever said to me. Or, um, texted at least." That bright laugh again.

Well, it was good to know that that one had made a hit. "I was afraid I'd gone too far with that one," Adam confessed.

"It made me happy the rest of the day!"

And then food started to arrive, and the conversation naturally turned to the food and what the ingredients might be. It was only after the plates were gone, and spiced tea was all that was left of the meal, that Rose turned the conversation back to important topics:

"About the boyfriend-girlfriend thing," she began: "we need to have... a serious talk."

"I can be serious sometimes," Adam assured her, "if I put some effort into it."

She laughed a little. "You make me laugh. See, Bradley never did that." She looked serious again. "He made me cry often enough, but he never made me laugh."

"Sounds dreary,"

"It was intense. That was the problem. Every time I saw him, it felt like being punched in the stomach."

"Oh, I know that feeling," Adam said, not adding, "It doesn't happen with you."

"Things moved so fast with Bradley. I moved in with him less than a month after I met him. I thought—well, I thought this must be love, didn't I? —because the feeling was so intense. But I was so miserable."

"Did, um, Bradley mistreat you?" Adam felt a chivalrous loathing welling up against any man who could abuse a thoroughly nice girl like Rose.

"I think we mistreated each other. I think that's what I'd have to call it. He was so possessive—he was even jealous of the time I spent with my girl-friends. And I suppose I provoked him, because I didn't like to be...possessed."

"You have a right to be trusted," Adam said. "Even if you're married, you have a right to be your own person."

"You're so sweet." She took his hand across the table. "Because of what happened with Brad, I promised myself I'd go slowly this time. Actually, I promised Alice, too, since she had to pick up the pieces last time."

"That sounds wise," Adam said, giving her hand a gentle squeeze.

She had been looking down at their joined hands, but now she looked straight into his eyes. "Are you disappointed?"

"Disappointed?"

"That I'm not...sleeping over tonight?"

Here was one of those tests that women devise, Adam thought. There might be no right answer, but there were plenty of wrong answers. He would have to steer between Scylla and Charybdis. "I think you're doing the right thing. It doesn't mean I'm not attracted to you, and I'd be a liar if I told you I haven't thought about being more intimate with you, but it's worth the wait and worth the trouble to get our relationship started right. And I do want a relationship, not just a fling."

Rose gazed into his eyes for a few moments, and then half-stood and leaned across the table for a gentle kiss. Then she sat back in her chair. "Being more intimate," she repeated. "You have a charming way of talking about these things. Bradley could only think of a couple of words for sex, and he always made me feel grubby when he talked about it. You make me feel... wanted."

"You *are* wanted. But I hope you feel respected, too."

She smiled brightly, as if the realization had just hit her. "I do! I feel respected. That's the difference. Thank you." Then she looked shy, which was very appealing, "Would you like to do something tomorrow?"

"I'd love to," he answered immediately. And then he remembered: "I'm busy in the morning, but if you'd like to get together around four..."

"Perfect. I'll pick you up."

And here at last was his chance to resolve all his internal contradictions and put everything in the open. How good it would feel to be completely honest with Rose! "In the morning," he explained, "I'm meeting an artist acquaintance at the Carnegie. But I can cancel if you think—"

"Of course not!" She smiled. "You have a right to be trusted."

Adam smiled, too, thinking he might tell her more about the artist, but she went on:

"Maybe you can introduce me to him sometime."

It's not a him, Adam thought of telling her, but she was finishing up:

"Are you ready to go?"

Since he'd finished his tea, he had no reason to say he wasn't ready.

Rose drove him home, and when she found a parking spot half a block from his duplex, she insisted on escorting him to his door. She kissed him, and then asked him again, "You're not disappointed?"

"You're worth it." There—that should convey that he was willing to take her at her own pace, but he was seriously attracted to her. Neither Scylla nor

Charybdis could get him.

Apparently it had the right effect. "If it helps, I really want to come up with you. It's just... I promised myself."

He smiled at her, but didn't say anything.

She appeared to reach a decision. "But remember this." She pressed her mouth to his and gave him a deep and memorable kiss.

That certainly was enough to make him feel as though the evening had been a success. And later, when he was in bed and just about to put out the light, his phone chimed. He opened the text to find a row of little red hearts—he counted thirteen of them—and an exclamation point.

And tomorrow morning he would see Fidessa.

BOOK III.

CHAPTER 11. FOR ART'S SAKE.

SATURDAY morning Adam woke up early, and hungry. He glanced at his phone. No new messages, but there were those thirteen hearts and one exclamation point, which made him warm and happy. Then he thought of meeting Fidessa, and he felt a strong contraction of the chest muscles. Or something in the heart region, anyway. Maybe he ought to call it off, since he now officially had a girlfriend. (Girlfriend! What a warm and happy word that was.) But to call it off would imply that he had been planning something deceitful in the first place, which he hadn't. He had been absolutely straightforward with Rose, except for the little misapprehension about the sex of the artist, which was hardly his fault. So he went and had breakfast at the bakery down the street, and after he had sacrificed two huge doughnuts on the altar of gluttony he was ready to ride in to the museum.

She was dressed simply and elegantly in black

and red. Adam did not know that there could be such a thing as an elegant sweatsuit, but this one was black with red piping, and the fit was perfect, and he had never seen a more desirable woman in his life. He had fortified his mind with Rose's kiss and her thirteen hearts in a row, but those didn't protect him from the bottom-dropping-out-of-the-stomach feeling.

"You are very punctual," said that precise and musical voice. "It is a virtue."

"I like to be on time," Adam said with stupid bland obviousness.

Fidessa nodded, and then stepped in front of Blythe's coal-seller. "Extraordinary, isn't it? Imagine how long Mr. Blythe must have waited, how long he must have searched for this subject. Imagine his elation when, by pure random chance, he saw this man in the street, and he said to himself, 'I shall make a masterpiece of this man.'"

"Do you think that's how it happened?" Adam willed her to keep talking, just so he could listen to the music of her voice, just so he could watch the ballet-like sweep of her arms as she gestured toward the painting, the subtly perfect rippling of her whole body as it emphasized the modulations of her voice.

"Oh, I'm sure of it. He might not even have known he was searching, but he was searching. A true artistic temperament is always searching. And he knew what he had found when he had found it. He must have felt the joy of a Balboa discovering the Pacific. He must have understood at once that here was the opportunity that would make him more, much more, than a mere caricaturist. Oh, an artist of his brilliance would have taken one look at that face and said, 'This will be my masterpiece. I shall be remembered for this.' And that is what has happened to me."

"Really? When did that happen?"

"When I saw you."

Adam was taken aback. It felt as though he had only just now understood the meaning of "taken aback" for the first time: the statement had sneaked up behind him and smacked him before he realized what had happened. He wasn't sure whether he understood her exactly, and he had to ask, "What do you mean by that?"

"I want to make a work of art out of you," she answered.

"You mean a portrait?"

"But more than a portrait, as this"—she indicated the Blythe painting with a flowing sweep of her perfect arm—"is more than a portrait."

Adam looked at the painting. "You want me to carry a shovel?"

Fidessa smiled indulgently, or at least Adam had

the strong impression that she was indulging rather than enjoying his attempt at a joke. "That would not be necessary." Then the indulgent smile faded into an expression of earnest hope. "Will you do this for me, Adam?"

"Why me? I mean, I'm not saving no, but why do you want me after all the portraits you've done?"

"Precisely because of that—because of all the portraits I've done. Oh, I have made a good living with my brush. A businessman wants a portrait to hang in the boardroom: he must look honest and decisive. I give him what he desires. A politician wants a portrait of his second wife to hang over the fireplace; she must look aristocratic and proper. I give him what he desires. And the politician's wife is a vapid former cheerleader, and the businessman is a dithering fraud. I serve the paying customer, and I am very good. But you—you have real character. Or at least you have—how shall I say it?—a foundation on which I can build."

"I'm like a pile of concrete blocks," Adam responded. He was thinking. There was absolutely nothing wrong—nothing he could think of, anyway —with allowing an artist to use his face to make a masterpiece. How often had he been told that his face was worthy of a masterpiece? Roughly once, counting today. He had been idly looking at the Blythe painting to avoid gawking at Fidessa, but now that he had something to say he turned toward her:

"What would you do—take a few pictures to work from?"

"No!" She was startlingly definite. "I do not work from photographs. Photographs never show character, because character is an event, a thing that happens over time, and a photograph must be instantaneous. There is no instantaneous character. I work from the living subject. I work *on* the living subject."

She moved closer to him, although the movement was so subtle and natural that it hardly seemed to be a movement at all; but she had passed the very subtle boundary that separated standing near him from standing close to him. He could feel the warmth of her body across the seemingly infinitesimal space that still separated them, and the deeper undertones of her voice, like quiet pedal notes from an organ, were audible to him for the first time. "It will take several sittings. I must come to know you very well. And of course it follows that you will come to know me very well. Will you do it for me?"

"Of course. I've always supported the arts."

She smiled. Her smiles were subtle, seldom tooth-baring, although she seemed to have perfect teeth when they were visible. "I was prepared to beg."

Adam very nearly asked, "What kind of begging were you prepared to do?" But that sounded too much like vulgar innuendo, which in fact would have been the way it was intended. Fidessa was not a woman to be amused by vulgar innuendo. Besides, he had a girlfriend to think of, though it was very hard to think of her in the intoxicating presence of Fidessa. Instead he told her, "No begging necessary. It will be a new experience. And after all, it's not every day someone looks at me and sees a potential masterpiece."

"When I've finished with you, everyone will see what I see." She was still standing very close; he could feel the light puff of her breath. And yet no one could have said she was standing improperly, indecorously, or impolitely close to him. She seemed to have calculated the proper distance exactly. At most a disinterested observer might have assumed that the two of them were a little better acquainted than they really were.

"When do you want me to start?" Adam asked.

"Now," she replied without hesitation. With her habitually precise speech, it sounded like a command, but Adam would not have resented a command from her. He would follow her anywhere. Except...

"I do have to be home before four."

"I'll have you back by three-thirty. Come with me."

Adam followed her. He didn't care where.

Adam was impressed to find that she drove a Lexus. He liked to think of himself as a man not easily impressed by cars—he didn't even keep one himself, having decided that the care and feeding of an automobile in the city consumed more of his limited income than any benefits could justify. Still, an artist with a Lexus must be an artist who is do - ing well for herself.

She drove him back to Brackenridge Avenue, and then into a little service alley that ran behind the historic district, and then into a small garage with spaces for about three and a half cars—the half-car space being occupied by a tiny French car that Adam thought ought to come with carrying han- dles. From the garage they walked through the back door of a stairwell, which—if Adam had to guess— he might suppose was the other side of the door- way he had seen her go into the second time he had glimpsed her on Brackenridge Avenue. Up the stairs to the third floor, and through a door into an- other world.

It was an artist's studio like the ones in nine- teenth-century paintings. Generously illuminated by skylights, it was strewn with paintings, easels, prepared canvases, and all the other marks of the working artist. Yet it was not a mess, not untidy in the least: Adam sensed at once that every piece, every seemingly stray item, had been placed with an artist's eye for composition. The place created an impression, and Adam could see at once how it would be an impression that would be exactly right for a paying client. A rich executive, flush with new money, would walk into this studio and immediately understand that here he could purchase the old-money respectability of a real portrait by a real artist.

"You are thinking," Fidessa said, "that I am a bit of a fraud."

"No!" Of course he wasn't thinking that. But he could understand how she could have interpreted what he was thinking that way—if she could hear what he was thinking, which of course she could not. "I was thinking that even your studio is...artistic."

"All art is fraud," she declared mildly. "The route to truth lies through falsehood. The artist lies, distorts, disguises the truth, because it is the only way to make the truth apparent."

"I like paradoxes. You must be a philosopher as well as an artist."

"I am a little of everything. That is what it means to be an artist."

"Epigrams and paradoxes," Adam said. "You must know my tastes. So tell me: why does the route to truth lie through falsehood?"

"You said that even my studio was artistic. You are correct. It is not an efficient arrangement. But it does look like an artist's studio. A wealthy client comes here, and he feels assured that he is in the presence of a capable artist. If I had arranged the studio for my own convenience alone, would he feel the same way? Yet I am capable. The arrangement of the studio, which is a lie, conveys the truth: but if my client were to deduce from an efficiently arranged studio that I was not the most competent portraitist he could find, then the unadorned truth would have told him a lie."

"Well," Adam said, looking at a portrait of a middle-aged woman who looked powerful and self-assured, "you certainly are a competent portraitist. This is—well, I should probably be prohibited by law from having opinions on art, but this is good. This is John-Singer-Sargent good."

"No," she said decisively. "That is competent. The foundation will be pleased, and it will hang in the lobby and be properly decorative. But it is dull."

Adam noticed—felt at first, then saw—that she was close to him again.

"You," she said, "will not be dull."

CHAPTER 12. THE MODEL.

THE first step in becoming an artist's model, Adam learned, was to eat. "I want you not to be distracted by the needs of the belly," Fidessa explained. "And I begin with some simple and inconsequential conversation. It is useful in coming to know your mannerisms." So Fidessa told him, and that is how Adam's gluttony at breakfast came to be supplemented by more gluttony in the middle of the day. Fidessa had prepared for her visitor: she had procured a whole box of French pastries, which were so uncommonly delicious that Adam just kept eating them. They were small, after all, and one brioche was so insubstantial that he might as well follow it with a tarte aux fruits, and perhaps one of those croissants, and maybe another croissant, and a napoleon. Fidessa encouraged him to take as many as he liked. She must have been pretty sure he would accept her invitation: a box of fresh French pastries like these could not be cheap, and she didn't appear to be eating any of them.

Meanwhile, she was asking him questions. They were just inconsequential questions—Where were you born? What do you do for a living? What music do you like? Do you have a wife or girlfriend? Adam's answer to that last one was "No—I mean yes," which amused Fidessa enough to produce one of her subtle smiles.

"Ah!" she said. "A new girlfriend. How delightful for you. So many possibilities before you. So much hope. Do you not find hope exhilarating? Some day she may be your wife. But you do not know. You can imagine it, but it's uncertain. And that is why you hope, because it's not certain."

"How about you?" Adam asked between bites of his third croissant. "Married? Boyfriend? Girlfriend?"

"No," she answered; and though Adam waited (with a mouth stuffed with croissant) for her to say more, she had no more to say on that subject. And Adam was not willing to say that his heart leaped when he heard that she was unattached, because of course he already had a girlfriend (he forced himself to recall the feeling of her open mouth glued to his, but it seemed distant and indistinct); but he did feel some strong sensations in the chest area.

"These croissants are just about the best I've ever had," Adam remarked after what felt like a little too much silence. "I've eaten too many already" (gazing at the two left in the box), "but..."

"Don't deny yourself an innocent pleasure," Fidessa responded. "I bought these for you."

With an almost-shrug, Adam reached into the box and pulled out the penultimate croissant.

Meanwhile, Fidessa was still watching him with a keen eye. There was nothing impolite about her observation—Adam wouldn't have called it staring—but it did make him very much aware that he was observed.

"Tell me about the new girlfriend," she said just when Adam's mouth was stuffed with croissant and he couldn't answer right away. Was she taking note of his reaction? She showed no signs of amusement, but her gaze was still quite analytical.

Adam swallowed the croissant a little too hastily. "Her name is Rose. She's English—well, half-Jamaican, but grew up in Sussex, so I suppose she's as English as anybody else. She's a graduate student working on a doctorate in theoretical physics. And —by the way—how did you know she was 'new'?"

"Your first response was 'no,' suggesting long habit. Your immediate correction suggested that you did not consider it a debatable matter. Therefore, a new relationship, not established long enough to break your settled habit of answering 'no' to that question."

"You're a psychologist, too, I see."

"An artist who is not a psychologist had better paint barns, not portraits. Tell me—what do you see in her?"

Once again she had managed to ask the question just after he had stuffed his mouth with croissant. It was some little time before he could answer, during which she did not take her eyes off him. When at last he cleared his mouth for other duties, he still hadn't figured out what to say.

"Rose is...very nice. She's intelligent but not opinionated. She... she's an interesting person. We sort of took to each other right away. And of course it's very nice to have someone to go out with, since you were right—I went a long time between girlfriends."

"So you have good reasons." She emphasized the word "reasons" just slightly. Then she leaned forward and spoke just a little lower. "Does she make your heart soar?"

"It's very early in the relationship," Adam said. Did he sound defensive? Why hadn't he just said "yes"?

Fidessa leaned back again with a subtle smile and watched as he stuffed more croissant into his mouth. Then, as he was chewing, she asked, "Have you had sex with her yet?"

"That's a bit personal," Adam said with his mouth

full, only just managing not to spew croissant in front of him.

"I ask personal questions because I am interested in the person. You are under no obligation to answer them." She let him chew for a few seconds, and then continued: "No sex yet, but you feel as if the relationship has... potential."

It wasn't a question, which might have been infuriating coming from someone else. It was slightly disorienting and slightly impressive coming from Fidessa. Why did she know everything about him before he told her anything?

After the eating (and the coffee—she made very good coffee, almost as if she knew his weakness for the stuff) came the sitting. All that was required of him was that he sit. Fidessa excused herself for about two minutes, and then reappeared in a voluminous men's shirt that came down to just above her knees. Her calves and feet were bare; Adam couldn't guess what was under the huge shirt, though it was fun trying.

Fidessa began sketching directly on the canvas. It was like watching a dancer. Every stroke was itself a work of art. Adam couldn't see what effect her movements had on the canvas, but their effect on her body—even in an enormous smock that was practically a tent—was mesmerizing. She was silent for long periods while she worked, and then she would resume the conversation without changing the pace of her strokes—a flurry of short ones, and then some long, fluid sweeps, and then more fine work. She never got paint on the smock.

"Are you thinking of Rose right now?"

"Yes." He had not been thinking of Rose; he had been watching the play of a stray ray of sunlight that tumbled through one of the skylights and landed in Fidessa's hair, bringing out astonishing highlights of golden bronze in what had appeared to be pure silky black.

"I have a suggestion," she said.

He watched her dancing arms for a while before he realized that she was waiting for a response from him. "What's that?"

"You might present Rose with a unique gift. This portrait will be my best work, if I have my way. I'll never sell it. But when it's finished, I might make a single copy in a reduced size—one that you could give to your girlfriend." Something about the way she pronounced the word "girlfriend" suggested private amusement, but with her subtly non-native inflection it was hard to tell. "It would be something no other boyfriend has ever given her. Instead of a washed-out selfie to carry around on her phone, she would have a portrait of her boyfriend in oils. A portrait by one of the leading portraitists of the day, because this portrait will certainly be my masterpiece."

"You keep flattering me. It'll go to my head if you're not careful."

"I mean no flattery. Nor boasting, though the work will be mine. It is an artistic judgment, and I am capable of making it. But it will take work— from both of us. I will work on you, and you must allow me a certain freedom in getting to know you better."

"Of course," he agreed. The reciprocal necessity of his getting to know her better was very much in his mind.

"Meanwhile, you might want to avoid mentioning the portrait to your girlfriend."

Adam's eyebrows went up a little. Fidessa explained: "It will be a delightful surprise for her."

Wells that certainly made sense. He had a good reason for not telling Rose he was sitting for his portrait, didn't he? What a present it would make for her if their relationship prospered! But he would have to keep these sittings secret from her.

❧

Fidessa spent about two hours on the portrait, first with a charcoal pencil and then with a paintbrush, and even when there were long periods of silence Adam never wearied of watching her. Her movements were so elegant, and the woman was just so impossibly beautiful, that he couldn't keep his eyes off her. Only twice did she ask him not to move. For most of the time, he had no desire to move. He had a perfect view just where he was.

At last she announced, "We are at the end of our time for today"—although Adam could have sat for two or three hours longer just for the reward of watching her work. She stopped painting and started putting the equipment aside.

"May I see?" Adam asked.

"It is not finished," she told him. "In a sense it's hardly begun. But if you wish to see it…"

Adam stood—he felt a bit creaky after sitting in the same position so long—and walked around the canvas for his first look at what she had been doing.

Maybe it wasn't finished, but she could have framed it and called it done as far as Adam was concerned. There was no background yet, but it was the best rendition of his face he had ever seen. It was far better than any photograph—Fidessa must have been right about character eluding the camera. Every instantaneous picture he had ever seen of himself looked unfinished and wrong in comparison with the face on the canvas.

It was a pleasant face—not handsome, he wouldn't go that far, but not hard to look at. It was a face he was used to, at least, and he thought it looked like the face of the pleasant sort of young man he imagined himself to be. The shape was squarish, or rather mildly trapezoidal, tapering a bit toward the jaw. The forehead was broad and smooth, with almost straight eyebrows that shaded rather widely spaced grey eyes. The nose was the feature Adam had always criticized most on his face: it looked a bit unfinished, as if the sculptor had just roughed it in and never got around to the final shaping of it. He was absurdly disappointed to see that Fidessa had rendered his nose faithfully, but of course he couldn't ask her to do something else with it, could he? Below the nose was a broad and almost straight mouth, and then a chin that was almost equally broad and nearly flat on the bottom. Altogether a pleasant, open face, such as ought to belong to a pleasant, open young man.

"It's certainly the best picture of me I've ever seen," Adam said after a minute's examination.

"It's rubbish," Fidessa declared, startling him a little. "It's no good. But it is only the first sitting. I will make a work of art out of you yet."

Then she excused herself, leaving Adam to contemplate what she had called rubbish for two or three minutes. When she reappeared, she was in the black and-red sweatsuit again. Even though he lived only a few blocks away, she offered to drive him home; and she left him with an appointment to meet her at the studio at ten the next morning.

Adam looked at the clock when he came upstairs to his apartment. It was 3:29— just time enough to get ready for Rose. Rose—he thought hard about Rose, and tried to think thoughts of not-Fidessa.

Rose picked him up a little after four, and they took a long walk in the park, holding hands, stopping for a kiss once in a while, acting like the young lovers they were. The woods were bright with spring flowers, none of whose names Adam knew except golden alexanders, which he took pleasure in pointing out to Rose. It was a delightful scene: the late-afternoon sun cascaded through the bright new leaves and landed in ragged patches all around them. Could anything be more...nice? Surely as he got to know Rose better she would make his heart soar.

"How did it go with your artist friend?" Rose asked as they strolled hand in hand down the carriage path. Adam had convinced himself over the course of the stroll that his future lay with Rose, so he answered her as honestly as he could without spoiling the surprise.

"We spent a lot of time talking about art."

That pleasant English laugh again. "I might almost have guessed that. What kind of artist is he?"

Now here was another opportunity to be completely straight with Rose and remove all taint of dishonesty. "He's a she, first of all. A little Chinese woman who paints portraits of rich people." There was nothing dishonest in that description, was there? Fidessa was only a couple of inches above five feet tall, and if she weighed more than a hundred pounds it wasn't by much. Something in the back of Adam's mind told him that his description of her conveyed a false impression, but the rationalizing part of his brain pointed out that every word of it was strictly and literally true.

At any rate, Adam told her enough about his conversation with Fidessa to make it clear that he had only an intellectual interest in her—which was true, wasn't it? He had decided it ought to be true. So he told Rose as much as she needed to know, and he kept the secret of the portrait, and he kept open his opportunity to get to know Fidessa better.

After a light supper, Rose dropped Adam off at home and left him with another memorably active kiss. Then he retired for the night: he ended up in bed before ten, and he lay there thinking about Fidessa. That is, Rose. Rose was the one he should be thinking about as he drifted off to sleep. It was true that Fidessa was desirable. But so was Rose, wasn't she? Eightieth percentile, remember? And, after all, he couldn't have both of them.

Could he?

CHAPTER 13. THE BAKERY.

"ALL I can say," Hope said, "is that you're a glutton for punishment. Or just a glutton."

In addition to his usual. coffee, Adam had picked out a cinnamon roll as big as his head, which Hope believed would give him sugar poisoning or "lardosis" or some evil condition he would come to regret later in the day. "I call it 'hair of the dog,'" Adam told her. "I spent all weekend eating French pastries, and I need to let myself down gradually." He didn't mention that he had been up a good bit of the night before with an old-fashioned bellyache, the strange effect of which was that, now that it was gone, he positively craved more pastry.

"Oh!" Her face lit up with a suggestive smile. "Were you taking somebody out to breakfast?"

"Hm? —Oh, no, it wasn't with Rose. We haven't got to the, um..."

"So no sex. But that was what we expected. How did it go otherwise?"

"Oh, we had a very good time. Three times."

"Three?"

"Our dinner Friday night, and then a walk in the park and supper on Saturday, and then dinner again on Sunday."

"Adam! I'm impressed. Third, fourth, and fifth dates. If you were going by my list, you'd be ex-hausted this morning. But how far did you get with her? I want details."

"Isn't that...personal?"

That didn't work with Hope any better than it had worked with Fidessa. "Hey, I set you up with her. This is my commission. Pay up."

"Well, there's not much to tell. The breakup was pretty bad, I guess, and so she wants to go slowly. We've been holding hands a lot, kissing—"

"Tongue or no tongue?"

"Tongue," Adam said, though it felt a little like breaking Rose's trust.

"That's good. It means she wants more. You'll still be living together in six months—if you don't mess up. So you're right on schedule."

Adam leaned back thoughtfully with a mouth full of cinnamon roll. What a sensation that cinnamon roll was! It was a primitive, almost animalistic pleasure. For some reason it made him want to talk about Fidessa, which he knew would be a difficult subject to deal with without setting off Hope's alarm bells—her irrational fear that somehow Fidessa was opposed to Rose. When in fact Fidessa was doing him and Rose a favor, wasn't she? All these sentences that passed through his mind and got questions tacked onto the ends—it must be a British habit he was picking up from Rose, mustn't it? That meant he was thinking about her a lot, didn't it?

"You remember that artist I told you about?" As soon as he said it, Adam knew he had brought up the subject in exactly the wrong way. His brain called all neurons to battle stations.

"You're not still stalking her, are you?" Hope's eyebrows had lowered to an alarming degree.

"I wasn't stalking her!"

"Then why did you bring her up when we were talking about Rose?"

"Because she's going to help me do something nice for Rose, that's why."

The eyebrows were still low, like storm clouds hovering over the eyes. "Even on my list, that doesn't happen till the ninth date."

"Why do you always... *What's* on your list for the ninth date?"

"Focus, Adam. You were about to tell me how you weren't cheating on Rose with the sexy artist chick, in spite of all evidence to the contrary."

"Okay, listen. Do you promise not to interrupt me

again till I've finished explaining what's going on?"

"No."

"Fair enough." He took a gulp of coffee to prepare himself. "I got a text from Fidessa saying she wanted to meet at the museum Friday night. Well, I said no, of course, because Friday night I was going out with Rose, but—"

"Good instincts there, at least." The storm clouds were still hovering.

"So I said how about Saturday morning, and..." At this point Adam realized that he had fallen into his usual habit of making a short story long, so he cut out the middle twenty chapters. "Anyway, it turns out she wants to do a portrait of me. She's doing it, in fact."

"A portrait?" The eyebrows rose considerably, but Adam still found them frightening.

"It seems I'm the subject she was looking for to make her masterpiece." He couldn't help the little surge of pride that oozed through him as he said that. "So I've done two sittings already."

The eyebrows were back in the lowered position. Ice was forming on them. "Did she make you take off your clothes?"

"No! For the love of... She doesn't do that kind of portrait."

Some of the frost melted a bit. "I see. And you were going to tell me how this would somehow be good for Rose."

He fortified himself with another gulp of coffee. "Well, actually it was Fidessa's idea. I told her I had a new girlfriend. I told her I was hoping this relationship would really go somewhere. So she said she could do a copy of the portrait, and it could be my gift to Rose. You know, like instead of a washed-out selfie, she gets a portrait in oils. How many boyfriends can do that for their girlfriends?"

"Not many," Hope admitted...frostily.

"So that's the scheme. But don't tell Rose if you see her. It's going to be a surprise."

"Of course," Hope said in a voice that suggested not so much assent as the confirmation of all her suspicions. "So what was Fidelia—"

"Fidessa."

"What was she wearing during these 'sittings'?" Hope didn't make little quotation-mark motions with her fingers, but it was easy to hear the quotation marks in her voice.

"A big smock while she was painting."

"Smock. And this 'smock' wasn't lacy and sort of see-through, was it?"

"No!" He put down the coffee and picked up the cinnamon roll. "A big shirt, practically a tent. I thought it was men who were supposed to have dirty minds." He bit into the cinnamon roll, and it felt as though his whole body was formed to ingest cinnamon rolls. What simple, elemental, primitive pleasure!

"You don't know much about dirty minds if you think women don't have them." She leaned back, teacup in hand. "Oh, Adam... Smock, huh? Like in grade-school art class? I had sort of pictured her at the center of a web, dressed in black with red trim."

"She's not a spider, and she wasn't wearing... uh... Look, I'm not dating Fidessa, okay? I'm dating Rose. I'm Rose's boyfriend now—she's telling her friends that—and it makes me feel good. She's sweet, she's cute, she's everything you said she was. Now I have a chance to do something different for her, something unique, something—something worthy of her, if 'worthy' is the word I'm looking for. Can't you see she's special to me? You've won. For once you told me what to do, and I did it, and it worked out perfectly. That's the story. There's no hidden agenda."

There was a long interval of silence, during which the other incidental sounds of the Wild Beans invaded Adam's conscious mind—china clattering, the hum of conversations, the occasional loud hiss of the espresso machine. Hope's face, to the accompaniment of that atonal music, went through a very interesting thawing and softening. When she did speak, it was hard to tell whether her expression was registering acquiescence or pity.

"I do care about you, Adam. You know that, don't you?"

"Of course." He had a very strong desire to bite into the cinnamon roll again, but he put it off because Hope was looking so serious, and might expect a few serious responses from him before she was through looking serious.

She leaned forward, setting down the tea. "If you lied to me, I'd be worse than angry. I'd be disappointed." She leaned back again in the attitude of one who has had her say.

With relief, Adam picked up the cinnamon roll. "Of course I'm not lying to you," he said. "Not unless I'm lying to myself." He bit into the cinnamon roll at last.

❧

There wasn't anything on his calendar for Monday night: a graduate student has to be a student once in a while, so Rose regretfully told him she couldn't see him till Wednesday. That meant there was no reason to hurry home, which meant that, after a leisurely supper at a cheap little Lebanese place, Adam ended up wandering under the great iron arch just after sunset.

Once again the shades of purple and violet and indigo mixed with the shades of sodium-vapor streetlight to create a surreal world out of time. Monday night was not the busiest night on the avenue, but there were enough pedestrians to make the place seem lively without interfering with Adam's sense of being by himself. He thought of Fidessa—Fidessa whose studio was coming right up on the left, just past the...

Well, that was odd. And interesting. The pretzel shop downstairs from Fidessa's studio was gone. Instead there was a thing called "Le Gourmand," which was quite clearly a French bakery.

Adam was pretty sure it had still been a pretzel shop the last time he had seen the place, which was just the day before. But then maybe it hadn't been. Maybe he just hadn't noticed the change. And come to think of it, that must be where Fidessa had got those French pastries, mustn't it? And the place was still open right now, though it was past eight-thirty, and it occurred to Adam that it wouldn't be a bad thing at all to have some French pastry after a good Lebanese dinner. Given the colonial and culinary history of Lebanon, he might almost say it would be appropriate.

So he went in.

There was no one else inside, not even behind the counter. But the door had a little bell on it, so Adam was pretty sure somebody would appear soon. Meanwhile, what a beautiful display of really deca-

dent things to stuff in the mouth! Each thing behind the glass counter had a little handwritten card
beside it with its French name, which Adam could
read but not pronounce. He would probably have to
pick his choices by pointing at them. But doubtless
the baker was used to that.

"Bon soir, monsieur," said a musical voice above
him. Adam had been concentrating so deeply on
the array of perfect little pastries that he had not
even noticed someone appearing behind the
counter. He stood up from his kneeling position
and saw Fidessa.

"Oh! I didn't expect you here."

Fidessa spoke with a French accent, which was
too musical and attractive to be comical. "Apologies, monsieur. I was in the back, and did not hear
the bell. Mais how may I help monsieur?"

Adam smiled. "Your French accent is delightful."

"Monsieur is most kind. I should have said that
my English accent was, you would say, atrocieux."

She was looking at him with a fixed smile, the
kind of smile a professional gives a stranger to
make him feel welcome. There was something
strangely…strange about it. It suddenly occurred to
Adam to ask:

"You do recognize me, don't you?"

Which was a silly question, of course, because if
anybody should have his face completely memo-

rized by now, it was Fidessa. But she replied,

"Apologies, monsieur. I do not believe so. But you see we are new in the neighborhood."

This was obviously a peculiar sort of joke. Fidessa's style of humor was a bit too refined for Adam to appreciate. But she was still glorious to look at in her little black dress, and Adam could see no reason not to play along.

"I suppose I must have been mistaken," he said with a smile. "But I did think I knew your face from somewhere."

"Perhaps it was a dream. Déjà vu. And now would monsieur perhaps like to sample anything?"

"It all looks impossibly delicious: Do you have a suggestion?"

"Oh, I could not presume to know monsieur's taste. But I could put together a box for you. A sampler, with a little of this and a little of that."

Adam didn't need to think about that very long. "That sounds perfect."

"Bon. Un moment, s'il vous plait." She turned and picked up a very large pastry box, which she assembled as if she had been doing it all her life, and then began to stuff with every conceivable style of pastry. She had picked out at least a dozen by the time she was through—Adam wasn't counting, and the things were all different shapes and sizes. Then she tied the box up neatly with string and placed it in front of him, saying, "Bon appetit, monsieur."

"Thank you. How much do I owe you?"

"Oh, rien du tout, monsieur. Please accept it with our compliments."

"That's very kind, um, miss, but I couldn't possibly ask you to do that."

"Oh, but you did not ask. I insisted. You will try our best work, you see, and you will develop a weakness, yes? Then you will return."

"A weakness." He chuckled. "I think I've already developed a weakness."

She smiled one of those not-quite-tooth-baring smiles of hers. "Bien! Then we attack you at your weak point, yes? And we win the victory."

So Adam walked out of the place with a box full of sugar and fat, a little baffled by the game Fidessa had been playing but rather pleased with acquiring more expensive French pastries than he could possibly eat tonight at no cost to himself. And, after all, he had a refrigerator. He didn't need to eat everything right away.

He didn't eat everything when he got home, but he did eat four of the bigger ones right away, and the next morning he had three more for breakfast. He had definitely developed a weakness for French pastry.

Tuesday evening after work he had another sitting with Fidessa; and when he got to her door, he noticed that there was no French bakery. The pretzel shop was there again, looking for all the world as if it had been there the whole time.

FIDESSA greeted him upstairs in her usual American-accented but not-quite-native English, and she made no mention of the incident of the French bakery. It was very odd, Adam thought, that there should be a bakery one day and not the next—that a whole patisserie should just vanish overnight, leaving the world with no patisserie-shaped hole in it. And when Adam saw that there was another box of French pastries waiting for him (from which he immediately took a tarte aux fruits: an afternoon of digestive distress had made him resolve to go easy on the pastries for a while, but when the things were right there in front of him, gluttony easily defeated prudence), he had to ask the question, even if it would spoil whatever game Fidessa was playing.

"What was up with that French bakery downstairs?"

"Downstairs?" she asked with a very convincing

show of incomprehension.

"Last night, where the pretzel shop is."

She still looked confused. "It's only a pretzel shop."

"It must have taken a lot of effort to transform it just for a few hours," Adam went on, even though she was still playing the game, whatever it was.

Fidessa looked him straight in the eye with a very grave expression. "I think you must be mistaken. Perhaps it was a dream." Then she smiled and winked, and turned and walked out of the room without another word.

Adam was not at all sure what the rules of the game were. That it was a game of some sort hardly admitted of any doubt—but of what sort? It was an expensive game, surely. To set up a whole French bakery, complete with the pastries, would have to cost a fair amount of money. It occurred to him to wonder whether he had wandered into the middle of something—something he wasn't supposed to be in the middle of. But what kind of something? His brain almost overheated itself trying to imagine what kind of nefarious plot or criminal conspiracy could force a harmless artist to pretend to be a French baker. Was she hiding from someone? But there must be cheaper and more effective ways to hide.

No obvious conclusion had occurred to him—in

fact, not even an unlikely but remotely possible conclusion had occurred to him—by the time Fidessa reappeared in the same oversized shirt she had worn for their past two sessions. He wondered why she bothered with it: there wasn't a spot of paint on the thing, and the way she worked, with such absolute command of her tools that they would hardly dare disappoint her with any slovenly dripping or spattering, made Adam fairly sure that she could paint for the rest of her life without a spot of paint on the smock. Perhaps it was a badge of office—a warranty, like the studio itself, of her authenticity as an artist. At any rate, he asked her no more questions about the French bakery: one wink had closed off that subject conclusively.

So Adam sat in the same chair as before, and Fidessa arranged her tools as usual. Then, as the daylight was fading, she pulled a floor lamp away from the wall and set it a few feet to Adam's left.

"Tonight," she said, "we shall add shadows."

"Shadows are important, I suppose."

"Oh, very much so. The painter works with light, but the shadows give the light its character. Most painters begin with the dark colors, and layer on the lights. But I prefer to work in the opposite direction. When I begin, the canvas is white—the color of pure light. Each stroke of the brush is, in a manner of speaking, a shadow. I make my art by taking away light. When I say that I work with light, therefore, I really ought to say that I work against light." She gave him one of her enigmatic smiles. "I am an angel of darkness."

❧

Adam walked out of the studio after dark that evening. Fidessa had offered to drive him home again, but he thanked her and said he'd rather walk. It had been tempting to prolong his time with her by five more minutes in her Lexus, but he wanted some fresh air and exercise. He wanted to think. On his way out the door he glanced at the pretzel shop and confirmed that it was still a pretzel shop and not a French bakery at all.

Two questions were agitating his mind. Why did Fidessa lie to him—and then wink at him, as if she knew perfectly well that he knew perfectly well that she was lying to him? That was the first question. The second was this: why did the mystery of her unaccountable behavior make her seem so much more desirable?

Was she a dangerous woman? It seemed like an old-fashioned term: who says "dangerous woman" anymore? A woman with a machine gun is a dangerous woman; a woman who is armed only with some sort of private joke can hardly be called dangerous. To what would she be a danger? The image of Hope scowling across their favorite table in the Wild Beans rose unbidden in his mind. Hope would think that somehow Fidessa was a danger to Rose, or at least to his growing intimacy with Rose. But had Fidessa given him the slightest encouragement in that direction? No, she had not, Oh, yes, he still got that bottom-dropping-out of-the-stomach feeling every time he saw her, but that wasn't her fault, was it? And he was a grown man. He could control himself. His mind could control his heart, and any other organs affected by Fidessa.

But he had to admit that, if things had been different—if there had been no Rose—he would have been pursuing Fidessa with every weapon in his arsenal. Not that he had many weapons in his arsenal: that was his problem, wasn't it? But he would at least have been making himself miserable over Fidessa. He would have fallen in love with her, and doubtless would have been rejected, and what a blessing it was that he had found Rose before he fell off that cliff! And though there was some very primitive part of him that cursed the world for not letting him have both at once—the comfortable companionship of Rose, the visceral thrill of Fidessa—still, it was a fact that the world did not allow a man to have two women at once. A man couldn't have everything he wanted. Well, there were some men who seemed to get everything they wanted, and there were some women who seemed happy in unusual relationships, but... But it was impossible to imagine Rose as one of them. And just the fact that he had thought that thought, Hope would say, was what made Fidessa dangerous. But was Hope right about that? Was it really true that he should abandon the portrait and stop seeing Fidessa altogether just because he was having a few harmless fantasies? No, that couldn't be right. He was seeing her for art's sake, after all. It would almost be a crime against art to abandon her when she had put so much work into him. And if he found her entertaining to look at, well, that was all in his brain and had nothing to do with his relationship with Rose. He could have his Rose and keep Fidessa: that wasn't too much to ask of the world.

His brain received a message from his stomach at about this point in the progress of his internal monologue. The stomach politely requested that he lay off the French pastries for a while, and threatened dire consequences if its very reasonable request was ignored.

❧

Wednesday was a day of gastric regret for Adam. He had obeyed his stomach's admonition Tuesday night, but by Wednesday morning there were still French pastries in the refrigerator, and he was feeling fine, and his mouth demanded pastries, and his stomach registered no objection at the time, and that just went to show that his stomach was a shortsighted fool.

He recovered enough by evening to enjoy his date with Rose. They went to a string-quartet concert in Synod Hall, and then to coffee afterwards, and it was getting rather late by the time they were heading back to Rose's car, and then a thing happened.

It was one of those things you ought to expect when you have a new girlfriend, but Adam actually hadn't expected it at all. It had never happened to him before; possibly he had been lucky, or possibly he simply hadn't had much experience with girlfriends. He and Rose were walking along the sidewalk hand in hand, feeling as if the evening had been a great success (or at least Adam was feeling that way, and Rose gave every indication of being just as happy as he was), when a man called Rose's name.

She turned at once, and it was clear that she recognized the man, and that she was not necessarily pleased to see him. "Hullo," she said, and it looked as though she might say more but then thought better of it.

The man was a bit taller and a good bit more muscular than Adam was, and he had an intense sort of expression that didn't at all match the tentative words that came out of his mouth.

"You been all right?" he asked in a recognizably working-class Pittsburgh accent.

"I'm doing fine," she replied in a tone that suggested she was defying him to tell her otherwise, Adam had never heard such a hard edge to her voice before.

"That's good," he said. He was looking at Adam, and his eyes kept moving down to their joined hands. It looked as though he meant a lot more than what he said.

"I should introduce you," Rose said, in the sort of tone she might have used to say "I should eat this disgusting fungus." "Bradley, this is my boyfriend" (the emphasis on that word was unmistakable) "Adam Mueller. Adam, this is Bradley Hart."

Adam started to raise his hand for a polite handshake, but he could tell from Bradley's face that no handshake was going to happen.

In fact Bradley was pretty much ignoring him, as if he were merely some unpleasant sort of growth on Rose's hand. "So you got over it pretty quick, huh?"

"I wouldn't say that," she responded quietly, but

he didn't seem to hear her at all.

"I wish it was like that for me. I wish I could just take those two years and say, 'Oh, never mind.' I wish I could just move on and get on with my life."

"I'm not stopping you," Rose said in a tone that, to Adam, sounded hostile-bordering-on-dangerous.

"But that's not me. I'm not the kind of guy who just throws up his hands and says 'Oh well.' That's not what I'm like."

"It was nice seeing you, Brad," Rose said with deliberate finality, and she started pulling Adam along.

Bradley didn't follow, but his voice did. "Yeah, nice seeing you. Hope your life is working out just the way you wanted. Mine sure didn't, but whatever."

"Good night, Bradley," Rose called out without looking back.

"I haven't had a good night in two months," he shouted; and Adam thought he heard, much lower, a derogatory term for human females, but he couldn't be entirely sure.

Rose sighed a resigned and somewhat relieved sigh. "That was Bradley."

CHAPTER 15. REVENGE.

"SOD it!" Rose suddenly said to the night at large, and Adam was surprised to hear that tone from her. "Why do I still let him get to me? It should be 'Hullo, Bradley,' 'Goodbye, Bradley,' 'Have a nice life, Bradley.' I shouldn't feel like I've been punched in the belly."

Adam didn't quite know how to respond. He had never actually walked out on a relationship the way Rose had obviously done. He had always been the one who was walked out on. So he resorted to platitudes, which he found useful when he had nothing to say but something still had to be said. "Breaking up is never easy."

"No," she agreed. "No, it's not—but then I suppose staying with him was harder. You're so different to him, Adam. You're—you're cultured."

"Like buttermilk."

There was that pretty laugh again. "And you make me laugh. Bradley was all beer and football.

He laughed at crude jokes, or people falling down,
Can you imagine him sitting still for Debussy? You
know, that was the first classical concert I've heard
since I've been in Pittsburgh. Bradley mostly took
me to bars."

"What did you see in him?" As soon as the words
escaped his lips, Adam regretted them. "I'm sorry. I
shouldn't ask a question like—"

"No, really, it's all right. I suppose the answer is…
It was physical, wasn't it? I looked at him, and…
Well, I suppose I learned that a good body isn't the
thing to look for in—I mean, not that you don't
have a good body—oh, bloody hell."

Adam put his arm around her shoulder, and she
wound hers around his waist, and that took the
place of conversation for the rest of the short walk
to her car.

There wasn't much talking during the short drive
back to Adam's duplex—mostly because Rose
couldn't really talk and drive, but also because
Adam's mood was more somber than usual. It was
painful to see Rose in pain: she was usually so
cheerful. And it was painful to think that the old
boyfriend was a superior physical specimen. Adam
was no judge of men's looks, but he was pretty sure
Rose hadn't picked him for his physical form if
Bradley was her standard of comparison.

Rose stopped on the street almost right in front

of his apartment and turned off the motor, She kept her hands on the wheel for a moment, staring straight ahead; and she was still looking forward when she spoke.

"I really feel like going upstairs with you and having my revenge." She turned to face Adam. "But, on the other hand, I don't feel very... I feel angry, not..."

What did she want to hear? Another test, Revenge sounded like a good idea to him, but she liked him because he was—because he was better than Bradley. "I want it to be because you love me, not because you hate him."

She smiled and took his hand. "You know exactly the right things to say." Then she leaned over for a kiss.

Adam retired to his lonely apartment and spent the next few minutes wondering what it would have been like if he had persuaded her to take the revenge option. Then, opening the refrigerator, he caught sight of the last of the French pastries, and he ate them while thinking about Fidessa behind the counter of the French bakery.

❧

"Old boyfriend." Hope was waving a chunk of cinnamon roll as she spoke. "Well, sometimes old boyfriends can be useful. She might want revenge."

"I wouldn't take advantage of her that way," Adam declared in his very high-minded voice.

"Yeah, but you have to learn to recognize when a woman *wants* to be taken advantage of." She stuffed the chunk into her mouth.

"I told her I wanted it to be because she loved me, not because she hated him."

"Mamph!" She hastily swallowed far too much cinnamon roll. "You mean she offered you revenge and you turned it *down?*"

"Didn't you tell me those cinnamon rolls would give me lardosis?"

"I decided to try gluttony and see how it works for me. So you mean that Rose wanted to spend the night with you, and you said no?"

"I don't think she wanted to. I think she was just mad at the old boyfriend. So I thought she might resent me later if I took advantage of her."

"Well..." She leaned back and looked at him with her head tilted. "Well, that was either brilliant or really dumb, and I can't tell which. Like a lot of things you do."

"I thought I was behaving as a gentleman."

"Yeah, that sometimes works."

She sipped tea; Adam sipped coffee. It was hard for him to think of something to say when everything he said might possibly be wrong.

"Flowers," Hope said at last.

"Same to you."

"Next time you see her, bring her flowers."

"Another rose?"

"Make it a dozen. That should persuade her to put the perfect-gentleman interpretation on your behavior instead of the he-doesn't-find-me-attractive interpretation."

"Do women build these minefields into the dating landscape intentionally? Is it some Darwinian thing to weed out men not fit to be boyfriends?"

"Darwin has nothing to do with it." She pulled off an enormous chunk of the cinnamon roll. "The minefields are art, not nature." She stuffed the whole chunk into her mouth.

"I wish it could be simple. Maybe arranged marriages were best after all."

"I arranged as much as I could." At least Adam was pretty sure that was what she had said with her hand in front of her mouth full of cinnamon roll. "Your job is just not to mess up."

"But messing up is what I'm best at."

"Well..." She swallowed. "I hope you're not expecting an argument there."

❧

Adam's next appointment with Fidessa was that evening—a warm, summer-like evening that made him perspire a bit as he walked under the iron arch just before sunset. He checked the pretzel shop and made sure it was still a pretzel shop; then he pulled open the next door and walked into the narrow stairwell. Up to the second floor, with its unmarked doors that doubtless led into sad little offices, and then around and up to the third floor and into Fidessa's studio.

Fidessa was waiting as usual, with more of the pastries on the usual side table. She was dressed for the warm weather in black shorts and a red tank top, and it was all Adam could do to keep from staring at her perfect legs. They were only legs, he told himself: machines for conveying her from here to there—elegant, sculpted machines, masterpieces of form and function.

The floor lamp was already in place, and—after a lemon tart-thing and a napoleon and some coffee— Adam took his usual seat in his usual position. Fidessa disappeared as usual and reappeared in the usual smock, and the art part of the evening was under way.

Adam was positioned so that he pretty much had to look at Fidessa, so he might as well take advantage of the arrangement. He could admit to himself that he enjoyed looking at Fidessa. It was harmless fun; it had nothing to do with Rose, who was still his girlfriend. Probably Rose enjoyed looking at men with well-developed muscles, like that ex-boyfriend of hers, and she was entitled to that little indulgence, just as he was entitled to an eyeful of Fidessa when he had a natural opportunity.

"You enjoy watching me paint," Fidessa said, breaking into his reverie. It was unnerving how she seemed to be able to pick up his unspoken thoughts, as if he were broadcasting them on her frequency.

"I— Well, it's very interesting watching an artist at work. I've never had a chance to do it before."

Fidessa's expression didn't change. "I think it's a different kind of enjoyment."

She was dead right, of course, but what could Adam say? He wasn't going to tell her, "I get a cheap, harmless thrill out of looking at you." So he said nothing, in response to which Fidessa spoke again:

"Did you want a liaison? Is that what you were hoping for?"

All sorts of thoughts exploded in Adam's brain at once: "Liaison" is a very odd word that no native speaker would use in that sentence, I've given her the wrong impression, we're on dangerous ground here, what does she want to hear?, and—somewhere way in the back—yes.

"I have a girlfriend," Adam said.

"Oh, but that is scarcely relevant. Men do not stop wanting more because they have enough. Men are gluttons. So are women, frequently."

She put down the palette and brush and started walking toward him. No—toward the floor lamp. She raised it a little and moved it back a little.

"We need to make the shadows a bit deeper," she explained.

❧

Adam had a slight moment of embarrassment at the florist's shop: his debit card was declined, and he had to use a credit card. He told the clerk he didn't know what the problem was, but actually he had a pretty good idea: he'd been spending more money than usual lately, and he had emptied his checking account. He always lived from hand to mouth, and even the modest dinners with Rose had sapped his reserves quicker than he expected. If he was going to have a girlfriend, he might have to find some way of bringing in some extra cash. Meanwhile, he stopped off at the teller machine and transferred some money from his meager savings.

But the embarrassment was worth it, because the roses were a big hit. Rose insisted on keeping them in their vase on the table all through dinner. "You're such a perfect gentleman," she told him with a smile and a kiss, and Adam made a mental note to pay attention to Hope's dating advice in the future.

"I thought you needed some cheering up after Wednesday," Adam explained; and then he wondered why he was apologizing for the roses, as if they would be an embarrassing faux pas without a sufficient excuse.

Rose smiled. "I thought you'd be the one who needed cheering up. I know you…gave up a lot by being a perfect gentleman." She took his hand and squeezed it. "You're so right for me. I can't imagine Bradley doing that. I can't imagine Bradley taking me to hear Haydn and Debussy, or reading ancient philosophers. Or having an artist friend. Bradley wouldn't even know what to say to an artist."

"Artists are just regular people," Adam said, which felt like as close to a direct lie as anything he had told her about Fidessa. "It's just interesting to talk about art with someone who knows what she's talking about."

"Does she have any portraits of hers on line? I think it would be interesting to see one."

"I don't know." But, he thought, it would certainly be good if Rose could see one of those impeccably respectable portraits. It would make his whole relationship with Fidessa seem impeccably respectable.

"I'll text her and ask." Which he did right away, sending Fidessa a message that asked, "Any portraits of yours on line I could show my girlfriend?"

Then dinner came, and Adam forgot about the text while the conversation spiraled off in other directions, until a few minutes later when his phone chimed. "Oh—that must be Fidessa," he said. He pulled out the phone, unlocked it, and opened the text.

It was a title: "Self-Portrait, Reclining." A picture was attached. Adam tapped the link, and a picture filled the little screen.

"Did she have any pictures to show?" Rose asked.

"No," Adam answered, frantically pounding the home button until the picture disappeared.

BOOK IV.

CHAPTER 16. THAT PICTURE.

IT WAS art, so at least arguably it was not meant to excite lust; but still, the right thing to do, Adam was pretty sure, would be to delete that picture at once. Or perhaps to keep it on the phone until he had a chance to ask Fidessa what on earth she meant by sending it to him as a thing suitable for showing his girlfriend. Or perhaps any number of other possibilities. But he was pretty sure the right thing to do wasn't to email it to himself so he could gawk at it on the big screen at home.

Especially when things were going so well with Rose. She had left him that evening with another memorable kiss, and then told him, "It'll be soon, I promise. I want to go slowly, but I'm not a tortoise."

Now, if that didn't give him enough to think about for one night, what was wrong with him? Nevertheless, there was Fidessa's "Self-Portrait, Reclining," at full size on the 21-inch monitor in front of him.

The rationalizing part of his brain stepped in at once to save the day. He had already admitted to himself that he enjoyed looking at Fidessa, and he had already done a considerable amount of looking, and yet he had not had any trouble keeping it confined to looking, not acting. Furthermore, Fidessa herself had sent him this picture, which meant she definitely wanted him to see it, so it wasn't as though he was doing something that wasn't strictly aboveboard as far as she was concerned. In fact she had thought it would be suitable for sharing with his girlfriend. Obviously she was thinking like an artist, and it wasn't her fault that the rest of the world was a little more prudish in its view of the human body.

Yes, it was quite reasonable to look at this picture. In fact, since he had another appointment with Fidessa Monday night (she had decided that she wanted to paint in the evenings now, because of the shadows), it was almost an obligation. He would be asked how he liked it; he ought to have something intelligent to say. Something more intelligent than any of the things that were going through his mind right now, which meant that he would have to spend some more time studying the work in question.

Fidessa might also ask him how his girlfriend liked it, and there he had a problem. What would he tell her? If he said he couldn't show that kind of thing to his girlfriend, then it would suggest that he had seen the painting not as art, but as...something else. And yet it would be very hard to show that picture to Rose and say, "This is my artist friend Fidessa. Isn't she interesting?" Perhaps he could show it to Rose and say, "This is a painting by my artist friend," and see what that led to. But if Rose put two and two together—he had called Fidessa a little Chinese woman, hadn't he?—then what? He couldn't tell her it wasn't Fidessa; he didn't feel as though a direct lie would be appropriate, or even sustainable. Rose was likely to meet Fidessa eventually if he kept seeing both of them. And he was going to keep seeing both of them, because of course Rose was his girlfriend, and on the other hand he was working with Fidessa on a masterpiece that couldn't possibly be abandoned now. And besides, he couldn't give up the simple and innocent pleasure of looking at Fidessa. Especially not now —not after seeing this.

The picture itself was something extraordinary. Even with his limited understanding of art, Adam could see that. It was not exactly obvious what Fidessa meant by it, and there lay its subtle interest. Certainly it was not obscene: it was far too beautiful, too well done, to be obscene. One couldn't call it photo-realistic, because it was better than any possible photograph. It was more real, in fact; and it had that sense of character that defined all of Fidessa's portraits. Yet though it was not obscene one could hardly say that it didn't put Fidessa in her most attractive light. It was clearly meant to show her as desirable, and it was very explicit about what she evidently thought the viewer would desire. There was no modesty about it. One had the impression that she thought modesty was useless when she was aware of her own physical perfection in every aspect.

And so there was nothing for Adam to do but enjoy what she had given him, and assure himself that there was nothing more to it than that.

Saturday he spent another very pleasant afternoon with Rose just walking around town, seeing things she'd never seen before, trying food from street vendors, and ending with ice cream. This was the sort of pleasure Adam had always hoped for from a relationship, and while he was out strolling with Rose he seriously thought about deleting that picture as soon as he got home. But after Rose left him he was back at the computer, looking at Fidessa and thinking to himself how amazing it was that he could personally know such a perfect woman as that—a woman who thought nothing of displaying her perfection to him. He had never thought of the possibility that something like that would happen to him. It was a privilege not to be tossed away lightly. There must be some way to integrate Rose into this thing, whatever it was, that he had with Fidessa. When he saw Fidessa, he would ask her for a more conventional portrait to show Rose, a sort of painting with training wheels to prepare her for the full Fidessa experience by gradual stages.

Sunday Rose absolutely positively had to work on a paper she was writing or it would never get done and she might as well forget about that degree, so Adam was left alone. There were some very pleasant texts from her imploring him to think about her in her drudgery, and of course he did think about her when he got the texts, and about Fidessa much of the rest of the time.

Monday morning Hope grilled him about how the weekend had gone, and he was able to give her a very satisfactory account. He told her all about the stroll on Saturday, with descriptions of little out-of-the-way shops and an especially rhapsodic tribute to the ice cream.

"And how are things progressing physically?" Hope asked, which was just the sort of thing she would ask.

"Well, she's a very good kisser," Adam said.

"That's it?"

"She says it will be soon. She says she wants to go slowly, but she's not a tortoise."

"That sounds promising. Just make sure you're ready."

"I'm pretty much always ready."

"I'll bet. But you know what I mean. And make sure you make her feel like she's special, like she's the most beautiful woman in the world, even before the time comes, because, trust me, that'll make the time come faster."

"How do you make a woman feel like she's the most beautiful woman in the world?"

Hope gave him another of her I-pity-you-for-being-you looks. "You could try telling her that."

"I don't…" He stopped, because he was just about to say "I don't want to lie to her," and he realized just in time that he wasn't supposed to say that. "That's trite, isn't it? I mean, everybody says that. She won't believe me, will she?"

"Everybody says that because everybody wants to hear it. Look, you've had a girlfriend before, right? Once upon a time? If she told you you were the world's greatest lover, did that offend you? Did you think, "Well, I guess I don't want this one, because she's an awful liar"? Or did you love to hear it no matter how often she said it, no matter how much you thought she must be exaggerating, no matter how much your brain told you, 'Well, I can't possibly be the greatest in the world, right?' "

"Yeah, top twenty, maybe, but not greatest in the

world. But you're right. I can tell her more about how beautiful I think she is."

"And keep it simple. Use words she can understand."

"We both speak English, you know."

"Rose speaks English. You speak pedantic philosopher. Sometimes you have to translate what you say so it makes the right impression. You can trust me on this."

"I'll do my best."

She gave him that look with the lowered brows that always made him feel more than a little uneasy. "You'll have to do a lot better than that."

❧

Monday was Fidessa night, and he wasn't quite sure what to do about that. He would go, of course, but what would he say to her? Would he mention the picture right away, or would he wait for her to bring it up? He didn't want to make her think he was offended, because by this time the picture had already become one of his most treasured possessions. On the other hand, he didn't want to leave the subject untouched. Or maybe he did. The difficulty was that he wanted her to know he had responded favorably, but maybe it wasn't quite exactly what he had asked for, and he didn't want her to think he was offended, but he didn't want to have to say he couldn't show it to Rose, but he didn't want her to think it was the sort of thing he had wanted to show Rose. In other words, he had no idea what he wanted her to think, because he didn't know what he thought himself. He still didn't know what he was going to do when he arrived at Fidessa's studio (the pretzel shop was still incontrovertibly a pretzel shop, by the way), so he ended up saying nothing and eating a couple of French pastries in near-silence. Not until he was seated in the usual chair, with the lamp casting its shadows across his face, did the subject come up. And then it was Fidessa who brought it up:

"So how did your girlfriend like the self-portrait I sent you?"

Adam took a good while to formulate a reply, during which Fidessa was painting furiously, as if she had to capture something before it disappeared.

"I didn't show it to her," he said at last.

"Ah," Fidessa replied, without sounding at all surprised. The painting slowed down now to a few slow, short strokes.

Adam was silent. He had planned on explaining why, although nothing could be more artistic than that painting, still he didn't feel as though it was the sort of thing one should show one's girlfriend to introduce her to the idea of one's having a friend who was an artist. But he couldn't think of any way of putting it that didn't make him sound like either a prude or a ditherer.

It was no problem for Fidessa. She would speak when she wanted to speak. At the moment, she seemed to be happy with the effect she had produced, because the slow, short strokes continued for some time.

The silence was long enough that her next question startled Adam slightly. "Did you think it would make her jealous?"

"Um," Adam said, and it was a long time before he could think of something to go after that "um." Fidessa was patient; she would wait and make use of the expressions that probably were passing across his face from moment to moment, even though he was doing his best to sit still with a neutral expression. At length he decided to tell her something like the truth, insofar as he understood the truth. "I thought it would come as a bit of a surprise to her, I guess you could say. I told her I had an artist friend who did portraits of rich clients, which is what you told me after all. I don't think she was expecting to see something like...that."

"It was the only portrait of mine that I was really proud of," Fidessa told him without slowing down the movement of the brush and colors. "Until this one is finished, it may be my only work of real art."

"Well, it was very skillful. And artistic. The composition was... I guess what you'd call it is... diagonal. And I realize that the artist sees the human body differently. I'm sure for you it's a matter of abstract beauty, not eroticism."

"You didn't find it erotic?"

"Uh," Adam said, because at least it was some variation from "um."

"I meant you to find it erotic."

"Then why did you send it when I said I wanted to show it to Rose?"

"I meant her to find it erotic, too." The pace of the painting was picking up again.

"I don't think she's..." Adam didn't bother to finish the sentence, because his mind was getting away from him.

"I do not believe in ignoring the sexual, or pretending that it is something else. You find me beautiful. I do not pretend that it is an aesthetic judgment; I know it means you desire me. Very good. We have a truth before us, and it informs my art."

Adam was at the point in this conversation where he instinctively felt that silence served him better than any attempt at speech.

"Art tells us the truth about ourselves. Some truths are too deep for words. My picture told you something about yourself. It might tell you something about your girlfriend. That was what I was thinking."

"Well, I..." Adam thought he ought to say something, but words were not coming out of his mouth.

Fidessa stopped painting for a moment. She seemed to reach a decision; she walked slowly and deliberately toward him until she was standing right in front of him; then she bent down and gave him a very chaste and friendly kiss on the cheek. Then she walked back to her painting.

"What was that for?" Adam asked.

"For atmosphere," she replied. "Oh, tomorrow we are going to add some very interesting colors."

CHAPTER 17. A PARTY.

TUESDAY evening, just after work, Adam's phone rang. He stopped on the sidewalk and pulled it out of his pocket, but then couldn't think of what to do from there, because it was Derrida-woman calling. He looked at her name in a kind of moral paralysis, and eventually it was too late to answer, and doubtless she was leaving another voice mail, and he really ought to listen to it as soon as it was ready. And there it was, the voice-mail chime; but he was standing on a sidewalk where other people might want to walk, and he shouldn't make an obstruction of himself, so it would be better to wait until he got home. And when he did get home he needed to eat something, though only a light snack because there would be French pastries at Fidessa's studio, Then, though there was still some time before he had to meet Fidessa, Adam suddenly found himself appalled by the condition of his apartment. He spent half an hour on a whirlwind cleanup that improved the place a good bit: when Rose was ready, she wouldn't be disgusted. Then he took a short rest and looked at Fidessa's self-portrait again, which was a very reasonable reward for the productive work he had done; and if it incited him to lust, it was a harmless, abstract lust that had no bearing on his relationship with Rose. And then—how time flew!—it was time for him to walk over to Fidessa's studio, so philosopher-girl would have to wait until he was done with his sitting.

It was a warm night, summery and humid, but the breeze was beginning to pick up. The sky was overcast, and by the time Adam reached the iron arch a dull purple twilight had spread like a blanket over the whole landscape. He reached the door to Fidessa's studio (the pretzel shop was still a pretzel shop), opened it, and stepped into the stairwell.

Muffled music was coming from upstairs—the bass line sounded slow and sultry and Latin, very appropriate for the weather. Someone must be having a party behind one of those nondescript doors on the second floor. Adam walked up the stairs, not looking up until he had reached the landing; and then he saw, waiting for him, on the second floor, Fidessa.

He could never see her without the bottom dropping out of his stomach, but the sensation was particularly violent this time. This was not Fidessa as she normally appeared for one of their sittings. This was Fidessa dressed to kill, or at least to maim, in a short red dress that was cut to show off the best aspects of her figure. Those perfect legs were right at eye level as Adam ascended the stairs. He tried not to gawk, but the dress was calculated to inspire gawking.

When Adam reached the second floor, Fidessa touched his forearm lightly and stood on her toes to give him a kiss on the cheek. "I decided to take a break from just sitting," she said. "So I brought in a few friends for a party."

"A party," Adam repeated. "If I'd known, I'd have—"

"You're perfect the way you are. I told you I need to come to know you better. Your full character can't reveal itself when you just sit in a chair. So we bring your character into a new situation, and perhaps new aspects reveal themselves to me."

She took his arm in a friendly sort of way (so there was no reason for Adam to find the mere touch of her fingers so thrilling) and led him to one of the nondescript doors, behind which he could hear a female voice singing some slow ballad in Portuguese.

"And I think you'll like some of my friends," she said as she opened the door and let some of the music out.

Behind the door was a rather larger room than he had expected. About two dozen people of all sorts were there, but the crowd was heavily skewed toward attractive young women—that was Adam's first impression. If she wanted to see his full character, Fidessa might have made a strategic error: the presence of multiple attractive women tended to make Adam withdrawn and stammery.

"Have a drink," Fidessa said, and as she said it a drink moved toward him in the hand of a particularly good-looking blonde whose dress could almost compete with Fidessa's. He took the glass with a quiet "Thank you."

"This is my friend Lilith," Fidessa said. "Lilith, this is Adam, the model I was telling you about."

Lilith gave him a very-impressed look. "I see what you meant," she said to Fidessa without taking her eyes off Adam. And then to him: "She's told us so much about you."

"Pleased to meet you," Adam said, and he realized his voice was very nearly inaudible.

"Now, you'll have your chance, Lilith," Fidessa said, "but I have to show him off to somebody else first.—Come with me, Adam. I've been wanting to make this introduction ever since I met you." She steered him to the other side of the room, where, in a corner under a Tiffany lamp that cast a mellow dim light on deep red walls, a middle-aged man with a striking pointed Vandyke and remarkably bushy eyebrows was holding court. That was the word for it: he was surrounded by half a dozen beautiful young women and two or three indistinguishable young men who seemed to hang on his every word. As Adam approached, he could hear the bursts of approving laughter—it was that peculiar laughter of approval that some intellectual sycophants bestow on their idols.

"Adam," Fidessa said as the crowd parted (she seemed to be the acknowledged authority here, something greater than a hostess and more like a cult leader), "this is Professor Nicholas Brent. Professor Brent, this is Adam Mueller, the man I was telling you about."

"Pleased to meet you," Adam said, and even as he spoke he was conscious that, as if they had caught some mysterious signal from Fidessa (he hadn't noticed it, whatever it was), all the young people surrounding the professor were moving away.

"Ah! So this is your model," the professor said with every evidence of delight. "She's told me a good bit about you, and I've been very interested to meet you."

"Professor Brent is an experimental psychologist, a well-known specialist in his field," Fidessa said with clear approval, the kind of approval that suggested she thought he was almost as worthy as she was herself.

"And what is your field, professor?" Adam asked, since it seemed to be expected.

"Sex," he answered. And then, after a moment, he laughed heartily. "I love saying that and watching people's reactions! It's like an ongoing experiment with the mechanics of a practical joke. It appeals to my curiosity and my sense of malicious fun."

"I'll leave you two to get acquainted," Fidessa said, and she moved off, leaving Adam's arm feeling uncomfortably naked without her.

"Malicious fun?" Adam asked. "Is that why people study psychology?"

"Oh, well, of course there are many reasons to study psychology. But, yes, malicious fun is one of them. One not often advertised to would-be students of the science, or perhaps we might get a better caliber of students." His glances around the room suggested to Adam that at least some of the other guests might be some of the students he was talking about.

Adam was not quite sure what one talks about with a world-famous student of sex. "So what do you find with your ongoing experiment?"

"Oh, well, you know how people are. The whole subject of sex in our society is surrounded by a veritable stockade of taboos. Even the mention of the word 'sex' raises your automatic defenses, doesn't it? You stand here in front of me—and, by the way, pull up a chair, won't you?—and think to yourself, 'What do I talk about with a sexologist?' And you wonder what I think when I look at you. You wonder whether all your secret fantasies are as clear to me as headlines in a newspaper. They aren't, by the way. Like most students of psychology, I spend most of my time with boring statistics. I can tell you what the probability is of your having a particular kind of fantasy, but I can't tell you that you do have it. I can tell you that none of yours would surprise me, but I can't tell you in what way I wouldn't be surprised. In fact, there's only one thing I can tell you about your fantasies."

He had paused in such a way that he obviously wanted to be asked the question. So Adam obliged him: "What's that?"

"Some of them involve Fidessa."

"What makes you say that?" Adam asked with what he himself recognized as a nervous chuckle.

"Everyone who knows her has fantasies about her." The professor smiled. "I certainly have them. And it doesn't take a deep knowledge of human nature, or a pile of dry statistics, to notice how you melt when she touches you. I think 'melt' is about the right word, don't you?"

"I, um—" Adam knew he wasn't coming across as a scintillating intellectual here, but he forged on: "I have a girlfriend, you know."

"Oh, monogamy!" the professor said with a dismissive wave. "The bane of our existence, but a full-employment program for psychotherapists. All our neuroses stem from this curious Neolithic notion that a man should be a woman's exclusive property, and vice versa. How we ever took it into our heads to impose absurd limits on ourselves like that is a mystery beyond even my specialized knowledge. But I can tell you that the idea isn't healthy. It infects all of us—even me—but it's a disease, and the sooner we recognize it as such, the sooner we can cure it."

"So you're looking for a cure for monogamy?"

The professor laughed. "Well, in a manner of speaking, I might say I've found it. And you can find it too, I think. Fidessa thinks you're a very intelligent man—intelligent enough, I'd say, to come up with the cure for monogamy without my help."

"Well," Adam said—still a bit nervously, because there was something about this professor that made him a little uncomfortable—"I suppose as a matter of logic, the cure for monogamy would be...infidelity."

"No," the professor said very definitely. "The idea of 'infidelity' presupposes monogamy. If you even use the word 'infidelity,' you are suffering from the disease. The cure for monogamy, of course, is pleasure. Where you find it, when you want it. It's a thing we can all understand, but we insist on making the question uselessly complex."

"So you mean it's not infidelity unless you take fidelity as the norm," Adam said. He thought to himself that taking fidelity as the norm didn't sound as unhealthy as all that, but then he wasn't a famous psychologist.

"Yes. Fidessa was right: you are intelligent. I know because you agree with me. She also said you were very attractive. I'm no judge of that, because you're not my type. But you're apparently hers."

"Oh," Adam said. And then he couldn't think of anything else to say.

"And all I can say about that," the professor concluded with a wink, "is that you're a very lucky man."

Adam thought he ought to have something clever to say in reply, but the epigram generator wasn't working. So he took refuge in his drink, which was really very good—a mimosa, obviously made with very good champagne and fresh orange juice. It was very easy to drink, and just the first sip turned out to be more like a gulp.

"Of course," the professor added after that interval of silence, "if she's not to your taste…"

"I never said that," Adam replied instantly.

CHAPTER 18. THE STORM.

ADAM had always thought of himself as the sort who didn't like parties. But that might have been because he had always gone to the wrong kind of party. This party was what a party ought to be: it was small enough to be manageable, it had music loud enough to enjoy without making conversation difficult, and it was well stocked with beautiful and apparently unattached women. He was still feeling a little wary about that last part, because he didn't want to betray Rose (although it was true that monogamy was hard to justify in the modern world, from a philosophical point of view); but he could hardly say he wasn't enjoying that aspect of the gathering.

And mimosas. Adam had always associated mimosas with Sunday brunches and croquet on some rich old lady's lawn, but they were just perfect for this kind of party. He didn't know exactly how much he had been drinking, because every time his glass got to the halfway mark Lilith appeared by his side, filling it from a pitcher.

"Are you one of Professor Brent's students?" Adam asked her when she appeared with her pitcher yet again.

She carefully topped off his glass. "In the day-time, yes."

"And what are you in the evening?"

"I'm an escort."

"Oh." Once again he had paddled out into much deeper conversational waters than he had expected.

"But tonight's my night off." She gave him a sly smile. "So anything I do tonight is on my own time."

"Must be..." He took another gulp of the mimosa. "Must be interesting work."

"Oh, yes. Professor Brent says it's the perfect laboratory."

"Hm," Adam said, and he took refuge in the drink again, which somehow had been refilled one more time since he last took a gulp from it. As soon as he lowered the glass, Lilith refilled it.

And then there was the pretty redhead who was a tattoo artist, whose body was her sample case. And there was the dark beauty from India who was a sculptor, and simply had to feel his face out of pro-fessional interest. And there was the lovely chest-nut-haired guitarist who was sure he must have undiscovered musical talent, just from the sound of his voice. There were men here and there, too, but —except for the professor—they seemed to serve mostly to occupy those unfortunate women who were not currently having their turn with Adam.

Warm fingers landed on his arm, and Fidessa was beside him again. He melted.

"Are you enjoying yourself?" Fidessa asked. Yes, Lilith was something to look at, but only Fidessa could make the bottom drop out of his soul like that.

"Oh, yes," Adam answered. "These momeesas are very good, by the way."

"Dance with me?"

Adam was about to tell her that he couldn't really dance; but then, thinking carefully, he decided that he probably could dance if he put his mind to it. So he allowed her to lead him to the middle of the room, and then she poured herself into a dancing position that maximized the contact of her body with his, and the two of them started moving to the slow Latin beat of the music. And it was absolutely true that Adam could dance if he put his mind to it, since dancing Fidessa's way was a matter of a tight embrace with just enough movement to be graceful on her part and not clumsy on his. It was just as well that it wasn't more vigorous, because Adam wasn't feeling very stable at the moment.

The position put Fidessa's lips at about shoulder

level below Adam's ear, a good position for quiet conversation that she almost immediately made use of.

"You made a strong impression on Lilith." The rich undertones of her voice sounded like another line of counterpoint in the music.

"How do you knew—uh, know?" It was possible that he had drunk just a little too much of that mimosa stuff.

"I might enjoy my little joke by telling you that we women have our ways. But the truth is that she told me. She finds you very attractive."

Yes, he longed to say, but how can I think of her when...you? And another part of his brain was saying "Rose," but his whole body was saying "Fidessa."

"So do the others," she continued. "You're a sensation." Her head tilted upward, so that her lips were that much closer to his ear, and she could speak even lower: "You could have any woman in this room."

A nervous chuckle escaped him before he could clamp down on it. "I think you're exaggerating."

"Any woman in this room," she repeated; and then, raising her head even higher, so he could feel the hot breath on his ear, "without exception."

The heat of her breath, the heat of her body, the languid movements of the dance, the rich Latin rhythm of the music—and yet the rational brain still managed to force one sentence out through his mouth: "I have a girlfriend."

She hardly spoke, or even whispered; it was more like an articulate breath. Yet he could hear every word: "I don't think that's relevant."

Adam didn't reply, but his brain was working hard. It was not as easy to think as it should be; it might be that the mimosas were too intoxicating, or it might be that Fidessa was. He kept dancing with her for a minute or two longer, until she stopped moving and whispered, "Come with me."

Now she was leading him toward the back of the room—past tattoo-girl, who winked at him—to a door, which she opened, and then through the door to a small bedroom.

The door closed, muffling the music and conversation on the other side, and Fidessa led him to the bed. With a gentle push from her he was sitting on it.

"What are you doing?" he asked, while another part of his brain prepared the Stupid Question of the Year award for him.

"Getting to know you better," she replied, and she bent down to kiss him on the cheek.

"I'm not sure I should—"

"Don't deny yourself an innocent pleasure." She sat beside him, and now her hand was on his thigh and her hot breath in his ear. "Would you like me to

ask Lilith to join us?" The hand was moving down
toward his knee ever so slowly. "You can have everything you want, Adam. All that you desire. And
the only thing that stops you...is you."

"It's very tempting, and, uh..."

"Temptation implies resistance. It's not temptation if there's no reason to resist."

Then she kissed him on the cheek again and
stood up.

"Wait here," she said, and she oozed through the
door that Adam guessed led to a bathroom.

He had to think, but it was hard. Thoughts
weren't thoughting themselves, and he was feeling
light in the head. There must have been somedrink
in that thing. A mimosa seemed like a very inocu-
lous thing, but there were two species of mimosa
that he could remember, Mimosa pudica or sensitive plant, and Mimosa somethingelsica, the tree
mimosa, which might not be a mimosa at all, and—
focus. Rose. If— He knew he wanted Fidessa, but
Rose. Rose, his girlfriend. By any other name. Rose
Rosa, a diverse genus. Rosa multiflora was the only
species he knew, because he really wasn't a
botanist, but now that he thought of it he remembered Rosa rugosa, the wrinkled rose, but Rose
wasn't at all wrinkled, but oh! what a perfect face
Fidessa had, and the rest of her—the rest—it really

not was a good idea to drink so many mimosas in a row, row, row, gently down the stream.

❧

Thunder; a flash, and more thunder, and it was loud and close. And there was the sound of hard rain outside.

Adam was aware that he was waking up, but it didn't seem at all fair. No one should have to wake up, least of all someone who felt like this.

In the dim light, he took stock of his surroundings. He was lying on his stomach on a bed in a small bedroom with a sash window to his right. He didn't have a shirt on, but there were pants. His joints seemed to ache. His stomach didn't feel very settled at all. There was an annoying itch he couldn't reach right between his shoulder blades, a sort of burning itch, like a rash, and it just figured that it would have to be where he couldn't reach it, didn't it? And his head hurt like anything.

Standing up would be a good idea, but later. Right now, he was remembering things. Fidessa—Fidessa beside him in that dress that exposed more than it covered, Fidessa about to change his life. Did he sleep through the central experience of his existence?

Where was she now? The thunderstorm was raging outside, but he couldn't hear any party going on. What time was it? No clock. Cell phone? In his pocket; he would have to move to get it.

Moving was worse than he had anticipated, but he did manage to retrieve the phone at last. It showed the time as 2:56. He must have been asleep for at least four or five hours.

Then she must have let him sleep, which was decent of her in some ways, and the question was how much he had done before he collapsed. His state of partial undress suggested he hadn't got very far, but he couldn't remember anything at all after she left the room. He remembered the rear view of her vividly, and then—nothing.

Experimentally he tried sitting up. The results were not pleasing; his head split right down the middle and all his brains fell out in his lap. Well, not quite; apparently that was only what it felt like, because when he put his hands on the side of his head to press it back together, he couldn't discover any openings that shouldn't be there. He sat for a minute and a half just holding his head together, and then he decided he would have to stand up.

Standing up was just as bad as sitting up, with the addition of a very real danger of failing down again. Once he felt stable enough to move, he made his way toward the door, supporting himself with walls and furniture. An exceptionally loud clap of thunder startled him enough that he almost lost his balance; but he recovered and opened the door.

The big room beyond was empty and clean. Not only had the guests gone home, but someone had been through and meticulously straightened up the place. so that there was no evidence left that there had ever been a party at all.

Only now did he remember that he still didn't have a shirt on. He would have to go back into the bedroom, which seemed like an improbably arduous journey, and find his shirt. And his head was still aching, and his legs were still wobbly, and his back still itched in an inaccessible place, and his brain was still full of cotton candy where neurons should be. But he did find the shirt: it was folded neatly on a dresser in the bedroom. He applied all his mental and physical resources to the task of getting it back on.

And then what? Fidessa was nowhere to be seen, so he ought to find her and—well, and apologize to her, because pretty much no matter what he had done last night it required an apology. Either he had gone way too far or he hadn't gone nearly far enough. And if Fidessa wasn't here, that probably meant she was upstairs in her studio, because of course she wouldn't just leave him.

But after the arduous ascent of the stairs—he had been able to make it only by inhaling his fill of oxygen at the base camp, and then pausing for a while to establish another temporary camp on the landing—he found no Fidessa. She didn't answer when he knocked on the door, and so he tried the door and found it unlocked, and explored the whole studio—for the first time seeing the back room where she stored prepared canvases and neatly organized supplies—but there was no Fidessa. The portrait of him she had been working on was nowhere to be seen; she must have put it away somewhere, but there was no evidence of it anywhere he looked.

And no Fidessa. As far as he could tell, he was alone in the whole building, which was not at all what he had expected. Fidessa was too well organized to forget about him.

It occurred to him suddenly that he had a cell phone. It was a consoling thought: the building might be empty, the thunder might be rumbling— more distant now, but still occasionally startling him with its violence—but in spite of the Gothic desolation of the scene, he was not alone, because the world was in his pocket. He could text Fidessa, and she would let him know where she was. And then he could apologize.

There were two texts waiting for him when he unlocked the cell phone. One was from Rose, just before midnight: "Good night, thinking of you," and three hearts. The other was from Fidessa, and it said it had come in at 10:07. "Sorry I couldn't make it for our sitting. Unavoidably detained. See you Thursday."

What?

Adam's brain couldn't process it. Two things were going on in his mind, two processes, each of which demanded all his processing power. What was the meaning of that text from Fidessa—as if she hadn't been at the party at all, as if she had thought he would be wondering where she was at seven past ten, when he distinctly remembered she was pressed close to him and moving slowly to a Latin beat? And then there was the other constant loop: What had he done to poor Rose?

He had to get home. He had to get out into the open air, even if it was raining, and think, if thinking was possible. He headed for the stairs and trotted down them, almost losing his footing three or four times, until he was at the front door. But it was locked, and the lock worked only with a key. He was locked in. Was this up to fire code? Was it legal? Then he remembered that there was a door to the back alley. He staggered back that way and found the door unlocked. As quickly as he could, he opened the door and burst through it into the rain and wind.

He was drenched almost immediately, but he was

outside. He looked right and left, orienting himself, and forced himself to remember that home was to the left.

He took one step in that direction, and his foot sank into a pothole filled with mucky water, and he lost his balance, and he fell forward, just barely breaking his fall with his hands, and he landed with a splash in the mud and muck at the edge of the alley. And now his hands hurt, too, and he was wet and filthy, and for the next several minutes he just sat there and wondered why something in the back of his brain kept saying, "Serves you right."

CHAPTER 19. PLAN B.

THE rain washed off some of the muck as Adam walked home, but not all of it. The mud and mire had penetrated every fold of his clothes; he had only just rescued his cell phone from the ill effects of it. The storm lasted long enough to soak him through to the skin, but not long enough to get him clean.

But the rain was sobering. It pelted him awake with relentless cold pounding on his face. By the time it stopped, Adam felt his head clearing, and thinking was possible again.

Possible, but not productive. He alternated between blaming Fidessa for leaving him alone and blaming himself for—what? Had he betrayed Rose by giving way to his own unreasoning lust? Or should be blame himself instead for being too drunk to enjoy his favorite fantasy?

By the time he got home, Adam was alert but exhausted. And filthy. He went straight to the bathroom, flung his clothes in a pile, and took a long hot shower. Then he fell in bed and slept.

He woke to the sound of his alarm, which apparently had been going off for an hour and a half. He wasn't going to make it to work on time, obviously, and he still felt dreadful. So he called in sick and told his boss it was "probably some twenty-four-hour thing," which was vague enough not to feel like a lie. His boss told him he sounded awful and should take care of himself. With a feeble "Thank you" (Was he exaggerating the feebleness for dramatic effect? Maybe), Adam hung up and turned over to go back to sleep.

But sleep didn't come back. He lay there tired and miserable—his head still hurt, his back still itched, the scrapes on his palms were sore, and his stomach was now demanding food that he was pretty sure it would reject as soon as the food went down.

And he was angry—angry at himself, and possibly at Fidessa. At least she owed him an explanation for leaving him alone like that. He texted her —"Where did you go last night?"—but hadn't got an answer after half an hour. Meanwhile the details he did remember kept coming back to him. He had come very close to being unfaithful to Rose. He might actually have done it if he'd had the opportunity. Who was he kidding? He would certainly have done it if he hadn't passed out. It would not have been possible to resist Fidessa. It would hardly have been possible to resist her friend Lilith. If they had attacked him on two fronts...

He shouldn't be thinking those thoughts. But nothing like it had ever happened to him before. The most desirable woman he had ever seen desired him.

Was that professor—the fellow with the beard like a cartoon Satan—right about monogamy? Maybe so. Adam couldn't recall any of the arguments against monogamy; he could recall only the sensation of being convinced by them.

But dishonesty was another thing. Wasn't it? He didn't think it could possibly be right to lie to Rose, even if all the professor's arguments against monogamy were sound. And Rose seemed like the kind who wouldn't approve of cheating. Of course it wasn't cheating if they agreed to an open relationship. But how likely was that? How do you bring up the subject in the first place? "I really like you, but I've found this girl who's a lot sexier than you, so if you don't mind..." That probably wouldn't work.

But if he was going to burn up with lust, then why shouldn't Rose be the one to put out the fire? Maybe his problem was simply that he hadn't been with a woman in so long. That must be it. The first woman who offered him what he wanted was bound to get his attention. But if he could get what he wanted from Rose, then surely he wouldn't burn for Fidessa anymore.

He was angry at Fidessa for leaving him alone last night—and the whole cycle of thoughts repeated itself. He tried calling Fidessa, but she didn't answer, and a generic recorded female voice said that her voice mail was full. So around the wheel of thoughts he went again, feeling overwhelmed by lust for Fidessa, wondering whether he could somehow have her and keep Rose, and coming back to the conclusion that a night of passion with Rose would solve his problems.

And tonight he had a date with her.

By noon or so, Adam finally admitted to himself that he wasn't going back to sleep. He got up and made coffee and had breakfast—or lunch—and actually felt a good bit better. His stomach didn't rebel against some experimental oatmeal, and his headache was mostly gone, and he could ignore the itch in the middle of his back some of the time. It was probably a mosquito bite, or a couple of mosquito bites. It would have to go away eventually. At any rate, he felt well enough to do some real apartment cleaning, with the idea that Rose should find the place welcoming if things worked out as he hoped. Meanwhile his brain kept replaying his dance with Fidessa. "You could have any woman in this room." Was it true? Was he attractive to women like those? Then he should be attractive to Rose. And, on the other hand, if Fidessa was lying to him, then what was she up to?

It all came back to the same thing. He needed Rose. She was already his girlfriend, and she was going to sleep with him eventually, so all she needed was a little gentle encouragement. Adam would have to be at his most attractive and seductive, and he wasn't sure whether he knew how to be attractive and seductive. Although he seemed to be doing all right last night. But something told him that Fidessa had more than a little to do with the way those other women saw him. With Rose he'd have only himself to rely on. He almost thought of calling Hope for advice—Hope, who must have missed him at the Wild Beans this morning—but that idea got squashed before it was fully formed. What would he say to her? "I almost cheated on Rose with the sexy artist chick I was stalking, but I passed out dead drunk before I could do anything, and now I'm feeling desperate, so I was wondering how you think I should go about seducing Rose." That was likely to earn him the kind of advice he didn't want. So there would be no emergency call to Hope.

No, he would just have to be himself, and see how that worked out.

✤

Well, she liked the dozen pink roses—a variation from red—so the date was off to a good start. But from there it wandered into territory Adam didn't quite know how to navigate.

"I got a call from Bradley last night," Rose mentioned as soon as the order was given and the menus taken away. She brought up the subject with a certain apprehension, to judge by the way she didn't look directly at Adam when she mentioned Bradley.

"What did he say?" Adam asked.

"I didn't answer it. He left a voice mail, but I can't bring myself to listen to it."

"I know what that's like." Adam said with unfeigned sympathy. He suddenly realized that this was the same little Moroccan place where he'd had his one date with philosopher-girl.

"I don't even know why I'm telling you, except that—well, I suppose I don't want you to think I'm hiding anything from you."

"I appreciate that." So if it was confession time, was he supposed to say, "By the way, I almost had sex with that Chinese artist I was telling you about"?

"I don't know why he's calling. And I don't know why it bothers me so much. I thought I was bloody well over him."

"And you're not?"

She smiled a weak, sad smile, reached across the table, and took his hand. "You're so sweet, and I do really like you. I wouldn't be telling you this if I didn't trust you, if I didn't want to be sure we trusted each other. Brad isn't right for me. I know that. But he has this effect on me. Just thinking about him does it. It's raw and animal. I know I'll get over it. It's just disappointing that I haven't got over it yet."

"Well..." Here might be his opening, but the food hadn't even arrived yet, and it didn't seem quite right to start the seduction until they were at least ready to leave the restaurant. So instead of saying "Maybe I could help you get over it," which were the words that almost came out of his mouth, he took refuge in a platitude: "These things take time."

"I suppose they do." She let go of his hand and sat looking out the window to her left. "Have you ever been obsessed with someone you knew was really bad for you?"

"I guess so. You could say that." Part of him wanted to tell the whole story of Fidessa right now, since confessions were in the air.

"What happened? How did you get over it?"

"Oh, you know. Time heals all wounds. Found someone new." The confession wasn't going to happen, it seemed. "I found you."

She turned toward him again, and her smile was much less sad.

Mint tea came then, and food started arriving shortly after that, and the conversation drifted into other avenues. Adam tried to be at his sparkling best, which he was afraid made him come off as unattractively artificial. But there was only so much he could do with the material he had to work with. He was nervous and hopeful and guilty all at the same time, and it didn't make his conversation come out any better.

But when dinner was over, and they had walked out into the cool evening air (those thunderstorms had been a cold front moving through, and the weather had turned from summery back to bracingly springlike), Adam decided that the time had come to begin the real program of the evening.

"I've been thinking," he began, and of course he instantly decided that it was the stupidest way possible to begin a seduction, but what was done was done. "Your obsession with Bradley—it's bothering you, I can tell."

Rose didn't say anything to fill the pause he left for her response, so he continued.

"Well, what I mean is this. You're the most beautiful woman I know." It was what he would call a permissible lie. "And I thought maybe... Well, you know how attractive you are to me, and I thought maybe if you could find a way to, you know, redirect your obsession...

Rose still didn't say anything, but she was smiling that weak, sad smile.

"I guess you know what I'm driving at. I'd really like it if you could stay with me tonight."

She squeezed his hand. She smelled the roses she was holding in her other hand. Eventually she said, "I can't."

Now it was Adam's turn to say nothing, because everything he thought of to say sounded whiny and childish in his mind.

They stopped walking, and Rose turned to face him. "I've been thinking so much about Bradley, and... It's going to happen, Adam. I promise. But it can't be tonight."

"I understand," Adam said. No, I don't, the selfish, primitive part of his brain insisted, but he squashed that back down into the depths where it belonged. "I don't want to push you into anything you don't want. I just thought... Well, you know I'll do anything for you."

And that was all he could think of to say. She gave him a kiss—a light and sweet one, not one of those hot and memorable ones he knew she was capable of—and asked if he wanted her to drive him home. He thanked her and said he'd rather walk.

So that was the outcome of his best attempt at seduction. Not a raving success. And his back was still
itching. He looked both ways to see that no one was
watching him, and rubbed his back against a traf-
fic-light post.

When Adam did get home, he decided it was time
to do something about that itch. He rooted through
his small collection of medicines and found some
old calamine lotion—the stuff doesn't go stale if
it's been stored for six years, does it?—and then
searched all over for his shaving mirror, which he
never used. Finally he found it under a heap of toi-
let paper in the hall closet. With the shaving mirror
in one hand and the calamine lotion in the other,
he headed into the bathroom.

Standing in front of the mirror, he took off his
shirt (and let it fall to the floor, because it wasn't as
though he was expecting visitors) and picked up the
shaving mirror to see if he could get a view of that
bite or rash or whatever it was. It took some awkward maneuvering to get the mirror in the right
position, but—

He stopped breathing and nearly dropped the
mirror.

Right in the middle of his back, just between the
shoulder blades, was a big red heart with an arrow
through it. And across the middle of the heart, in
ornate script easily legible in the double reflection,

was the name "Fidessa."

He moved the shaving mirror. He tried it in the other hand. He put down the shaving mirror and tried to see his back by turning around and looking at the bathroom mirror over his shoulder, which was not a great success, but at least did show that the thing was there. It wasn't his imagination.

While he stood in that awkwardly twisted position, a text came in. He ran out to the bedroom where he'd left the cell phone, ready to give Fidessa more than one piece of his mind if she was by her phone. He had a lot of choice words for her, short and sharp ones.

But the text was from Rose: "I'm downstairs. Let me in?"

CHAPTER 20. SOME EXPLANATIONS.

THIS was not exactly what Adam needed right now. It was not possible, though, to tell Rose to go away. He quickly texted back, "Coming 3 min," and then indulged in a bit of panic. He picked his shirt up off the bathroom floor and put it away and headed for the stairs; then he realized that he wasn't wearing a shirt and ran back to get the same shirt and put it back on; then he decided that that shirt wasn't clean enough and threw it off and got a different one and put it on. Then he headed for the stairs, and then he realized he had thrown the first shirt on the floor and ran back to put it in the laundry hamper.

So it took pretty much the whole three minutes for him to get downstairs and open the door for Rose, who was standing there looking—well, a bit shy, and very cute.

"May I come up?" she asked.

"Of course," Adam said, with his heart pounding.

He thought Rose must be able to hear it.

He led the way upstairs; she followed him into his little living room, and he showed her to one of the two comfortable (though slightly bedraggled) armchairs that he definitely wasn't going to tell her came from the Salvation Army.

"This is a big apartment," she said in a making-conversation-to-put-off the-inevitable tone.

"It's amazing what you can get in this end of the neighborhood," Adam replied, also putting off the inevitable, whatever it was. "I like having an extra bedroom for an office, and that kitchen is twice the size of the one in the house I grew up in." When she didn't reply right away, he felt as though he had to fill the silence with something: "Of course the house I grew up in was tiny, so, you know..."

"Adam," she began. Then she stopped. But it wasn't appropriate, Adam thought, to fill this silence. This silence was meant to be awkward.

Rose was looking down at her own feet—cute feet, Adam was thinking, just as Hope had said—and obviously trying to formulate some words. When she did speak, she didn't look up at first.

"I drove home and parked, and then I sat in the car." More silence, in which she continued to look at her own feet, and Adam looked at them too, because it seemed as though looking directly at her face might be cruel when she was so obviously avoiding his gaze. She took a breath, and then didn't continue; then she took another breath and did continue. "I sat in the car and thought about what you said, and about what I said, and I felt—I felt so selfish. I felt like I had messed everything up. I felt like I'd just told you I—" She stopped and wiped a tear from her eye. "I felt like I'd just told you I didn't love you. And I didn't mean to tell you that. And then I got terribly angry with Bradley for a while, and then I was sad again, and then I realized that I was letting Bradley control me, which was just why I left him in the first place."

More silence, but her hand was resting on his now. Adam looked up, and she gazed into his eyes. "Gazed" was just the right word for the wide-eyed, steady, slightly tear-fogged look she was giving him. Adam had never seen Rose look more appealing, had never felt closer to being in love with her, not even when she had rescued him from philosopher-girl.

"So," she continued, and then another pause, in which she substituted squeezing his hand for words. "So I started the car again and drove back here again, and..."

Adam kept his gaze fixed on hers, which gave his mind the leisure to indulge in a spiral of panic. This conversation was probably heading in only one direction, but—but the tattoo. What would he do when she saw the tattoo?

"So I decided not to let Bradley control me anymore."

He could tell her it was an old girlfriend. A failed relationship from the distant past. But he had told her the artist's name was Fidessa. How many women in the world are named Fidessa? He had heard of exactly one.

"And I came here..."

She couldn't see the tattoo. It was fresh and bright. She would know it was recent. She would know he had been lying to her. Which he hadn't, except that...

"And..."

He had to stall. He had to wait until he figured out some way to erase that tattoo. Or at least get rid of Fidessa's name from it. He wished he knew more about tattoos.

"And I'm ready."

And low could he delay without destroying the relationship he'd worked so hard for? What could he say? What excuse could he give?

"I want to make love with you tonight."

She had said it. Now it was his turn—on, hell, now it was time to refuse the thing he wanted most from her. He cursed Fidessa in his mind. What had she done to him? How had she known?

"Rose..." He placed his other hand on top of hers.

"Ever since I met you, this is what I've wanted." Absolute truth. "From the first I thought you were the most beautiful woman I'd ever seen." Permissible lie. "And believe me, I never thought that more than I do tonight. But—" and here it came: with that one word "but," he could feel the muscles in her hand contracting involuntarily. "But tonight—tonight you're worrying about me. I mean, you're thinking about what I want, and not about what you want, and I can't take advantage of you that way."

Her gaze became perceptibly more intense. "Believe me, Adam, this is what I want."

"It's what you think you want now." Desperation was not producing his best reasoning. "It's... It's... It comes down to this. A gentleman has to have a code about these things. I'm not like Bradley, you know—I don't just demand what I want. It has to be... It has to be completely mutual. It has to be something we're doing for each other, not something you're doing for me. It has to be... It has to be some time when your mind's not full of how angry you are at Bradley."

Rose withdrew her hand and didn't say anything for a while. When she did speak, it was in a strangely detached voice. "This has never happened to me before."

Adam desperately wanted to tell her it wasn't happening now, but obviously it was happening.

She wasn't looking directly at him anymore. "I suppose you really are different from Bradley. Most men... Usually when I offer a man sex, I don't get an argument."

"Believe me, it's not because..." Adam wanted to marshal all his best arguments; perhaps it was still possible to make this some kind of victory. "It hurts me more than I can tell you to do this, but I just..." Well, that wasn't exactly his best argument, was it?

"It's all right, Adam, Really. I think I understand. You really are a gentleman, and it's just—it's just that I've never been with a gentleman before. Says something about my taste in men, doesn't it? So I'll say good night, and I...suppose I'll see you Friday,"

And so Rose went down the stairs without kissing him goodbye, and Adam watched her drive away from his living-room window. Then he threw himself on his bed and beat his pillow senseless.

Two minutes later he was asleep.

❧

Thursday morning Adam was not his usual self at the Wild Beans. He had already texted Fidessa twice and called her once, but no response either way, So he sat at the usual table so sullenly that Hope was finally moved to ask,

"Is everything all right with Rose?"

"I don't want to talk about it," Adam said.

Hope set her tea down with a clank and leaned back with a despairing expression. "Oh, hell."

Adam was still silent.

"You're not messing this up, are you?"

"I can mess up my whole life if I want to," Adam said without looking at her. He was finding the surface of his coffee intensely interesting.

"Yes, but if you mess up Rose's too…"

Adam didn't say anything. He really wanted to tell someone the whole story, and who better than Hope? But he couldn't bear the blame that he knew he deserved.

"Well," Hope said, "my date went well. Not that you'd be interested."

Wait—Hope was dating someone? Was that allowed? If she attached herself to some other fellow, what would happen to the morning confessional at the Wild Beans?

But it did give him a way out.

"I'm sorry," he said. "Of course I'm interested. I'm just suffering a little from, you know, aftereffects of the virus or whatever. Don't mind me. Tell me all about the date."

So Hope did tell him, and he didn't hear a word of it.

❧

All day Adam tried to get Fidessa on the phone. He even tried calling her number from his work phone, on the theory that she might be avoiding his calls. But she didn't answer his calls, or his texts, or his desperate pounding on his desk with his fist.

But he did have an appointment for a sitting in the evening, and even though he didn't think there was much chance she'd keep it, he was determined to show up.

In fact he was about twenty minutes early, because he wasn't able to think about anything else. The door to the stairwell was open, and he dashed up the stairs two at a time. He flung open the door to her studio, and there she was, in a silk robe with her hair still a bit damp, sitting in the chair he usually sat in, reading some old leather-bound book.

"Where have you been?" Adam demanded, almost frightened by how angry his own voice sounded.

"You're quite a bit early," Fidessa answered, very calmly.

"I mean since Tuesday. Since the party where I passed out and got a tattoo on my back."

"I've been out of town. A little emergency. You mentioned a party?

"Look, I don't know what game you're playing, but you had a party downstairs with all sorts of gorgeous women, and a professor who looked like

Satan in a suit, and then..."

She was looking at him very calmly, but a little speculatively. It was infuriating that she could be so calm.

"It sounds like a dream," she said.

"A dream? How can you sit there and tell me it was a dream?"

"Were all the women exceptionally beautiful? Did they all find you unaccountably attractive? Were all the men indistinguishable ciphers, except for this professor you mention? It sounds like a dream."

Adam flung off his shirt and turned around. "Does that look like a dream to you?"

She didn't say anything. Adam stood with his back to her, until suddenly he felt hot, soft fingers in the middle of his back and Fidessa was right there beside him. Fidessa in silk.

"It's very flattering," she said. Her hand was gently passing over the area between his shoulder blades in what Adam might almost have called a caress.

"Flattering?" Adam wasn't quite sputtering; he would have sputtered if Fidessa's delicate warm hand hadn't been on his bare back.

"But it's coming off."

"Coming off?"

She took his arm. "Come with me."

And because he couldn't think of anything to say, Adam suffered himself to be led into Fidessa's bathroom, which was amply provided with mirrors that would allow her to admire her own perfection from every angle. Between two mirrors, he could easily see the tattoo on his back. It seemed to be breaking up.

"It's a temporary," she said. "Anyone with a computer can print one. They stay on in water, but they start to come off after a couple of days. They are great fun for lovers."

Adam stared at the image of himself and Fidessa in the mirror—himself with no shirt, Fidessa only in a short silk robe. Red with black trim.

"I can't do this anymore," he said at last.

"Can't do this?" Her hand was on his back again, the palm flat, the fingers spread, as if she were thoroughly enjoying the sensation of his bare flesh.

The only way to resist her would be to make a clean break. "Whatever you're doing, I can't do it. I don't know what's going on here, and I don't know what your game is, but it's going to ruin my life if it keeps going." Adam felt as if he had just made a very brave speech, but he didn't make any movement to dislodge her warm, soft hand from the middle of his back. "I've passed out drunk, which I never did before. I've ruined my big chance with my girlfriend, and I don't know what it's going to take to salvage that relationship. And the tattoo itches."

"They do that sometimes." Her hand was still on his back, making slow caressing movements that nearly melted Adam into a puddle.

"I'm not coming back," Adam said very definitely. "I'm going to leave now, and I won't see you again." Just as soon as her soft, warm hand was detached from the pleasure centers of his brain.

"I think that would be a bad idea," she told him very calmly.

"No, it was this whole...thing... It's been a bad idea letting you get away with... whatever." All his power of articulate thought was being sucked out through his back into her hand.

"It would be very bad to abandon the project now. It would be a crime against art." The hand was sending him the real message: Everything will be all right if you just let me touch you.

"I have to," Adam insisted, melting further into her hand. "I can't keep my sanity and still keep see-ing you."

He watched her in the mirror as she inched closer, pressing her silk-wrapped body against him. Her hot breath was on his shoulder. "I could make it worth your while."

But that had been just a little too far. Adam sud-denly found the strength to break away from her. "No," he said, leaving the bathroom and yanking his shirt on as he crossed her studio toward the door. "I'm making a clean break."

She was following him. "I'll double your fee."

Adam stopped. "Fee?"

"Well, you didn't expect that I'd take all this time from you for nothing, did you?"

Actually, that was exactly what he had expected. He hadn't even thought about money when he agreed to sit for her.

"This portrait is worth a great deal to me," she continued, by his side again and reestablishing contact with her fingers lightly on his arm. "I was going to pay you ten thousand dollars, but I could make it twenty."

Adam didn't say anything, but he was thinking of his drained bank account.

"Thirty," she said after not very much pause. "It will be written off as a business expense anyway."

Adam stood thinking for what seemed like a very long time, but was probably only ten seconds or so. Finally he pulled his arm out from under her fingers and headed for the door. "I'll think about it," he said.

BOOK V.

CHAPTER 21. WANDERING.

So ADAM thought about it. It should be easy to decide: it was a simple appeal to his greed, nothing more. But it wasn't easy at all. He wandered through the back streets in the silence of the early evening thinking about Fidessa, Rose, and thirty thousand dollars, and the thoughts would not sort themselves out. It was a cool and pleasant evening, the kind of evening that was just made for walking and thinking. The moon was high in the sky, a day or two before the first quarter; Jupiter was shining brightly, and a few of the brighter stars poked through when Adam was between streetlights. A strong scent of honeysuckle occasionally wafted from the back alleys.

Thirty thousand dollars. Was it really so easy for her? He had thought Fidessa was irresistible, but finally he had gathered together all his strength of character, all his prudence, all his courage, and managed a brave resistance even when she was wrapped in only a little bit of silk and looking more appealing than... Well, he shouldn't dwell on it. He had broken away from her, which had taken extraordinary resolution.

And then...thirty thousand dollars.

It would make a difference. It would make a big difference. It was more than half his annual income. Adam was not very proud of his annual income: the fact was that he just barely made enough to keep himself comfortable, and certainly not enough to keep two people comfortable.

How did she know? How could she find his weak spot so easily?

Of course it was possible that he was being ridiculously suspicious. It was possible that all she cared about was her art. If that was true—

If that was true, then she was telling the truth about the party, and the French bakery, and even about seeing him on Brackenridge Avenue, and Adam must be mad—a possibility he was more and more willing to admit.

Suppose Fidessa was telling the truth. Suppose she had no knowledge of any party on Tuesday night. Suppose she had not tried to seduce him. Then what had happened?

Something had happened. The evidence was there in the middle of his back. He couldn't have put that heart there himself. But the simple fact that the something had happened while he was drunk made everything suspect. Adam had no previous experience with being so drunk that he passed out. He'd never done it before. He didn't know how reliable his memory would be when he woke up from his stupor. He certainly seemed to have a vivid memory of that party, but then... Gorgeous women, all fixated on him. A cartoon Satan spouting philosophy. An erotic interlude with the object of his most obsessive desires. It did sound like a dream, didn't it?

And if that was a dream, then how much of the rest was a dream? Was the French bakery a dream? Was the offer of thirty thousand dollars a dream? Was he dreaming right now?

Adam stopped walking for a moment and looked around him. Beside him was a house built of orange brick, two and a half storeys, with a front porch—obviously a later replacement—made of blond brick that clashed with the brick of the house. The lights were on in the house: he could see green curtains in the living room or parlor in front. On the porch was a grey cat, long-haired, with a puffy tail that looked almost as big as the rest of the cat. The cat was eyeing him speculatively, and when Adam still didn't move, the cat stood, stretched, and came down off the porch toward him. It rubbed itself on his right leg and looked up; meeting no disapproval, it rubbed again in the opposite direction.

Almost automatically, Adam leaned over to pet the cat. Its fur was soft, probably brushed smooth, and it was already vibrating with a loud purr.

If this was a dream, it was a very real one.

And that was the problem with dreams. He could remember the sensations of dancing with Fidessa very clearly; he could remember how it felt at each point of contact between her body and his. But he could also remember the sensations from the dream he had had some time before that, the dream he had rebelled against waking up from. They were as vividly lodged in his mind as the ones from the party; they were as real at the time as the feeling of this grey cat rubbing against his leg, of his hand stroking the smooth fur.

The cat rolled over in front of him and lay with its legs pointing up in the air.

Adam scratched the cat's belly, which provoked the cat to grab his hand with its front paws. The claws didn't dig into him very deeply: it seemed more an affectionate gesture than a defense.

If this was a dream, then nothing was reliable anymore. And perhaps the only answer to that was to treat his dreams as if they were as true as anything else in his life.

His dreams, and therefore his nightmares as well.

✤

After an hour and a half of wandering, Adam finally found himself back home, still no closer to having any idea what he was going to do with himself. Would greed or prudence win? Or, would prudence or stubbornness win? That was the problem: he couldn't tell on which side of the question prudence weighed in. It would be a lot easier if someone could explain that part to him; then he could just take the prudent course and be done with it.

Rose. Rose was the prudent course. What did that mean? Which would be more likely to give him a future with Rose—kicking Fidessa out of his life and scaling back his expenses, or going ahead with Fidessa's portrait and earning thirty thousand dollars?

Well, that was assuming that he hadn't blown it with Rose completely and irrevocably. He decided to send her a text: 'Thinking of you a lot. Still sorry about last night."

It was absurd how much he worried in the next minute and a half, but his pulse raced and his breathing grew shallower and more irregular until at last a reply came in:

"No need to be sorry. See you tomorrow."

So she was still planning on their Friday date, which was good. On the other hand, Adam couldn't help noticing the absence of little pictures. A heart, or even a smile, would have made him feel a lot better.

Rose didn't send any more texts. Adam thought of replying, but couldn't think of anything to say.

Now... Thirty thousand dollars. What did he have to look forward to without those thirty thousand dollars? He ought to have a clear picture of his financial situation, which shouldn't be hard, because with trivial exceptions his financial situation consisted of one checking account and one savings account. So he sat down at the computer to get a clear picture, and immediately thought about Fidessa's self-portrait, which was a very clear picture indeed. So he looked at that for a while. But no, he thought, he should really be thinking about thirty thousand dollars: she had appealed to his greed this time, not to his lust. So he closed the picture and brought up his bank accounts instead.

The news wasn't encouraging. His checking account was down to about $73, if he rounded up to the nearest dollar. His savings account was down to $208.14 precisely. Pay would be coming in next week, but Adam knew that he could and would spend those accounts down to nothing over the next few days. Of course there was the credit card, which was a cruel trap worthy of Fidessa: a high limit, low monthly payments, and absurdly high interest. As a long-term strategy the credit card was not sustainable unless suicide was part of the plan.

Then perhaps he ought to cut down on his expenses. Where was he spending the most money? Well, dates with Rose were expensive by his standards. Of course there was no reason he had to pay all the time: she had always offered to pay, and he had always refused, because he had some primitive masculine pride that insisted on preventing him from allowing the female of the species to pay for a meal—a trait doubtless inherited from Adam's paleolithic ancestors, who lived in an era when sexual selection favored the males who could prove they were good providers by paying for mastodon a la reine at a fancy restaurant. And right now he was at the point in his relationship with Rose where he expected to spend more, not less. If he was to overcome the Wednesday disaster, he needed to make himself much more appealing, not to cut back on his generosity.

The Wednesday disaster. Perhaps it could still be overcome. Perhaps she would spend the night with him after tomorrow's date. But what about the tattoo? The Internet would know how to remove a temporary tattoo.

Mineral oil, it said. The drug store on the corner was open till midnight, so Adam ran out, picked up the mineral oil (he had to ask the clerk where it was, and the clerk had no idea that there was such a thing as mineral oil, and had to ask the one other employee on duty, who didn't know either, but while they were parading up and down the six aisles of the little store trying to find it for him Adam happened to spot the stuff on a shelf), and brought it back. Then he spent a good hour and a whole towel, which could never be used again, rubbing the tattoo off, which left his arms aching from the awkward twisting he had forced them into.

And now it was past midnight, and he really ought to get to bed. He had made no decision on the matter of Thirty Thousand Dollars vs. Conscience of Adam Mueller, and he put off the decision till tomorrow and retired to dream of Fidessa in silk.

CHAPTER 22. CREDIT.

FOR the first time in recorded history, Hope was not waiting for him when Adam walked into the Wild Beans Friday morning. He ordered the Guatemalan, and one of those enormous cinnamon rolls, and sat at a table in the middle of the room because the usual table wasn't available because Hope had inexplicably failed to show up at opening time and reserve it. Time was out of joint, etc.

She finally appeared—finally!—five minutes after Adam had sat down and resigned himself to a morning without her. She was looking a little less put together than usual, a little hurried, and a little tired. But she was also looking quite content with herself.

"I was afraid you were going to forget all about me," Adam said as she plunked her briefcase down in the chair opposite him.

"You mean like you did to me Wednesday?" she responded.

"Uh... yes," Adam said.

She just smiled at him, then turned to walk up to the counter. Adam enjoyed the rear view while she ordered and waited for her tea and coffee cake. When she returned to the table, she set the tea and pastry down and then carefully placed the briefcase beside her chair so she could sit down herself.

"So," Adam said, "what kept you this morning? I hope you weren't feeling sick, too." "Feeling sick" was still his official story about what had happened on Wednesday, and after all, it was perfectly true. It simply didn't specify the cause, which was nobody's business, and which he didn't actually know himself anymore.

"It was my fifth date with Ralph last night. I'm kind of worn out."

"His name is Ralph?"

"Lots of people are named Ralph," she said a little defensively.

Adam had to agree that lots of people were named Ralph. He was feeling absurdly annoyed, though, that one of them was making so much progress with Hope. Why annoyed? No good reason. He had no possessive interest in Hope. Had he? Was he really so selfish that he resented any other man's success with any other woman?

"So," Adam said in a light, conversational tone to mask his unjustifiable annoyance, "it sounds like things are going well with Ralph." He couldn't help pronouncing the name "Ralph" as if it tasted like castor oil, but otherwise he hoped he managed to sound neutrally cheerful enough.

"Going right down the list," she said with a sly smile. "And we're having our sixth date on Saturday. Hey, you don't know of a good equestrian shop that's not too far out of town, do you?"

"No…" It was a drawn-out syllable that suggested considerable distraction.

"Well, I'll look on line. So are you feeling better about Rose?

"Rose? —Oh, yes, we're having a date tonight, so I'm looking forward to that." With considerable dread, he didn't add.

"That's good." She was breaking off an enormous chunk of coffee cake. "Yesterday I was afraid that things were going sour. You sounded gloomy."

"Nothing to do with Rose," Adam insisted. Was it a lie? Well, that depended on how you defined "to do with." It was mostly to do with Fidessa, and Rose was just caught in the crossfire. "I was still feeling a little sick yesterday. And I've been worried about money." Why, his brain immediately demanded of his mouth, did you mention money?

"Oh. Anything in particular?" She looked genuinely concerned and sympathetic, and Adam suddenly thought that maybe mentioning money had been a good idea after all. It distracted her from more difficult subjects.

"Just not enough of it," Adam replied. "Somehow it goes out as fast as it comes in. Except that now, with Rose, it goes out twice as fast as it comes in."

"I know what you mean. We don't make much at the peon level, do we? With all the wisdom of a very expensive education behind us, we can't figure out how to make as much as a garbage collector. Lucky for me Ralph makes good money, and he's such a perfect gentleman that he pays for all our dates."

"That is lucky," Adam agreed. He really didn't want to think about Ralph.

"I bend over backwards to make it worth his while. And forwards."

"I didn't need to hear that."

She was still holding that enormous chunk of coffee cake. It was building up a little bit of suspense: when would it go into her mouth? And would it fit? Not yet, anyway, because now she was leaning forward a little to speak more confidentially: "Really, Adam, you know that I don't have much, but if you're in trouble, I can..."

"I'm not in trouble," he said instantly. Actually, the rational part of his brain feebly objected, I'm in every kind of trouble there is. But the paleolithic part of his brain told him not to show weakness in

front of an attractive woman, even if it was only
Hope. "Actually, I think I've figured out a way to
bring in a good chunk of cash."

She looked a little suspicious. "Legally, I hope.
You're not devious enough to be a drug dealer."

"Nothing like that," Adam said with a slight
smile, although part of his brain was telling him
that it would be more honest to be a drug dealer
than to be whatever he was right now.

"Oh, I know!" Hope said with sudden inspiration,
pointing at him with the chunk of coffee cake. "You
can moonlight as an artist's model." Then the chunk
went into her mouth, and, contrary to Adam's private prediction, it did fit.

"Something like that." And since she was attack-
ing her coffee cake, he decided it was time to deal
with his cinnamon roll.

❧

For the date with Rose he bought a dozen yellow
roses. He had already given her red ones and pink
ones, so yellow would make a nice change. He
could, of course, pick some other kind of flower,
but roses had worked so well the past few times
that he felt a superstitious dread of attempting car-
nations or even orchids. Better to stick with what
worked. Naturally he paid for the roses with his

credit card; he was going to pay for everything with his credit card until he had actual money in his account. Of course he was only building up debt for himself in the long term, but in the short term he was making an investment in his relationship with Rose.

She picked him up at half past six and drove him to the very nice little Italian restaurant they had agreed on. Rose appreciated the roses, and she was in fairly good spirits as they sat down and ordered. In fairly good spirits, but a little distant. It was almost as though all the progress of the last few dates had been wiped out, and they were starting again from square one. Once again Adam cursed Fidessa silently, and once again his mental curses brought up the mental image of Fidessa in silk, which his mind insisted on dwelling on even with Rose right across the table from him.

After a little bit of a lull in the conversation, Adam felt compelled to bring up the subject he didn't want to bring up.

"Once again, Rose, I'm really sorry about Wednesday. You know I—"

"We don't need to talk about it, Adam. I understand."

And she let awkward silence hang over the table until a basket of bread came out, and then the freshness of the bread gave them something neutral to talk about.

So dinner went well, as dinners go; the conversation was reasonably bright, and Rose made no accusations that Adam would have to duck. And at the end of the evening, when she dropped him off at home, she gave him a kiss. It was a light and almost chaste kiss—again, as if the relationship had been rewound to the beginning. There was no talk of her going upstairs with him. Rose didn't bring up the subject, and Adam thought the time was probably wrong to suggest it. He would let her repair the relationship at her own pace.

So he went upstairs alone and spent some time thinking about money, which didn't lead to any productive conclusions. But at least he had had a date with Rose that didn't end in disaster, and she was expecting to see him again tomorrow. On the whole, things had gone better than he had expected.

Of course, with the flowers, he had spent $200. A quick calculation told him that $200 amounted to about a quarter of his weekly income, so that two dates a week with Rose would eat up half his income before taxes. And here he was thinking about money again, which led by simple association to thinking about Fidessa in silk.

❧

Saturday morning Derrida-woman called again, and this time Adam was sure he knew exactly what to say to her. But the phone somehow didn't get answered anyway, so she left one of her growing collection of voice-mails for him, and he would have to get around to listening to them eventually. Adam was almost motivated to listen this time out of sheer curiosity: what could such an extraordinarily persistent woman have to say for herself after four or five or six (how many had it been?) unreturned phone calls? Curiosity did not outweigh dread, however, and the voice mail lingered there in the log with the rest of the collection.

And wasn't it strange, Adam thought, that, with all he had to worry about, philosopher-girl could still be an object of dread to him? It would get rid of her very efficiently if he just called her back and left a very impolite message, but of course he wouldn't do that. He might be a sinner, but he was still a gentleman. So he told himself, and he partly believed it.

Then there was his date with Rose this afternoon. This was a cheap one, because on Saturday afternoons they usually—surely that was a good sign, wasn't it, that there was a "usually" in their relationship?—they usually took a walk in the park and finished with a light supper from some little food stand or ethnic restaurant. One that would take credit cards, because cash was short at the moment.

So the date with Rose went all right, but something unpleasant came up in the conversation:

"I got a call from Bradley last night." Rose brought it up as they walked through the woods, and the late-spring flowers were giving way to the early-summer flowers, and a gentle breeze was moving the bright green leaves, and everything ought to have been right with the world. But everything wasn't really all right, because she was looking straight ahead and not meeting Adam's eyes at all.

"He's still bothering you?"

"I answered this time."

She let that hang in the air and be buffeted by the breeze for a while.

Adam decided at last that she wanted some kind of response. "What did he have to say?"

"Nothing...useful." She took a deep breath and let it out; then she took another deep breath. "He just wants to... He just wants to pretend we can get back together if he just doesn't give up. And I told him he needs to give up. He needs to be... He needs to give up."

"Do you want me to talk to him?" Oh, please say no.

"No. No, it wouldn't do any good. It would make him angry, and he wouldn't listen to you anyway. I

have to deal with it myself. I just— I wish it didn't
upset me so much. I wish I could just ignore him.
Why do I still feel so... so... Why do I still have any
feelings for him at all?"

Adam took her hand. Last week they had been
walking in these woods and their hands had been
practically glued together; now, Adam realized,
they had hardly been holding hands at all. "When
you have a strong emotional reaction to someone,
you can't just flush it. Every time you see that person or talk to him, you're going to feel strongly. I
guess that's a silly thing to say, isn't it? But sometimes we have to say the obvious things, because
they're not always obvious. —I should probably
shut up before I dig myself a hole I can't get out of,
shouldn't I?"

Rose gave his hand a gentle squeeze, and then
withdrew her hand and continued walking beside
him without looking at him or saying anything
more.

Adam was not ready to say that the date was a
bust—Rose gave him another light but pleasant
kiss when they parted, and she didn't seem to be
annoyed with him in any way—but the shadow of
Bradley hung over the whole afternoon, and it was
painful to Adam to see Rose in a blue mood. He
liked the cheerful, smiling Rose he had seen when
they first met. Actually, he liked the sad and wistful

Rose, too: he just wished he could do something to make her less sad and more happy. He wished she could feel about him the way she had obviously felt about Bradley. He wished he could feel about Rose the way he felt about Fidessa. He wished life could be simple and not complicated, but his life seemed to complicate itself whether he liked it or not. Surely it was just bad luck and nothing he was doing to make life complicated. Right?

It was still a warm and sunny early evening when Adam found himself back in his lonely apartment —should he have invited Rose up? No, probably not time for that yet—wondering what to do with himself. Eventually he decided to take a walk. It ended up being a long one, because there were lots of thoughts to sort out. Not that any of them got sorted: by the time it was twilight, Adam still had his thoughts in just as confused a state as ever. But as the dark purple tints suffused the landscape, he thought again of Fidessa—Fidessa in silk, Fidessa with thirty thousand dollars. He lusted after that money in almost the same way he lusted after the woman herself. No wonder she was dangerous.

And here he was on Brackenridge Avenue, and there was the iron arch.

Something told Adam that no good could come of walking under that arch. It was a portal to some alternate world, and now he was convinced that evil lurked beyond that portal.

And then he stopped in his tracks. Evil! What kind of superstitious medieval peasant was he, anyway? Twenty-first century men don't believe in demons and evil eyes and magic gates. He would walk right under that gate and show it he didn't have anything to fear from it. And if he met Fidessa, he would show her he hadn't anything to fear from her, either.

The street was its usual twilight self, and Adam walked along the sidewalk with an increasing apprehension. Something was going to happen.

But nothing did.

He reached the door to Fidessa's studio—right next to the pretzel shop, which was still a pretzel shop. If anything odd had been planning on happening to him, it would have happened here. But no: it was just a door with no markings on it except the street number. No demons leaped out at him; no strange adventures awaited him in the pretzel shop, which was closed for the evening. He stood in front of the door and smiled. His reflection in the glass smiled back at him. And Fidessa's reflection beside him smiled, too.

The bottom dropped out of his stomach. Warm fingers landed on his arm, and he melted. And that soft, seductive, musical voice spoke in his ear,

"Did you come back for thirty thousand dollars? Or do I have to make it forty?"

CHAPTER 23. FIRST NATIONAL BANK
OF FIDESSA.

"I HAVEN'T decided," Adam said immediately. He was proud of himself for coming up with a reply so quickly. He was decisively indecisive.

"Perhaps this is a negotiating tactic?" Fidessa suggested. "It might work. Your price might go up. You have cornered the market on you, after all, which is the only commodity I can't do without."

"I'm negotiating with my conscience."

"A skilled negotiator, I'm sure. Come upstairs and let me give you some of the best arguments I can think of."

Adam turned to face her. She was wearing all black again, which made her look a little dangerous. "I don't think that's a good idea."

"I think it's a very good idea. You have nothing to be afraid of from me. I don't think I could over-power you in a fight." She was smiling that sugges-tive little smile that made her look so appealing, and Adam thought how very easy it would be for her to overpower him without striking a blow.

The smile faded, and she looked very serious. "If I promise not to overpower you by other means, will you come up for ten minutes and talk to me?"

"How do you *do* that?" Adam demanded. It seemed very unfair that she could know what he was thinking without his having to say it.

"No one has studied your face as thoroughly as I have."

Adam stared into her infinitely deep eyes and wondered again what they saw in him. A fascinating subject? A potential lover? Or a toy?

Fidessa met his gaze with one just as intense, but the smile came back. "I give you my word of honor that I will not seduce you."

Part of him wanted to tell her, "No, it's all right, you can seduce me if you like." But his intellectual faculty was gloating over the victory it had just won. He had resisted her and forced her to keep the conversation straightforward and out of the danger zone. "Ten minutes," he said very definitely, implying with his firm voice and stern gaze that he would not be detained a minute more.

Fidessa nodded and opened the door, which apparently hadn't been locked (Did she leave it unlocked all the time? Did she trust her powers of seduction to keep burglars out of her studio?). She

walked ahead of Adam up the stairs to the second
floor, and then around past the nondescript doors
(no music was coming from behind them) and up
the stairs to her studio. Just as she reached the top
of the stairs, she stopped and turned around suddenly, forcing Adam to make an equally sudden
stop right in front of her, with his eyes exactly on a
level with hers.

"Just so we're clear on the extent of my promise,"
she said, "I did *not* promise not to succumb if *you*
make advances to *me*."

For a very long three or four seconds she stared
right into his eyes with that dangerously subtle
smile on her lips. Then she turned and led the way
into her studio.

The place was dimly lit by a couple of floor lamps
—the one by the chair where Adam usually sat (for
the first time it occurred to him to wonder whether
she didn't have any other projects going at the moment) and the other by her easel, which was empty
right now. Shadows enveloped the rest of the room,
making mysteries out of the artistically arranged
canvases and piles of frames. It was a strangely
gloomy place by night, quite different from what it
was in the day. But it was an attractive, almost seductive gloom.

"Sit down," Fidessa said, indicating Adam's usual
chair. He sat and watched her intently as she

brought a light but very elegant Eastlake side chair from its place by the wall and deposited it right in front of him. Then she sat in it, and the rational or cynical part of Adam's mind noted that she was rather close, her knees not quite touching his, as if she had calculated the exact proximity he would tolerate.

"Now we talk business," she told him. "Art is not merely business, but I have learned that without the business end the art end suffers. I have something I want from you, which is to finish your portrait. I am prepared to pay you for your time, which is only right and fair. Shall we say fifty thousand dollars?"

Adam swallowed and thought hard. Fifty thousand dollars was exactly two thousand dollars more than his worthless job paid him in a year.

"I am asking only a few more sessions," Fidessa continued. "Not a bad rate considering the work involved. A few evenings of your time, and you make a year's salary."

Adam was still silent, but the question of how she knew these things was running through his mind again. Had she been looking into his financial affairs?

"No, I haven't been researching your finances," she continued after a moment of quiet. "Each number I quote produces a different effect on your face.

It is really quite an amusing hobby, reading your face. If I had infinite time, I could do a study of the effect on your face of everything I say, and everything I do." The subtle smile again. "I'm sure I could produce some very interesting expressions."

Adam wondered whether he ought to remind her of her promise not to seduce him, but of course she could legitimately claim that she had said nothing that overtly tended in that direction, and if he was adding interpretations to her straightforward statements that was nothing she could help. So he still said nothing, even though it seemed more and more obvious that it was just about the time in the conversation where he would have to make some definite statement. Her ten minutes would be up soon (he hadn't been timing her, which was a mistake, because the expiration of the ten minutes would have given him a good excuse for terminating the interview without making a definite decision).

Fidessa was never at a loss for words, however. Somehow when Adam left awkward pauses in the conversation, the awkwardness never rubbed off on her. "Or," she continued after fifteen seconds' silence, "are you holding out for a more advantageous arrangement?"

"More advantageous?" He was struggling to imagine what could be more advantageous than a year's salary for a few evenings' work. Two years' salary, maybe.

"You'll have guessed by now that I live in comfortable circumstances. Under certain arrangements, there might be no practical limit to how much of that comfort I shared with you."

Another few seconds of silence while Adam tried to process that suggestion. It had definitely made the bottom fall out of his stomach. At last he tentatively asked her, "Is that a proposal?"

Her slight smile was a little higher on the right side than on the left, and she let a few moments pass before she spoke. "No. I'm not interested in a monogamous relationship. Just...an arrangement."

"So you want, what, a kept man?"

"I prefer uncomplicated pleasures. I can be very generous in every way."

Adam's brain was trying to come up with the proper reaction, but he had never been in this sort of situation before. He felt as though he had suddenly become the heroine in a Victorian melodrama, and Fidessa was playing the role of the mustache-twirling villain. But she didn't have a mustache, and no melodrama villain had ever been so irresistible.

Fidessa continued: "And I'd have no objection to your keeping your girlfriend Rose. If you like. What we did would be between us."

Adam suddenly stood up. "I think you've crossed the line we said you weren't going to cross."

Fidessa didn't stand. "I'm just proposing an equitable arrangement. If I'd wanted to seduce you tonight, believe me, I could have made it a lot more difficult for you to resist."

"And the ten minutes are up," Adam said. "I'm going." He headed for the door.

Fidessa stood and turned, but didn't follow him. "That's fine, but the next time the price may have gone up again. I may offer you sixty thousand. Or seventy-five. It may get embarrassingly high. Perhaps you'd better take my offer soon, while you can still convince yourself that greed had nothing to do with it."

Adam was already out the door and at the top of the stairs, but he felt as though the situation demanded some sort of witty and definitive retort. "I'll think about it," he said, and he began his descent. Apparently he wasn't destined to be witty this evening.

Out in the cool evening air, nothing was as clear as it ought to be. There was a fresh breeze, and the moon was bright, and the back streets—Adam headed away from the business district as soon as he could—were quiet and pleasant as usual. But Adam's thoughts wouldn't organize themselves the way he thought they ought to organize themselves.

Why didn't he just give in to Fidessa? What was he afraid of? Surely she was offering him exactly what he wanted. In fact, two things he wanted: herself and her money. Why not just take both and enjoy himself?

But Rose. He had a certain obligation to Rose. Unlike Fidessa, he wasn't ready to say that what Rose didn't know was none of her business. And Rose wasn't the sort to appreciate an arrangement like the one Fidessa was proposing, was she?

But the real problem with Fidessa was that he was afraid of her. And that was absolutely ridiculous, wasn't it? She was five feet two inches tall, and she could blow away in a fresh breeze. But of course it wasn't physical terror she inspired: it was —what should he call it?—supernatural dread. It was not that she could physically force him to do anything; it was that she was involved in something deeper than he could understand—that she could in some way turn his own mind against him.

Or, of course, there was the possibility that he was mad, that he had taken vivid dreams for reality. In which case, since it happened only around her, he still ought to stay away from her, the way he would avoid the edge of a bottomless pit, not because it was malevolent but because it was innocently dangerous.

It was rather late when, having wandered in circles mentally and physically, Adam found himself near the cheaper end of Brackenridge Avenue, where the lower-class bars were. And that was when he heard a voice from nearby saying, in a strong Picksburgh accent, "Hey, you're Rose's new boyfriend, right?"

Adam turned to face the voice and saw the old boyfriend, Bradley.

"Um, yes, that's right," he said. He was calculating his chances of either running away or standing his ground if Bradley decided that a fight was what he wanted.

Bradley looked him up and down, almost as if he were making the same calculation. Then he smiled what was probably meant to be an ingratiating smile, although Adam thought he could use a little more practice before he was really ready for a public performance. "Want a drink?"

Adam thought about it. Either he could be unfriendly and refuse what looked like a gesture of reconciliation, or he could say yes and possibly get a free beer out of it. And right now he would not object to a free beer at all.

"Sure," he said. And he followed Bradley into the nearest bar.

CHAPTER 24. BRADLEY.

It wasn't precisely a dive bar. In fact, it was technically at least partly a restaurant, so there was no smoking inside, which Adam was grateful for. Still, it wasn't the sort of place he usually frequented. He wasn't the sort who went into bars to get drunk, and he got the impression that most of the other patrons didn't come in for any other reason.

"What are you drinking?" Bradley asked.

"Just a beer, I guess," Adam replied.

"Two Arns," Bradley told the bartender. To Adam he said, "It's a good time for beer." Presumably he meant that a quarter past eleven was a good time for beer, although he might have meant something else.

The beers came, and Adam expressed his thanks awkwardly. Bradley was not the sort of person he felt comfortable talking to. He was the sort of person who might take a mention of Aristotle the wrong way and punch somebody out.

"So I guess I sort of wanted to apologize," Bradley said, and Adam realized that it was just as awkward for Bradley to talk to him as it was for him to talk to Bradley. "I mean, the other night, I was kind of drunk, and I didn't... Well, I mean, there wasn't no reason for me to act like that. I shoulda kept my mouth shut is what I mean."

"Apology accepted," Adam said. "I know how it is." He didn't really know how it was, but it sounded like the thing to say.

"I'm Bradley, by the way." He held out his hand, and Adam gave him a firm handshake. "I didn't know whether she told you who I was.

"She did. I'm Adam Mueller."

"Well, now we know each other. No hard feelings, I hope."

"No hard feelings."

With that Bradley seemed to have exhausted the possibilities of conversation for a while, and the two men retreated into their beers.

The silence lasted long enough that the sound of Bradley's voice was startling when it came again. "Are you in love with her?"

"With Rose?" Adam asked, and instantly he realized what a stupid question it was.

"How many other women you got?" Bradley asked with a sardonic smile, although he probably wouldn't have known what the word "sardonic" meant.

"I'm…not sure I should be talking about that."

"I mean, it's a simple question. I mean, you know the answer, right?"

"Yes, but it's personal. It's between Rose and me."

"See, I always wanted to tell the whole world I was in love with her." He drank more beer, and Adam felt a little ashamed of himself for not having been more definite and enthusiastic from the start. It was too late for that now, though, wasn't it?

The silence was thick for a while until Bradley spoke again, apparently continuing the same thought that had been revolving in his mind on a constant loop. "I mean, I couldn't help it. I was in love with her, and that was it. You know what I mean?"

Adam nodded and took refuge in his beer. It had been a mistake, coming into the bar. The conversation was getting awkward quickly.

"God, I'm still in love with her," Bradley continued. "You know? I just can't give up."

Adam was sipping beer very slowly, hoping to avoid the obligation of a reply. The conversation couldn't get much more awkward than this.

"I mean," Bradley added, "I used to think I didn't like black women. But Rose…"

All right, so it could get more awkward.

"Does she make you feel like that? Like you couldn't give up on her, no matter what?"

Adam realized that Bradley was looking straight at him, and it was no longer possible to avoid a reply. "Look, I care very much about Rose. I do. Much too much to be pouring out my feelings in a bar."

"Oh, you think you're better than me? I bet you went to college and got some degree in English literature or something."

"No! No, I mean, I'm not better than you. I'm different. It's okay for us to be different. You have your way of expressing your feelings, and I have mine. And my degree's in philosophy." Adam hated being mistaken for an English major.

"You're right," Bradley said. "Sorry. My fault. I guess it's just... Rose has all this education, you know? And I always felt like she wished I did, too, and I don't. I just get defensive."

"You have your kind of education, and I have mine. It's just different, and there's nothing wrong with people being different." Adam realized he was taking refuge in platitudes again. Was that why he had majored in philosophy—so he could be sure of having a platitude for every occasion?

Bradley set down his mostly-empty beer glass and brightened up a bit. "You know what? You're right. We're different, and that's all it is. You're a nice guy, Adam."

"I try."

"I'm not. I've never been nice."

"Oh, I'm sure you have your own way. I mean, Rose liked—"

"Rose wasn't looking for nice. I mean, you know how she is in bed, right? She's an animal. That's what it was. But now I guess she's looking for a nice guy, and she has you."

"Yeah," Adam said. "She has me." Funny how completely inadequate Bradley had just made him feel.

"But here's the thing." Bradley leaned over a bit, but it wasn't easy to tell whether it was to impart a confidence or just because the beer, on top of how- ever many other beers he'd had already, was getting to him. "I'm not giving up."

"Not giving up?"

"I'm going to try to get Rose back. See, a nice guy wouldn't do that to you, but like I said I'm not nice."

"Oh," Adam said. He couldn't think of any better reply than that, so he took refuge in his beer again.

"So now you know how it is."

"Now I know how it is," Adam agreed. And that seemed to be about all there was to say, except, "Well, thanks for the beer."

❧

Sunday Rose was busy with one of those papers graduate students are always having to write, so there was no afternoon date. Adam texted an affectionate message with a heart at the end, and eventually got a moderately affectionate reply, so perhaps all was well on the Rose front.

So there was nothing to worry about except Fidessa and money. Money would definitely help Adam deal with the expenses of maintaining Rose in the style she deserved. On the other hand, Fidessa was becoming more and more frightening.

Every once in a while—say, every five minutes or so—Adam thought about just giving in to her completely. If she wanted a liaison, as she quaintly called it, then why shouldn't she have it? Because of Rose, of course. But he had to admit to himself that he had never desired Rose as much as he desired Fidessa every time he saw her.

That was the frightening thing, though. Fidessa wanted to use him up and throw him away. If he could persuade her to love him, everything would be different. But was Fidessa even capable of loving him the way he loved her?

Every time Adam caught himself thinking about loving Fidessa, he forced her out of his mind and told himself it was Rose he ought to love instead.

Rose, the poor graduate student, who had nothing, and was living on student loans. She was much better suited to him than the wealthy and mysteriously beautiful artist who drove a Lexus and could offer him fifty thousand dollars as easily as he could offer Rose a samosa from a street vendor.

And wasn't it funny how, as soon as she failed to grab him through his lust, Fidessa immediately appealed to his greed?

Adam really ought to make a decision about the money soon, because he had his usual Monday evening sitting coming up, and he ought to have something definite to tell Fidessa—either he was taking her up on her offer, or he was not going to see her again. But after hours of mental dithering, no decision came to him. He finally went to bed at about ten, leaving Rose a goodnight text to which she didn't reply.

Monday morning Hope was at her usual spot in the Wild Beans, which made Adam feel better. All must be right with the world. Maybe she had even given up on her silly infatuation with this Ralph person. —No, that was a mean-spirited thing to think. He would make it up to her by asking her how the date went.

"How did the date with Ralph go?" he asked, as soon as he sat down with his usual oversized cup of Guatemalan.

Hope shifted a little in her seat. "Perfect—sixth date, just as scheduled. By the way, when we get to work, you don't happen to have an extra pillow or something, do you? Something I could, you know, put on my chair to sit on."

"I don't think so, but I'll look. Maybe a sweater or something?"

"Might help. So if you need to know, Luskins' Saddlery in Allison Park is easy to get to, and they don't ask awkward questions like 'What kind of horse are you planning on using that on?' "

"I see."

"Way better than going into one of those tawdry 'adult stores.' "

"Do I really need to hear this?"

"No, but I really enjoy watching you go all pink. It's so cute."

"And I gather you're really stuck on this Ralph." It was still irksome to him that Hope could have a boyfriend. He couldn't think of any good reason for feeling that way, which made it all the more irksome.

"Ralph is sweet and gentle, except when I persuade him not to be, and he's...reliable. I know where I stand with him. I like him a lot."

"That sounds like a lukewarm endorsement."

"Hey, don't knock lukewarm. There's a lot to be said for a relationship that's comfortable. And I can make it hot when I want."

"So you're giving up on romance?"

"I'm managing my expectations, and I think I'm doing a good job of it. I've been hit with Cupid's arrow before, and the wound just gets infected. So I've decided to make my own passion from safe, reliable ingredients."

"That's very cynical of you."

"I've earned this cynicism. I used to be a hopeless romantic, you know, but I let somebody crush that out of me."

"Oh." The idea of Hope suffering a romantic disappointment suddenly struck Adam as something very sad, and he wished he could have spared her the pain. It was very odd how seeing her in a romantic context, even with this Ralph he hadn't met yet, made him think of her as a woman and not just a friend. "You know, Hope, you can always talk to me when you're feeling down."

"For all the good that does."

"Really. I'm here for you, you know."

"No you're not. You're a nice guy, Adam, but you're selfish and oblivious. Just so you know."

Adam was a little surprised. "Um, I'm sorry if I—"

"Oh, Adam, I shouldn't have said anything. I didn't mean it at all. It's nothing to do with you. It's just that—it's just that these freaking benches are so hard."

CHAPTER 25. THE RIVAL.

So HOW do you decide whether you really want fifty thousand dollars? Or more?

It should be easy, shouldn't it? Fifty thousand dollars for a few days' work. It doesn't sound like a complicated decision. But how would he do it without betraying Rose?

And what was he afraid of anyway? Away from Fidessa, Adam was pretty sure he could handle her. She couldn't make him do anything he didn't want to do. But of course that wasn't strictly the problem, was it? The problem was what he did want to do.

These were the questions that kept revolving in Adam's brain while he was supposed to be working, so that all the copy he wrote came out listless and vague, and he was pretty sure he would have to throw it all away and start over again when he came in the next morning. But it couldn't be helped; inspiration, he told himself, was a tricky thing. Socrates didn't always have his daimon at his beck and call. He just needed to work until the inspiration came, and if it didn't come for a whole day that in no way indicated that he was a lazy slob.

Every so often he thought of asking Hope for her advice. She was just a few cubicles away, and she was always willing to give advice. But he had the notion that she would give him advice he didn't want to take. She had been unreasonable about Fidessa from the start, hadn't she? Or perhaps she had been entirely reasonable, and Adam didn't want to listen to reason.

So Adam left without talking to Hope about his problem, and he still wasn't any closer to solving it. Which was a difficulty, because he had a sitting with Fidessa scheduled for that evening, and he would either have to agree to keep going or tell her he was bailing out. Or—and this option seemed very appealing the moment he thought of it—he could tell her he was still thinking it over and needed more time, and then not make a decision tonight at all.

But something else came up while he was walking home. His phone rang, and it was Rose.

"Hello," he said hesitantly. He had been thinking of "Hello, darling," or "Hello, my love" (no, that was formal and ridiculous), or "Hey, babe," or something affectionate like that, but his indecision paralyzed him, and it ended up just being a trailing-off "Hello..."

"Um," she said, which was rather charming—she was as hesitant as he was. "Um, hi. Do you have some time to talk?"

"Of course."

She sighed in a way that was almost deafening over the poor cell-phone connection. "I have something to tell you."

The way she said it made Adam a little apprehensive. "I'm listening."

"It's nothing bad. I just want to be... I just don't want to hide anything from you, right? So I felt like I had to tell you that I, um, I saw Bradley last night."

"I see," Adam said, which was his usual response to something he didn't really know how to respond to.

"Nothing happened," she added very quickly, which of course immediately made Adam think that something could have happened if things had been slightly different. "He just talked to me, and I told him we weren't getting back together, and that was all."

This would definitely be a conversation that would work better face to face. "Do you want me to come over?"

"No." Her response was quick again, and almost sounded a little panicked. "I mean, there's no reason. Really, I'm all right." There was another deafening sigh; in the back of his mind the primitive, selfish brain was telling Adam that if she really cared about him she'd warn him when she was going to do that. "It's just..."

Adam waited for the end of that sentence, which was a long time coming. He decided to duck into the back street, where it was quieter, so he could hear it better when it came.

"It's just that he makes me so angry."

That wasn't really much of a climax to have waited for all that time. "Did he say anything nasty or mean?" And what would Adam do if Bradley had said something nasty or mean? Offer to beat him up?

"No. Not at all. It's just that he won't give up. And..."

Adam held the phone away from his ear, and, as he predicted, the roaring puff of air came next.

"I still...respond to him," she continued. "I hate him, but I can't stop feeling... Bloody hell, I don't know what to tell you, Adam. I called you because I wanted to be honest with you, but when I'm honest with you I make myself sound like such a bloody fool. I *am* a bloody fool—that's the problem. I can't stop feeling things. Urges. Why does he get to me that way?"

"Look," Adam said. He was used to the idea that

every problem could be solved, or at least sidestepped, with words, but maybe more than words would be needed to deal with this one. "It's natural. I'm going to tell you a secret. You know that artist friend I was telling you about? When I first met her, I felt this intense physical attraction to her." This was going to be as close to a confession as Adam would get, so he had better make it good. "I can't explain it, and I know it's not going to lead to anything. But it's there. It's a fact. It doesn't mean I'm a bad person, and it doesn't mean my future is bound up with her. I met you, and I knew you were the type for me, and she wasn't. But that doesn't mean I'm not physically attracted to her. And of course you actually did have... have a relationship with Bradley, so it's natural that the attraction would still be strong, even when your brain is telling you he's wrong for you." He sighed, and then wondered whether right now she was holding the phone away from her ear. "But I can see that I did the wrong thing last Wednesday, and I know I disappointed you."

"No. No, you were a perfect gentleman. I'm not good enough for you, but you were a perfect gentleman."

"Don't say you're not good enough for me. I'm not good enough for you. You're more than I deserve."

For the first time in the conversation, he heard

that pretty laugh. "We make a fine pair, don't we? I'm not good enough for you, and you're not good enough for me. We must be perfect for each other."

"I think you're right. And..." This next part was always tricky, but under the circumstances it was even trickier. "And I'd like to see you tonight and, uh, make up for Wednesday's mistake."

Adam didn't get the phone away from his ear in time, and he got the full impact of the sigh. "I should do it. But I can't. Not when I feel so...dirty. I think you were right. I can't do it when it's not really about us."

"I could make it about us," Adam said, which didn't make any sense at all, and he realized it as soon as the words were out of his mouth.

"Soon," she said. And then, obviously to end the conversation, "See you Wednesday?"

"See you Wednesday," Adam replied, carefully filtering all the frustration and annoyance out of his voice.

So there he was slowly ambling down a back street with rows of modest but comfortable houses on both sides, with a silent phone in one hand, and the real world closing back in on him—and in spite of everything he had told Rose, he was very much worried about Bradley. The one thing he hadn't told her was that he had seen Bradley himself. He knew Bradley wasn't going to give up on her.

Some part of him said that was okay—Bradley could have Rose back, and he would take Fidessa.

But Fidessa didn't love him. He wondered whether she ever could. No, his best chance of happiness was still with Rose. And in order to deal with Bradley he would have to be very appealing to her. What did he have that Bradley couldn't have? He was a nice guy, and Bradley wasn't—Bradley had said that himself. But do women really want nice guys? It had always seemed to be more of a handicap than an advantage.

However, women, his cynical mind told him, like nice guys with money much better than nice guys without it. And he felt strangely free now that he had confessed his attraction to Fidessa. Not that it had been a confession that really meant anything— it hadn't told her anything about how dangerous Fidessa was—but he had confessed. And she hadn't said anything about it. So he didn't have to feel guilty about seeing Fidessa. So...

So he turned back toward her studio. She wasn't expecting him till eight, and she might not even be there, but he had made his decision. If she was there, he would tell her right away, before he lost his conviction. He would take the fifty thousand dollars. No—here a sudden inspiration hit him. He would take sixty thousand dollars. If she was willing, as she had hinted, to raise the price to sixty thousand, then he would take it. If not, he would decide that it would have been the wrong decision, and walk away. He had never been a tough negotiator in business before—in fact, he was about as transparently bad a negotiator as anyone he knew. But he felt good about his decision. He had something she wanted, and he would set his own price.

It was only ten more minutes' walk to Fidessa's studio, and he reached it just a little after six. The pretzel shop downstairs was just closing, but the door to Fidessa's stairway was unlocked. As a courtesy, he stopped and texted her, "I'm coming up," and then waited for a reply. It came in thirty seconds: "Welcome." Sort of a strange reply, although Adam couldn't really figure out exactly what was strange about it. So he walked in, up the stairs, around past the nondescript doors to the next flight, where he had to step aside for a man who was coming down.

He looked like one of those men's fashion models you see in magazine advertisements, and there was something insufferably smug about him, like someone who had just... Well, that was something Adam didn't want to think about. He walked up the stairs and into the studio.

Fidessa was in that short silk robe again. She hadn't just taken a shower, but she looked like she'd had a workout. And she was smiling that smile of hers. She greeted Adam with a kiss on the cheek that lingered just long enough to be more than friendly without being obviously anything other than friendly.

Who was that man?

"You're early," Fidessa said. "Does this mean you've made your decision?"

"Um, yes. Uh, was that one of your models?"

"No. I hope you weren't expecting me to pine while I waited for you. So what is your decision?"

"I'll do it," Adam said. "I'll do it for sixty thousand."

"And have you thought about the alternative arrangement I suggested?"

"Sixty thousand," Adam repeated. Oh, yes, he had definitely thought about the alternative arrangement, but he was going to be firm. Especially since... who was that man?

"Well, I'm sorry," Fidessa said, "but that offer is no longer valid."

"Oh?" What kind of trick was she planning? "Well, you can..." He stopped: would it really be wise even to reject thirty thousand dollars? But his pride was involved.

Before he could continue, Fidessa stepped in. "The price has gone up to an even hundred thousand. Take it or leave it."

"Um..." Adam was sure there was supposed to be

something more coming out of his mouth, but he couldn't think of what it was supposed to be.

"Fifty now," Fidessa continued, "and fifty when we're finished."

Adam swallowed hard. Fifty thousand right now would be very helpful. "You'll write a check?"

"It's already in your account," she said. "You haven't been to your bank today?"

"No..."

"I was fairly sure of your decision."

"And...and what if I had taken the alternative arrangement?"

"Then it would have been a nice little gift for you. And I could have told Derek not to come back tomorrow."

Adam stood mute. Fidessa stood perfectly still too, but—was it his imagination, or had she somehow willed her robe to expose a little more leg?

And now he was fifty thousand dollars richer— somehow he absolutely trusted Fidessa when it came to money—which was more money than he had ever had at once in his life. But all he could think of was how much he hated Derek, whoever Derek was.

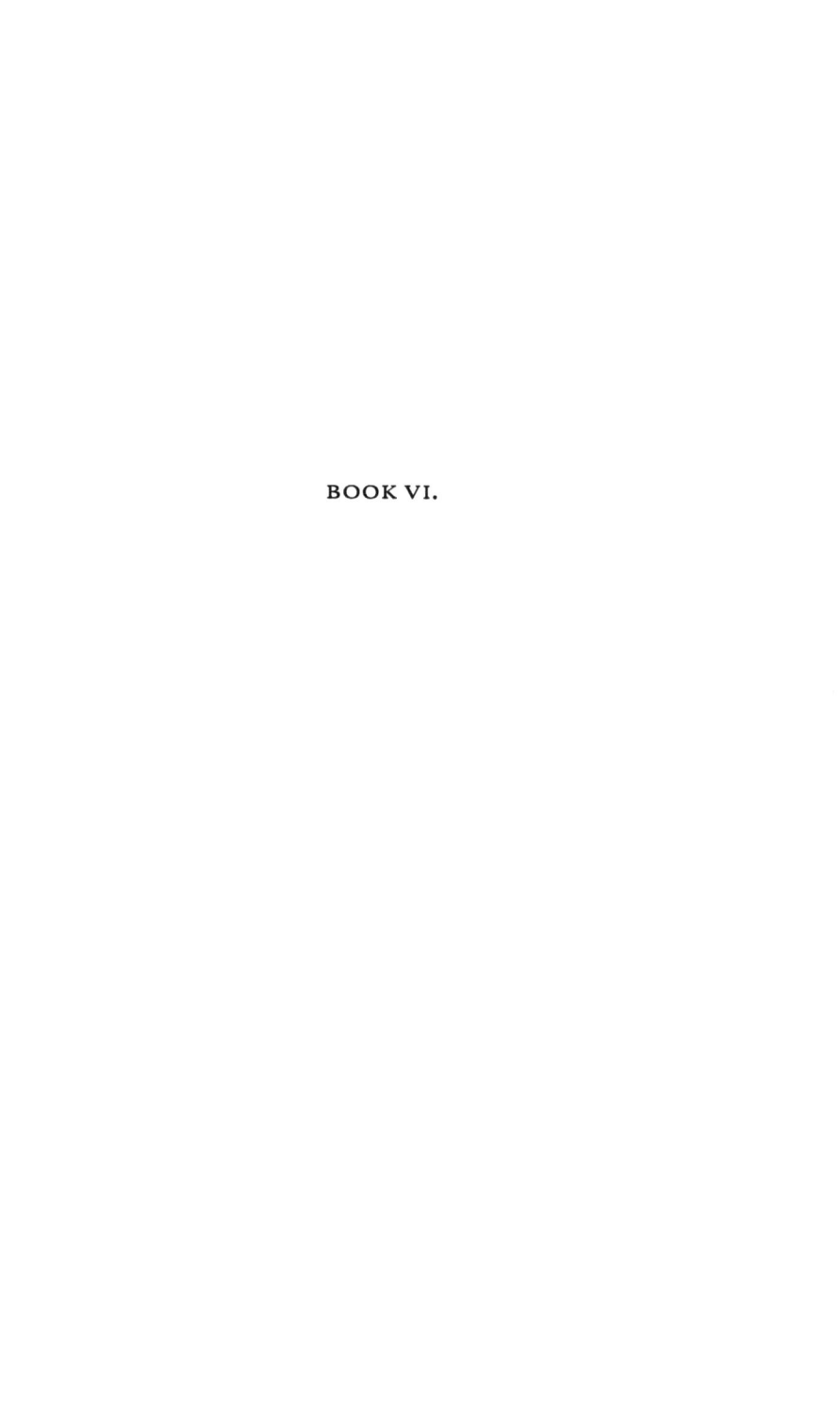

BOOK VI.

CHAPTER 26. RALPH.

SOMETHING absolutely unprecedented happened when Adam walked into the Wild Beans on Tuesday morning. Someone was sitting in his seat. There was Hope, next to the wall as usual, and there was some unidentified male sitting opposite her. Adam didn't know what to do. Obviously Hope was talking to the unidentified male, so it wasn't as though he had engineered a hostile takeover of the seat. Yet...it was supposed to be Adam's seat. Adam was almost ready to turn around and walk out, and then maybe walk back in again to see whether the universe had rebooted and come back to normal operating parameters, but then Hope noticed him and said something to the unidentified male, and both he and Hope stood up to face Adam, and Adam realized that this must be Ralph. He felt an absolutely unjustifiable wave of envy rolling over him. How could a man like that deserve a woman like Hope?

"Adam!" Hope was saying. "This is Ralph. Ralph,

my friend Adam."

Ralph was extending a hand, and Adam would probably have to accept it rather than punch the man, which was what he really wanted to do. Ralph looked...nice. He was tall, maybe a little overweight but not much, and he had a head that seemed too big for his body, accented by unruly black hair—a valiant attempt had been made to comb it, but it defied combing—that puffed into a dark nimbus.

So Adam took his hand in a firm and friendly grip and said, "I've heard a lot about you."

"Nothing good, I hope," Ralph said with a socially correct laugh, and Adam deducted a few more points.

"Any friend of Hope's," Adam said, not bothering to complete the sentence. Any friend of Hope's is my mortal enemy?

Hope turned to Ralph. "Call me at lunch, babe." Did she call him "babe"?

And then they kissed, which was really painful to watch, and Ralph said, "See you later, wild thing," and walked out.

"Wild thing?" Adam repeated, as if the words had got stuck in his mouth and he was trying to spit them out.

"His pet name for me," Hope said with a smile that looked a little sheepish.

"Wild thing," Adam repeated again.

"Hey, I've been working hard to deserve it."

"I really need some coffee."

He turned and walked up to the counter to order the usual Guatemalan, and discovered that it had run out again, which would just about make it a perfect day, wouldn't it? So he decided to try something from Kenya instead, because if there wasn't Guatemalan, he might as well give up on that whole corner of the world. And he decided to get a cinnamon roll, which might help drown out the taste of inadequate coffee. Cup and plate in hand, he returned to Hope's table, sat down, and repeated once more, "Wild thing."

"You don't have to listen if you don't want to hear it," Hope said, a little annoyed.

"Sorry. It's just...not the way I usually think of you."

"I know. Believe me, I've figured that out."

"So things must be going pretty well with Ralph," a name Adam couldn't pronounce without flattening out the A contemptuously.

"Pretty well," she confirmed.

"So here you are, madly in love. I guess that's good, isn't it?"

"It's very good. Um, I wouldn't really say madly in love, but that's part of what's good about it."

"What do you mean by that?" Adam had been about to bite into the cinnamon roll, but now he stopped. She wasn't in love with Ralph?

"It's comforting to be with someone who actually cares about me more than I care about him. I think that's the recipe for contentment."

"You mean you're happy being with someone you don't love?"

"I didn't say that. I do love Ralph, you know, in a way. Maybe I'm not *in* love with him, but he's in love with me, and that counts for a lot. And anyway I'm not looking for happiness. I gave up on that. I'm looking for contentment. I want to live without drama, without heartbreak, without pain. That's all. And... And Ralph thinks I'm sexy, and you have no idea how good for me that is."

"Well, of course he does. I mean, he probably never thought he'd get a woman anywhere near your league."

She looked at him over her tea with an expression of puzzled thought. "That's actually the nicest thing you've ever said about me, and yet it sounds like an insult somehow."

"Sorry. I didn't mean it as an insult." Not to you, anyway, Adam thought: he really meant it to insult Ralph.

"You know how good it makes me feel to be the star of somebody's fantasies? I mean, you must feel the same way with Rose, right? And I've felt so... so neglected. So if I can be Ralph's 'wild thing,' it makes me feel good about myself."

"It's just strange thinking of you that way."

"Yeah. Imagine me being a desirable woman. Who would have thought?" She took a sip of her tea, and Adam thought to himself that of course she was a desirable woman, although really he couldn't say that to her, because it might give her the wrong impression.

Adam wrote what he thought was some savagely good copy for the Masterpiece Inn account. A magazine ad that would make you believe that all those other hotels were infested with roaches and rats and possibly grizzly bears—it was perfect. It was funny, and it made the point the client wanted to make that the hotels were unusually clean and well-kept, and it would give Hope a lot of fun working on the design. He had accomplished it by imagining Ralph as the desk clerk at one of those other hotels, and then imagining that he ran the hotel the way he combed his hair.

He took a printed copy over to Hope—he always liked to read his copy on paper, which was very retro of him, Hope always said—and she liked it, too. He didn't tell her what had inspired it, but all the time they were talking he was thinking to himself that there was no way a man like Ralph deserved a woman like that.

In the evening he had another sitting with

Fidessa, but first he had some shopping to do. He had paid every outstanding bill and reduced his credit-card balance to zero, after which he still had $47,021.27 in his account. So he went to the wine shop and bought a bottle of real champagne for some special occasion—Rose's first night sleeping over, he hoped. Then he went to the grocery store in the neighborhood and bought as much good food as he could carry home—not cheap nutrition, but food he would really enjoy eating. And then it was time to see Fidessa, so he shoved everything into the refrigerator and walked out again.

Fidessa was her usual self. She still made the bottom drop out of his stomach; he had been thinking about Hope all day (that was odd, wasn't it?) but Fidessa drove every other woman out of his brain. Yet she wasn't playing any of her tricks—no attempts at seduction, no appearances in that little silk robe (Adam had been secretly hoping for the silk robe when he showed up fifteen minutes early, but no luck). She seemed especially focused on the portrait this time. She still wouldn't let him see it yet, but she seemed pleased by its progress. If indeed she was still working on the same portrait. For all Adam knew, she might be starting a different picture every time he sat for her. She had certainly accomplished a lot in their first session. Maybe she was making a dozen different portraits—the many moods of Adam Mueller.

"Are things going well with Rose?" Fidessa asked after at least a quarter hour of silent painting. She had stopped painting for a moment and was staring intently at his face. Then, as he worked to form a reply, she started working furiously with the brush.

"I think so," Adam said. Why hadn't he been more definite? Was it because he had spent most of the day thinking about Hope instead of Rose?

"You don't know?"

"Don't count your chickens... I mean, I'm sure things are going just fine. We have our usual Wednesday date coming up tomorrow."

"But you haven't had sex with her yet." She studied his reaction and painted it—he was sure that was what she was doing.

"That's still a bit personal."

"I'm paying a hundred thousand dollars to know you personally," she replied. But she didn't press the issue any further. She had already got her answer.

Adam, meanwhile, was trying to direct his thoughts back to Rose, but not succeeding. Fidessa was occupying his mind now—Fidessa in that oversized shirt, with her bare legs sticking out. She wasn't trying to seduce him, and yet he was more seduced than ever. Maybe she knew that. She was good at figuring these things out.

Even the ballet of her painting was...seductive. She obviously took such sensual pleasure from the movements of the brush, which involved her whole arm and made her whole body sway, that Adam couldn't help keeping his eyes glued to her the whole time.

Maybe, he thought, it wasn't too late. Maybe he could still tell her he wanted the alternative arrangement.

As soon as he thought that thought, he turned his mind, by a supreme effort of the will, back to Rose. Rose was the one he was supposed to be thinking of. Not Fidessa. She could have that fashion model, that Derek or whatever his name was, who was pretty and empty and probably stupid and completely unworthy of her, and Adam would take Rose.

"By the way," Fidessa said without breaking the rhythm of her painting, "my other offer still stands. The alternative arrangement, I mean."

How did she do that?

CHAPTER 27. JULIE.

WEDNESDAY afternoon Adam got a text from Rose saying she wouldn't be able to make it for their date that evening. "Can't make it. Paper due." That was what she wrote, and Adam didn't have any reason to suspect that she had any other reason than what she told him. Graduate students have to write papers, after all. She was probably up to her knees in test tubes or something right now. No, she didn't work with test tubes. It was worse. She worked with math. She was up to her knees in equations. Poor girl.

That left Adam with an unexpectedly free evening, and he spent the early part of it eating Cambodian food—that same Cambodian restaurant where he had taken Rose for their second date, but this time he ordered something rather expensive and just enjoyed the food without worrying about how he was impressing someone across the table from him.

And Hope, as he knew from this morning's conversation, was out with Ralph on their eighth date, followed, doubtless, by something, whatever was on Hope's list, that would cement her reputation in his mind as a "wild thing." He wondered whether Ralph would ever figure out that she didn't really love him. He wondered whether, under the circumstances, Ralph would care. He definitely envied Ralph.

Did he have to purge his mind of Hope, too? What was the matter with him? Why was he sitting here thinking of Hope, and how much he envied Hope's new boyfriend, when... Rose? "Ralph thinks I'm sexy," she had said. Well, of course he did. Everybody did, right? Adam certainly did. Although he would never tell her that, of course, because she might take it the wrong way.

But he should be thinking about Rose, who was also very pretty. He decided to give her an encouraging little text: "Missing you tonight," and a little heart. She liked little hearts. As it turned out, she didn't respond, so she must have turned off her phone or something so she wouldn't be interrupted in her work. Very sensible. Especially if she was doing math, which was hard.

After the Cambodian food, Adam decided that what he really needed was a new computer. His old desktop computer was on its last legs. He hadn't thought that before—he had thought it would last another three or four years—but then he hadn't had $46,893.06 in his account before. He went to the big office store and picked one out—not the low end of the range, but the middle, which was a first for him—and paid a little less than $600 for it without batting an eye.

On his way home, he had an interesting adventure: interesting in the sense of harrowing and embarrassing. He was just walking toward the bus stop when he ran straight into Derrida-woman. Not really ran into: more came into the sights of, and then she was on him like a leopard.

"So you're still alive," she said with a voice that rained sarcasm. That was the first he had been aware of her: she had seen him before he had seen her, or he might have avoided the encounter.

"Um," he said, and then he added, "Hi."

"So is your phone broken? Or did you just forget how to call back a number in your call log? It's right in your call log."

"I, um..." What was her name again?

Her sarcasm continued. "Or were you just too busy to pick up the phone and touch the screen? Or maybe you have one of those complicated phones where you have to unlock it first."

He remembered a name. "I'm sorry, Julia, I—"

"Julie. It's Julie. God, I hate it when people call me

Julia. Not that it would matter to you."

"I didn't—"

"I called you six times. It's enough, isn't it? Did you want me to call seven times? Is seven your lucky number?"

"Well. I—"

"Oh, that's fine for you to say. But it's too late now. I've *got* a boyfriend now. That's right. You missed your chance."

"I'm glad—"

"You could have been the one, but no. Too late. Sorry. You blew it. So now you're out of luck."

"Then—"

"And you know what? I'm glad I found out in time. What do you think of that? I'm glad. It makes things a lot simpler."

"Yes, it—"

"So goodbye, Andrew, and have a nice life. That's all I have to say. You don't have to worry about me anymore. I'm doing just fine, thank you very much."

"I'm sure I—"

"So if you see me around, you can just forget it. I'm busy for the next sixty or seventy years."

She turned around and walked away. And Adam thought to himself that, on the whole, the encounter could have gone worse. But it could have gone a lot better. And a primitive part of the brain was thinking that she looked awfully good from behind as she walked away in her tight jeans. He envied the new boyfriend.

Oh, he really had to clamp down on that primitive part of the brain.

❧

"How did I let it go that long?" Adam mumbled half to himself in the Wild Beans Thursday morning.

"Gee, Adam, I don't know," Hope replied. She was using her sarcastic voice.

"I mean, it was embarrassing, is all. It's not like it makes any real difference."

"No, of course not. You have Rose, right?"

"Yes." He took a sip of Guatemalan—the world was much better if the day started with Guatemalan—and then repeated it like an affirmation: "Yes, I have Rose."

"How did the date go last night?"

"Hm? Oh, I didn't see her. She had a paper due. You know, like you do when you're a student. I used to have papers due all the time when I was in college."

"But you talked to her?"

"Yes. Well, texted."

"And everything's all right between you?"

"I think so. Why shouldn't it be? I mean, she saw her old boyfriend, but—"

"What do you mean, 'saw'?" Hope was suddenly very alert, like a German shepherd who has just noticed a suspicious movement in the hedge.

"He came and talked to her, I gather, and she told him to bug off, and that was the end of it."

"Oh." She looked a bit mollified. "So you're not messing it up."

"Don't think so."

"Good. Because..." She leaned forward. "I really don't want you to mess this up."

"And how are things going with Ralph?" That should deflect her a bit.

"Oh, just fine. He's in Dallas the rest of the week, but we talk every night. And he'll be back Saturday, and it will be our ninth date. And so I'm planning something big for him, you know. The list. And I was, um, wondering, um, well... How well do you know that artist friend of yours? Does she, you know..."

Adam waited for the rest of the question, but it didn't come. Instead, Hope just said, "Never mind. There's got to be one of my friends."

Now he was really envying Ralph. He took a long, slow sip of his coffee to compose himself.

In the middle of the morning, Adam took some time out to compose a text to Rose: "How's the paper? Missing you." Then he went back to work, but every few minutes he checked his phone to see whether she had texted back. It was unnecessary, except that he might after all have missed the text sound, and the truth was that he wasn't getting any work done anyway, because he kept thinking about Hope and Fidessa, which made him feel guilty, and then he would check back on Rose. But she didn't reply. Maybe her phone had run out of batteries.

Rose didn't reply in the afternoon, either. He sent another text: "Hope all's well. Call if you need a break." But apparently she didn't need a break.

Finally, after an unproductive day of not writing anything useful, Adam had a modest dinner (he was eating out again because he had money now), and then made his way over to Brackenridge Avenue just as twilight was descending on the city again. Under the iron arch, the street was its usual self, with Thursday-night crowds still shopping and restaurants and nightclubs doing a good business. But as he approached the door to Fidessa's studio, Adam felt a curious sense of foreboding. Something was different.

It was the pretzel shop. There was no pretzel shop; its absence had made a subtle change in the streetscape. Instead, in the same little storefront, some new business had popped up. As Adam came closer, he saw the sign—simple, elegant, etched in wood with the letters picked out in gold: "TRUTH."

And through the plate glass he could see the

darkened interior. One light was on: a spotlight that shone on a simple desk in the middle of the room. And seated behind the desk—of course—was Fidessa.

CHAPTER 28. TRUTH.

ADAM stood outside for about a minute and a half looking through the window at the little pool of light inside. There was Fidessa, sitting behind a desk, looking very professional. She was watching him with a bland smile on her face, as if it made no difference to her whether he came in or went on his way. And the spotlight made the whole tableau into something oddly unreal. She seemed to be floating in infinite space—just Fidessa, a desk, and emptiness. She was dressed professionally, too, at least the part he could see above the desk. And yet she had, as always, managed to choose something that made her look enticingly perfect. Once again he thought of how much he envied that Derek person —the man he had seen exactly once on the stairs, but for whom he had built a whole personality, a very unattractive one, in his mind.

Surely this whole charade was for his benefit. How much had she spent on it? How much time had gone into it? And should he really allow her to go through with it? He could derail the whole train right now by just walking away. It would serve her right. He would walk away. He would smile, wave to her through the window, and turn around and walk away. That was just what he'd do, and it would be delicious to think that for once he had flummoxed her instead of vice versa.

And while he was thinking that very comforting thought, he found that he had opened the door and walked in.

She waited until he had taken a few steps toward her. Then she greeted him very politely and professionally: "Good evening, sir. How may we help you?"

"What's the deal?" Adam demanded.

"We have several attractive deals at the moment," Fidessa said, still with her bland and professional smile.

"You know what I mean. What's the scam? What little show do you have for me tonight? What special offer are you offering that I couldn't possibly resist?"

"Our business is a very simple one," Fidessa explained. "For a price, we can tell you the truth."

"Well, that's novel, anyway. The truth about what?"

"About anything, sir. About whatever there is

that you've been wondering about, whatever you have a deep longing to know. Whatever secrets have been kept from you, they can be revealed."

He had come to the front of the desk now, but he was very much aware that he was still standing in complete darkness, while she was flooded with light. "And why should I believe anything you tell me?"

"A very good question," she responded, as if she were reading from a script. "Naturally, the prospective buyer will want to be assured of the quality of the goods. That is why we insist on a free sample. When you have verified the truth of it, you will know that our service is reliable and legitimate."

Adam laughed slightly; it came out as a sort of snorting noise. "What kind of free sample of truth will you offer me? Maybe you'll tell me the capital of North Dakota? It's Pierre, by the way. I already know that one."

"Pierre is the capital of South Dakota," Fidessa told him with calm disinterest.

"Really?" He wasn't sure now. "Then what's the capital of North Dakota?"

"Bismarck," she said.

"Are you sure?"

"But these are questions you could answer with Wikipedia. Our answers are more personal. We can tell you the truth about yourself. About your own life. About the things you fear most, about your deepest hopes, about your secret desires. The things no one else could tell you. For a price, you can have absolute and reliable certainty."

"And what am I supposed to ask about?"

"Why, anything, of course. Naturally, our price will depend on the depth, so to speak, of the question. For easy answers, our prices are very reasonable. For more difficult ones, the price goes up proportionately. However, you can have one answer free. What question will you ask? What will you find out about yourself? Give yourself some time. Think carefully. Then ask your question, and it will be answered. And the answer will be the truth. Take as long as you need to verify it, and you will be assured of our veracity."

"What do you know about me that I don't know myself?"

"It doesn't have to be about you. Loved ones, family members—anyone who is part of your life can be the subject of an inquiry."

"So I could ask you my maternal grandmother's birthday, and you'd tell me the answer?"

"It's more common to ask about more sensitive matters. Things that have to do with desires, longings, hopes, dreams. Love."

Adam decided to end the charade. He didn't know what the game was, but he was tired of being a pawn in it. "Why don't you tell me something I don't know? Something I could verify, but something I don't know until I've verified it. Something that's personal to me, that isn't common knowledge. If you can do that," Adam concluded smugly, "I might actually believe you."

"Your new girlfriend slept with her old boyfriend last night."

Adam stared at her, not sure whether to give her an angry denial, a contemptuous dismissal, or—or just to turn around and leave. "I don't believe you," he said at last.

"Of course not," Fidessa said blandly and professionally. "That is why we insist on the free sample. That was your free sample, and now you must verify the truth of it yourself. Then you will be convinced, and of course you will be willing to pay our very reasonable prices for other inquiries."

Adam's phone chimed, but he ignored it for the moment. "Reasonable prices. What kinds of prices are we talking about? An arm and a leg, I suppose."

"The prices depend entirely on the depth of the inquiry. Some inquiries are very simple. Others take us into deep waters."

"For example," Adam said, leaning on the front of the desk, "suppose I asked you about my artist friend Fidessa Hao. What's her game? What is she up to? What's she involved with, and why is she do-

ing all these things to me? How much would it cost
to find those things out?"

"Oh," Fidessa replied, looking very serious. "Oh,
those are very deep waters indeed. You might not be
able to afford to ask that question. It might cost you
a great deal more than you would be willing to pay."

"So...an arm and a leg?"

"Shall we say your immortal soul? That seems a
fair valuation." Then she smiled that subtle and
dangerous smile of hers. "You ought to have picked
that as your free question."

Adam stood straight. "I'm leaving."

"Will you be going upstairs for your sitting?"

"Well, what would you advise? You are the
guardian of truth, after all. Should I go upstairs?"

Fidessa leaned back from the desk slightly. "I
think you have a text that needs your attention. You
might come back Saturday evening."

"I might have a date with my girlfriend Saturday
evening."

"You might," she agreed amiably. The bland and
professional smile was back. Adam felt as though
he was being dismissed. Without another word he
turned and walked back into the darkness toward
the door.

Fidessa's voice followed him: "See you Saturday
evening." He opened the door and walked out.

He needed the open air. Adam had never been

claustrophobic before, but that little storefront had given him symptoms of something like claustrophobia. It seemed to close in on him, and he realized now that his heart had been beating faster, and there was a high, sharp sensation in his nose, as if the air itself had been too thin to breathe.

He walked briskly down the avenue and turned into the first side street he came to, putting as much distance between himself and the business district —and especially Fidessa—as he could. He felt a need to escape. To escape from what was a question he couldn't answer, a question for answering which Fidessa had said she would charge him one immortal soul. She had a peculiar sense of humor.

And there was a text waiting for him.

He didn't look at it until he had put three blocks between him and Fidessa. Then he finally felt secure enough to take the phone out of his pocket and unlock it.

The text was from Rose, and there were only two words: "I'm sorry."

CHAPTER 29. A LONG WALK.

OF COURSE Rose could have been replying, finally, to his last text. It was there in the text stream: "Hope all's well. Call if you need a break." Yes, she was probably replying to that, telling him she was sorry she hadn't replied earlier. Or something like that. He sent a reply right away: "Do you need to talk?" He wished the text from Rose had been more detailed, less ambiguous, because his mind was uselessly inflating it into high drama. Fidessa's little game had had its effect on him. She knew exactly what she was doing, didn't she? Just plant the seeds of doubt, and watch them grow into a lovely waving field of angst and depression. Adam began to see the wisdom of Hope's low-drama approach to relationships. He envied her her tranquility. He envied Ralph for the fun he was having. Here Adam was with a girlfriend and a Fidessa, whatever she was, and all he had to show for it was a racing heart and a few beads of sweat on his forehead.

Rose wasn't replying to the text. Of course, to be fair to her, Rose had had only a few seconds to reply. Adam's racing mind had gone through quite a number of revolutions in that time, but if Rose had decided to send a text of more than three words, she must still be thumbing a reply. And that was even assuming she was replying right away. People don't always reply to texts right away, do they? Adam hadn't replied to Rose's text right away. She could be in the shower, or typing an important paragraph in her paper. She could be in front of the phone right now, thinking over her reply. It was a simple question, to be sure, but still Adam often started and erased a text several times before he got it the way he wanted it.

Well, there was no point in just standing in one spot and waiting for her to reply. He could walk around and wait for her to reply. He started moving again, ambling down the quiet street with no destination on mind. Certainly not home—not yet. It wasn't time to go home. At home his thoughts would be confined in the walls of his apartment; out here they could expand, and perhaps escape, which was what he really wanted. He didn't want to be stuck inside with the dread pressing in on him. He felt as though the dread would be more bearable if it had more room.

Of course—Adam thought as he walked slowly

across the cross street and into the next block, still holding the phone in his left hand—of course it was always a possibility that Fidessa had been right. Bradley wasn't going to give up, and Rose had admitted that she was susceptible to him, and Fidessa had this way of knowing things she wasn't supposed to know. It could be that Rose had succumbed to temptation, and it was all over, and it was all Adam's fault because he had got drunk and ended up with a temporary tattoo that he thought was permanent, which had happened because he was too susceptible to temptation himself.

And if that was true—

Well, if that was true, then it still didn't have to be all over with Rose. If she was sorry, then—then he could forgive her. He could forgive her, and then ask her to forgive him for something. For Fidessa, because he had come so close to doing the same thing. He could even confess about the party, telling her the whole story, and then they would be even.

Adam stopped walking for a minute, because another thought had just occurred to him, and it rather startled him. If Rose had taken a night with Bradley, some childish part of his mind insisted, then she owed him a night with Fidessa. Then they would be even, not before. One night of his ultimate fantasy, and then Rose could have the rest of his life if she wanted it. She owed him that much, right?

And that was the danger of Fidessa. She made him think things that... She made his mind into a... a thing he couldn't trust.

But all this was predicated on an assumption that was doubtless false. There was no reason to believe Rose had betrayed him. She had told Bradley to bug off. It was just one of Fidessa's tricks. One of her completely unaccountable tricks. And he would know that as soon as he talked to Rose. She hadn't texted him yet, but maybe she would answer if he called her instead of waiting for a text. He unlocked the phone and brought up Rose in the contacts and pushed the green phone icon, and the phone was dialing.

Rose's voice came on right away: "You've reached Rose Middleswarth. Leave a message after the tone, and I'll get right back to you." Then a beep.

That was the problem. Someone must have called her—maybe her parents in Suffolk or Sussex or wherever it was—and she was talking. Therefore she couldn't text. Adam left a quick message: "Hi, it's Adam, Call if you get a chance." Then he resumed his walk, convinced that he had done his best.

Convinced intellectually, but...

His stomach hurt. He wished he could be Ralph—

Ralph whose life was cheerful and uncomplicated, Ralph whom Hope would do anything to please, Ralph who didn't have to worry about anything. Ralph who had the ideal girlfriend, except for the little detail that she didn't really love him, which if he was lucky he might never find out.

It was dark by now, except that the western sky was still a deep indigo that glowed without shedding any appreciable light on the ground. Up and down the street, in all the neatly kept city houses, the ordinary domestic business of life was going on. Husbands and wives were telling each other about their days at work, or eating a late supper, or trying to make their kids do homework. How did they find each other and live happily ever after? Had they all gone through what Adam was going through? Had anybody in the history of the world gone through what Adam was going through, or was Fidessa an absolutely unique experience reserved for him alone?

A loud television was playing a sitcom behind somebody's open window. Adam couldn't hear the dialogue, but the rhythm of it was obvious and almost reassuring—line, line, laughter from the audience. Line, line, laugh. Occasionally it was line, line, line, laugh, which hit him like a badly constructed verse that wouldn't scan in a poem by a snobby teenager. Did Aristotle permit the rhythm to be interrupted like that in a situation comedy? The trouble with entertainment today was that it had no respect for the unities.

It was about time to try Rose again, so once more he poked her number. Once more she didn't answer. But if she was talking to her parents, for example, then that was perfectly normal, and in no way an indication that Fidessa was right. He hung up and kept walking. It was still a beautiful evening, and Adam still didn't want to be home right away.

He didn't get home until about ten, and by then he was very tired. Slow ambling seemed to be more exhausting than brisk walking, at least when there was something preying on his mind. He had called Rose four more times with no response. Either she was talking for a very long time, or she had turned off her phone, or she was ignoring him, or she was busy. He didn't like the images that popped into his head when he thought about "busy."

So Adam undressed and went straight to bed and turned out the light. and then he sat there and stared at the ceiling. There's no such thing as darkness in the city; there's only more or less light. A streetlight from the next street over made an expressionistically distorted projection of the window on his wall and ceiling. Adam stared at it for a while and tried to work out the geometry of it, but he couldn't think of the word for a figure that had two sides parallel and two sides not, and it was too frustrating to think about, so he gave up and closed his eyes.

What he saw when he closed his eyes was Fidessa. She was smiling that smile of hers, the one that seemed to be so full of meaning, so full of I-know-something-you-don't-know. He kicked that image out of his head by force and substituted the image of Fidessa in that little silk robe that left her perfect legs perfectly displayed. Then he realized that he was still thinking of Fidessa when he ought to be thinking of Rose, so he thought of Rose and immediately imagined her wrapped around Bradley in a very discouraging manner. He wished he could call Hope and talk to her, but when he thought of Hope he thought of the image of her kissing Ralph—an image that for some unknown reason had burned itself into his visual memory with indelible colors. That was a very discouraging image, too, although there was no real reason he should be discouraged, was there? He should be happy for Hope, except that she didn't love the man, and she deserved someone she could really love, didn't she?

For hours Adam's mind went though the same cycle: Fidessa, Rose, Hope, ceiling. Fidessa, Rose, Hope, ceiling. After a while the images became a bit more surreal, and Adam drifted off into a dream of Fidessa floating in space, smiling at him and telling him he could have anything he wanted as long as he didn't want it very much. And he thought that was a very odd offer to make, but she merely repeated it and smiled, and Adam told her that what he wanted was her, but she said he wanted her too much and he could have this toaster instead.

❧

With only three or four hours of fitful sleep, Adam wasn't in very good shape when he showed up at the Wild Beans the next morning. They were still out of the Guatemalan, and Adam asked for "whatever," and apparently they gave it to him because that was what it tasted like.

"If you're going to make faces like that," Hope said, "maybe you shouldn't drink that stuff."

"I'll survive," Adam said, making another disgusted face.

"Yeah, but you'll wear your face out. And I have to look at that face every morning, don't forget. You need to keep it presentable. You owe me that much. You owe Rose that much."

Rose. He wanted to tell her how worried he was, but he didn't know how to start that conversation. He still hadn't heard from Rose, and he had tried texting her again this morning. But... but it wasn't really anything to worry about, was it?

"What's the matter, Adam? No sarcasm this morning? Usually the wrong coffee fills you with sarcasm, like it's a digestive function or something."

"Sorry. I didn't sleep too well last night. So how are things going with Ralph?" That should keep her occupied for a while.

"Fine. He's in Dallas still, but he'll be coming home tonight, and then we have our ninth date to-morrow. I may have to deviate from the list, though. I've been calling everyone. I mean, you think you have a lot of friends, but then you just ask one little favor and see where it gets you. 'Oh, gee, I don't think I know your boyfriend well enough,' says the girl with the new boy toy every week. Or 'I've never done anything like that.' Like you've never been to camp."

"I'm worried about Rose," Adam said suddenly. He surprised himself as much as he surprised Hope.

"What do you mean, 'worried'?" She set down her tea and looked very concerned.

"I'm sure it's nothing." He wanted to talk about it, but he didn't want to talk about it. Not actually by moving his mouth.

"If you're worried, you're worried about something. It might be nothing, but it's definitely something."

"That's just what Immanuel Kant used to say."

"Don't Kant and Hegel me now. Tell me what's on your mind."

Adam looked down into his coffee and considered taking a sip of it before he went on. But the coffee wasn't worth it. He set it down and leaned on his elbows. "I'm sure it's just because I'm tired, and there's nothing to worry about. It's just that Rose has been hard to get in touch with since Wednesday, and, you know, she's usually not hard to get in touch with."

"Well, that's…" She leaned forward. "I'm sure it's nothing, like you said. I mean, she didn't give you any reason to think there was anything wrong, did she?"

"Not really. Just, you know, the old-boyfriend thing." He wanted help sorting out Fidessa's contribution to his worries, but what could he say? My artist friend opened a truth booth downstairs from her studio and gave me a free sample, and…

"You're way better than the old boyfriend. She's got to see that. I mean, she told me about the breakup, and that was when I told her I'd introduce her to you, and she said, 'Well, he's got to be better than Bradley.' So she's probably working on her paper, just like she said."

"You're probably right. That's what I've been telling myself."

"Do you want me to call her?"

"No," Adam said immediately. The one thing he was sure he didn't want was for Hope to find out Rose had betrayed him before he did. Somehow he couldn't handle the mortification of that.

Hope looked thoughtful for a moment. She picked up her tea and took a sip, and then set it down and said, "Here's what you do, then. Turn up the romance. Show her how much better you are than the old boyfriend. Even if nothing is wrong, it'll make you feel better. And it might move things along a little faster, which can't hurt, right?"

"Right," Adam agreed. It certainly couldn't hurt after the disaster of the tattoo.

"Flowers, soft lights—"

"I bought a bottle of good champagne."

"Champagne! Perfect. If that doesn't smooth the way, nothing will. Hope it didn't eat into your funds too much."

"Hm? —Oh, no, I kind of solved the money problems for a while. Just a bit more in the account now."

"Good news. How'd you do that?"

Adam smiled. "Moonlighting as an artist's model." And Hope took it as a joke, just as she was supposed to do, and so he hadn't had to lie to her.

✤

No texts or calls came from Rose in the afternoon, and none in the evening, and Adam really didn't know what to do with himself. He called four more times, and he texted three times, each time trying to sound casually concerned but not in any way desperate, but he didn't hear anything from her at all. Eventually he went to bed, and this time he did sleep, with dreams of Fidessa as usual.

Saturday morning he got up and made coffee and resolutely, superstitiously, avoided trying to call or text Rose. And at about eleven o'clock, there it was: the text chime. He seized his phone from the little side table in the living room and dropped it on the carpet and banged his head on the table retrieving it, but finally he had it unlocked, and there was a text from Rose. It said, "I need to see you."

He immediately replied, "Sre you OK?" and sent it, and then noticed the mistake. But she had already replied:

"Need to talk. Your apartment, 1:00?"

He replied, "OK," and then sat down and enjoyed the peculiar sensation of his heart lifting and sinking at the same time.

CHAPTER 30. ROSE.

FLOWERS. He had a little less than two hours to get flowers, and get the apartment ready, and get himself ready. First Adam ran downstairs and out the door toward the florist up the street, which was expensive but close. There he bought a dozen red roses and a vase, because he didn't have a proper vase, and it wasn't cheap but it might be worth it. Then he ran—well, walked briskly—back home and set them on the little table in the living room. And then he made a whirlwind cleanup, making sure the bedroom was attractive, because he was definitely going to pull out all the stops this time. He double-checked to make sure the champagne was in the refrigerator, and then dashed into the bathroom for a shower. And then he dithered for a while over the choice of clothes, wanting to look casual but attractive, as if he were a true gentleman born and bred, whatever that was. And then it was 12:30, and he waited five minutes, and then ran

back and changed his clothes because he had decided he looked like a clown. Then he brought the
champagne out of the refrigerator and set it on the
little table beside the roses, and then fetched his
dollar-store champagne flutes, which had never actually seen real French champagne before, and set
them beside the bottle. Perhaps it was all a little
elaborate for a Saturday afternoon at one, but Rose
was worth the effort.

So there was nothing to do but wait. And as the
clock came closer to one, Adam felt more and more
fidgety and nervous. By the time it was 1:04 and
still no Rose had appeared, he was feeling quite a
bit of panic.

But there was a knock downstairs at 1:07, and
Adam nearly tripped on his way down to get the
door before she gave up.

She was looking pretty and a little distracted. It
had been Adam's intention to greet her with a kiss,
but she sort of slipped past him before that happened, so he followed her up the stairs and into the
living room.

She stopped just inside the door from the stairway, and then walked in more slowly, saying, "Um,
this… This isn't why I'm here."

"Flowers make any occasion brighter," Adam
said. He sounded like an advertisement for some
trade association of florists, he thought. A very bad

advertisement. He was supposed to be a better copywriter than that.

"Adam," she said. She didn't say anything more.

"I, uh... I have some champagne, too, if you'd like."

She turned around to face him. "Adam, I slept with Bradley."

There were six or seven seconds of silence, and then Adam said, "I kind of thought so."

She looked a little surprised, but probably not very surprised. "Why?"

Oh, well, it was my free sample of Truth. That was what he didn't say. "You told me he'd been coming to see you, and you were still attracted to him, and then I didn't hear from you for a couple days, except that one text that said 'I'm sorry,' and... I thought all sorts of things, actually, but that was one of them."

"I suppose it wasn't all that hard to figure out. Not for anyone but me. I thought I was so bloody over him."

"Why don't we sit down and talk," Adam suggested. It would give him time to think of something else to say, anyway.

Rose nodded and moved to one of the Salvation Army chairs. Adam took the other one. She was sitting near him, but her eyes weren't meeting his.

She began to talk in a much flatter, less expressive tone than she usually used. "I want you to know this isn't your fault. It's completely my fault, not yours."

"We don't need to talk about 'fault'..."

"Of course we do, Adam. I cheated. It's my fault. That's simple enough."

"The important thing," Adam began, having no idea what the important thing would turn out to be, "is that... you came and told me."

"The important thing is that I'm not good enough for you," she said with an oddly detached expression. "The important thing is that you deserve better, and I deserve... I deserve what I keep getting."

"That's not true. You deserve the best there is. I'm not the best—I know I'm not—but I can keep trying to get better. If you'll let me, I'll work hard to be worthy of you." He actually believed every word he was saying right now. The emergency had brought out a single-minded focus he didn't think he was capable of. He wasn't thinking about Fidessa right now at all. He was thinking about Rose, as he would realize much later on when he recalled this little conference.

"I think you *are* worthy, Adam." She actually did meet his eyes now for the first time. "I think you're the worthiest man I know. You've been as sweet, as kind, and as considerate as any woman could possibly want. But I'm not as good as you are. I'm just...

I'm not a good person, Adam."

"Of course you are."

"No. No, I'm not. At least, not when it comes to—to love. The problem is, is that you're everything I should want if I were a good person. But I have these needs. I'm ashamed of myself, but I do. I can't control it. I know Bradley is bad for me. I'm not stupid. But every time I see him, every time I think about him, it's like the bottom drops out of my stomach or something. It's a feeling I can't describe. If I were a good person, I could get over it. But I can't."

Words were the only weapons Adam had, and they seemed dreadfully inadequate right now. But he couldn't give up—partly because if he did he would lose Rose, and at least as much because Bradley would win her. "I'm not perfect, either. I told you about my artist friend Fidessa—"

"Yes, you were attracted to her. You told me. That's sweet, Adam. It's almost cute. It's not news that men get attracted to good-looking women, Adam. I think women know that as a general rule. It's not quite the same as falling into bed with her when you already have a girlfriend."

"You made a mistake. We can get over it."

"That's not the point! Oh, Adam! I— Adam, I don't want to tell you this, because I've never known anyone nicer than you. But I didn't fall in love with you. I thought I could, I thought it had to be inevitable, but... But there was Bradley. I knew what falling in love was like, and it was like that. And my brain tells me I'm stupid, but my heart is so powerful, Adam! It makes me so miserable when it doesn't get what it wants. And my heart... My heart wants Bradley. It wants him so much! And I'll be sad and miserable for the rest of my life, because he makes me so unhappy, and maybe he'll leave me someday, and I'll just die. And I still have to have those moments, those times when I feel that hot thrill all the way down to my shoes, because... because I'm stupid and weak, and I can't do without them. I'm an addict, Adam. I need my fix all the time. I don't think you can possibly know what it's like to be addicted to a thrill like that, so that you have to keep coming back for it even when you know it's leading you straight to hell, so completely helplessly addicted that you'll throw away your best chance at happiness to get it one more time. But that's me. I'm throwing away happiness and taking misery, Adam. And I hate myself for doing it, and most of all I hate myself because I'm hurting the kindest man I've ever known—oh, Adam, when I think of how I've hurt you, I think I should just kill myself. But I know if I stayed with you I'd end up hurting you more. The longer I stayed, the worse it would be when it came. So there's just one thing to do, and... Adam, I can't see you again."

Adam was calm and quiet. He knew it had been leading up to this, and now that it came, he was going to force himself to accept it rationally and sedately, no matter how much raw fury was building up inside him—raw fury with no real object other than himself. "Is that your final decision? Because I can wait. But if—"

"It's my final decision. God help me."

Adam sighed very quietly, the way a soft cushion sighs when a kitten sits on it. "Then I suppose I... I guess I just have to appreciate the time we had together, and... and wish it could have turned out differently."

"I know. And that's why I feel so miserable. Because you even took this like a gentleman, Adam. My one chance at a gentleman! It makes me want to cry." (But she wasn't crying.) "I'm such an idiot. But I know now what kind of idiot I am."

"Would you like any champagne? As a goodbye toast, maybe?"

For the first time she smiled, although her smile was sadder than the dully neutral expression it replaced. "Save it for the girl who's really worthy of you."

"Rose, don't think you're unworthy," he said very calmly. He would not let her see the rage that was building up more and more inside him. "Just tell yourself we had some good times, and it ended, and we both went on."

She stood up. "You're right. I'll go now. And I hope... I hope you have the happiness you deserve. That I couldn't give you. I hope you have better than what I did give you. And I'm so sorry, Adam. I'm so sorry."

He stood up and gave her a kiss on the cheek, which she accepted. And then she looked over at the little table.

"Bradley never bought me flowers," she said. "Not once."

And then she was gone. She walked down the stairs, refusing Adam's offer to see her to the bottom of the steps like the perfect gentleman she thought he was—an illusion he was going to maintain for her to the last. He watched out the window as she walked across the street, thinking how much he wished he could be Bradley. Then she stepped into her little Honda and started it and drove away, and that was that.

And the rage was still boiling, with nothing to restrain it now.

Adam looked at the vase of roses. He stepped over to the table and picked it up and turned it slowly. A terrible calm rationality had descended on him: he was observing his own anger, his boiling rage, like some interesting natural phenomenon, thinking to himself, "In a moment this vase will be flying across the room, with regrettable results."

He felt his arm pulling back, and the tension of the contracting muscles as he heaved the vase toward the wall. It shattered with a loud crash, and bits of glass flew everywhere. Some of them narrowly missed hitting him.

He would have to be more careful when he threw the champagne bottle.

BOOK VII.

CHAPTER 31. RAGE.

THE champagne bottle refused to shatter. It took a wedge out of the plaster, but then it just bounced off the wall and rolled on the ugly green carpet. It should have broken with a satisfying explosion followed by a spray of fizz. Its refusal to cooperate made Adam even angrier than he was before.

What else was there to throw? His cell phone was handy. It would probably be a bad idea to throw it, because it was rather expensive, but Adam could see that it was going to be thrown whether it was a good idea or not. Yes, the muscles were contracting again, and here came the heave, and there it went across the room, hitting the wall and splitting into three pieces that Adam recognized as the main body, the back, and the battery pack. Perhaps it was still salvageable. Perhaps he ought to try again.

But the little table was right here, and there were still two unthrown champagne flutes on it. They would certainly shatter with a satisfying little crash. He picked one up by the stem. It was a bad idea to fill the living room with shards of glass this way, but it couldn't be helped. He could see that it was going to happen whether it was a bad idea or not. Yes, there went the glass flying toward the wall, and there was the crash, with glass flying in all directions. That would take some sweeping and some careful vacuuming. The other glass followed it with nearly identical results.

And then there was the table itself. It was light enough to lift with one hand by one of its three legs, and it would certainly not be a good idea to heave it across the room, because if it hit something along the way it could do some serious damage. But apparently it was going to be heaved against the wall anyway. It cut another wedge out of the plaster, and Adam wondered to himself how easy it would be to do the plaster repairs, or whether he would have to hire someone to do them. He certainly wasn't going to call the landlady about them.

Now what was he going to do? He looked around for other things to throw. His apartment was actually full of projectiles. Strange how he had never thought of it that way before, but it was amazing how many of the things he owned could fly through the air and shatter against the wall. Perhaps it was just as well that the idea had never occurred to him before. The results were going to be a lot of dull and annoying work to clean up.

He stopped himself—it seemed that his rational mind was regaining some motor control again—and breathed heavily. Throwing things was hard work. And cleaning up would be harder. Perhaps it would be best to retreat to the bedroom where, on the whole, objects were softer, and where he could throw himself on the bed and sulk. It seemed as though sulking was a good alternative to blind rage.

But as soon as he made it to the bedroom, the rage returned, and pillows and blankets started filling the air. At least they didn't damage the plaster, although they did incidentally break a pot in which he'd been trying to start a sprig of variegated ivy. At least the window behind it was still intact. It would have been very annoying to have to replace that.

And then, just as suddenly as it had begun, his tantrum was over. The rage wasn't gone; it was still a dull roar in his ears, like the roar of the ocean in the distance. But now it was time to sulk, not to throw things.

Adam threw himself on his mostly stripped bed. He wished it still had at least one pillow, but the pillows were both on the other side of the room, and immobility was the only proper state for a good sulk.

Fidessa. Fidessa had done this to him. Rose

couldn't fall in love with him because she needed to feel the passion. She would have got plenty of passion if it hadn't been for that tattoo. He still didn't know how the tattoo had got there, because he didn't remember anything from that drunken stupor. But he was absolutely positive that Fidessa was the reason it was there. Who else would do that to him? Unless he had done it to himself—well, no, that wasn't physically possible, was it? But he could have told somebody to do it to him. That tattoo artist, for example. And if he did, whose fault was that? Well, his own, obviously, but ultimately Fidessa's. Everything was Fidessa's fault.

And yet there was still the other half of his brain —the half that told him, All that is irrelevant. Fidessa is Fidessa. She is the most desirable woman in the history of the world. She is Cleopatra and Helen of Troy and Lillian Russell and Marilyn Monroe multiplied by ten. And it doesn't matter what the rational half of your mind tells you about her, because you will always want her more than life, and now, by the way, you don't have a girlfriend to worry about.

You've lost her. Yes (it was like a tennis match, and the ball was in the rational side's court now), he had lost Rose, and he would eventually have to tell Hope about it. And Hope would be so very disappointed, because she had put so much work into getting him and Rose together. She had tried so hard to make sure this relationship worked out for him. And why? Only because she wanted him to be happy. In spite of her sarcasm, she was his one dis-interested friend, the only one who really loved him. In his state of strange hyper-rationality, he could see that now. No one had ever loved him as much as Hope had.

If only she could have been in love with him—if only she could have wanted him that way—then none of the rest of this would have happened. Fidessa might still have been attractive, but with a beautiful woman like Hope who really loved him, wouldn't he have been satisfied? But no, he always had to make sure she knew he wasn't interested in her that way, because... Because of the tests. Be-cause she kept asking him...

She kept asking him why he wasn't going out with her. She kept asking him why he wasn't at-tracted to her. She kept asking him why he didn't want her for a lover.

They had all been tests, and he had failed every one.

It was as if his head had been ripped off and put on forwards for the first time. The rage had cleared the clogs out of his brain.

It must be true. It had to be true. He wanted to throw something again, but there was nothing on the bed to throw unless he got up and removed the sheet, and he wasn't ready to get up. He was feeling sick to his stomach. There was one true friend in the world, one woman who really loved him, and he had completely missed it—misread her clear signals, cowered in front of her obvious begging for his attention. His brain was all cleared out by the anger now, and he saw things the way they really were.

And what good did it do him? She had a Ralph now. A big-headed boyfriend who called her "wild thing," which was more and more disgusting the more he thought about it.

But then—she didn't love him. She had said as much. She had been hit by Cupid's arrow, but not this time. No, she hadn't fallen in love with Ralph. She had fallen in love with Adam. And what was he going to do about that?

It was another test. All this time she'd been going out with Ralph, but all this time she'd been dropping the hints right and left—telling him she didn't love Ralph, telling him she had loved somebody else, telling him she had realized he didn't think of her that way, and sounding disappointed. Disappointed! And he had shied away every time she had mentioned love. Every time she had hinted to him that she really wanted him, not Ralph, he had decided this was one of her tests. And it was. But he was getting the answers all wrong!

The rage was building up again. Had he really ruined his chance at the one woman who was really suited to him—the one he knew better than anyone else in the world, the one he loved with a strong and comfortable love that could carry him through the rest of his life? He thought he had lost Rose, but Rose was only a symptom of the big mistake, the life-ruining mistake.

And Fidessa... Was it really worth all this just to follow that stomach-inverting thrill? Fidessa had done this to him, he said to himself; and then he immediately corrected himself, because he knew that Fidessa had done nothing except bring out the worst in him—the worst that was already there.

Was it too late for redemption? Was it too late to confess his sins and beg for forgiveness?

All the facts were in front of him, and they all pointed the same way. Hope still loved him. Hope still wanted him. Hope was despairing because he wouldn't respond to her love. She was so desperate she had taken up with this Ralph character, a man she didn't love.

He would rescue her. He would rescue himself.

He suddenly jumped up and headed for the living room, which was a dreadful mess and needed immediate attention. But he could find the three pieces of his cell phone, and when he put them together, the screen lit up and the thing started booting up. It still worked.

How long could it possibly take? The same time it always took to boot up, obviously. But that was too long. His whole life was at stake here. The logo was still on the screen. Then at last it vanished, and the home screen appeared, still lazily reconstructing itself.

At last! It was ready to be a phone again. He found Hope's number in the contacts—the thing seemed deadly slow, but it might not have been any slower than usual, just measured against his racing heart—and pushed the green phone icon.

A ringback tone. Another ringback tone. Please don't let it go to voice mail. Another ringback tone.

Then Hope's voice, a beautiful voice even on the telephone, saying, "Hi, Adam, What's up?"

"I really need to talk to you," he said.

"Sure."

"In person. Do you have time to meet me?"

"Um... okay. Is everything all right?"

"I'm just figuring some things out. I need to talk."

"If it can wait two hours, I'm totally free."

"How about Schenley Park?"

"Okay," she agreed. "By the Greek lady?"

"Hygieia?"

"That's the one. See you at four-thirty?"

So it was agreed. She would meet him, and Adam

would pour out his heart and pray—it was worth praying for—that he was right about everything at last.

But first he had an appointment with a broom, a dustpan, and a vacuum cleaner.

CHAPTER 32. HOPE.

THE bus was two minutes late, which was enough to bring back waves of anger that washed over him while Adam stood helplessly, almost outside of himself, and watched them roll by. But then the bus did come, and it would be all right: he would make it on time if he walked fast.

He started walking fast as soon as he stepped out onto the sidewalk, adroitly making his way through the university crowds, and it was just as well for them that nobody seriously impeded his progress. The crowd thinned out as he crossed the Junction Hollow bridge, and he began to relax a little. He was going to see Hope. Hope always made him feel better. Why had it taken him so long, and so much pain, to realize that Hope was the only human being in the world who always made him feel better?

The temperature was perfect for walking. The sky was overcast with beautifully textured watercolor-wash clouds in artistic shades of bluish grey, and a gentle breeze tossed the leaves of the ginkgo trees without bending their branches. He was walking along the front of the conservatory now, and the summer flowers were just beginning to fill in, and it struck him that on the whole the world could be a delightful place after all, because life could be simple. It wasn't necessary to worry about love, the future, or even the impossible attraction he still felt for Fidessa. It was only necessary to accept what Hope had been offering all this time, and the other problems would take care of themselves.

And there she was, waiting by the statue of Hygieia, reading something on her cell phone, looking pretty and summery in jean shorts and an arts-festival T-shirt—pretty, summery, and uncomplicated. Adam felt a surge of affection for her—almost like infatuation, but deeper and more substantial. He had cried out for help, and she had answered his cry. All the anger he'd felt—he realized now that he was angry at himself, angry that he had missed the one friend who really loved him. But he had one more chance. If she really wasn't in love with Ralph —if all her hints added up the way he was sure they did—then he could still have a happy ending. And so could she, which mattered at least as much. He was rehearsing his speech in his mind one last time as he approached her. Then she looked up and saw him, and the expression of combined relief and concern on her face was more endearing than all of Rose's pretty smiles.

"Are you all right?" was the first thing she said to him. "You sounded so..."

"I just wanted to talk. I need to talk. I'm... Take a walk with me?"

"Of course."

He led her across the drive and then down the steps to the woodland trail in the hollow. Neither said anything as they descended; but at the bottom of the steps, Hope told him, "For someone who had to talk, you don't have much to say."

They started strolling down the trail in the whispering forest, and Adam still didn't say anything. For all the rehearsing he'd done, he had only just realized, he'd never come up with a beginning to his speech. He'd been rehearsing the middle, and especially the end.

Hope continued, since he wasn't saying anything yet. "If it's money, I meant what I said. I'll help you as much as I can. I'll find a way."

"It's not about money." The winding trail seemed to go deeper into the woods and farther away from civilization, so that the two of them might have been the only human beings left on the planet. And that would have been all right. A cardinal was singing somewhere nearby, and gentle puffs of cool air rolled out of the dim recesses of the forest.

Adam sighed and began with the bad news: "It's over with Rose."

"Oh, Adam! Oh—oh, I'm so sorry. But do you—I mean, have you really given up? Is it something you said or did? Maybe if you—"

"She's gone back to Bradley. She says she just had... She had to follow her heart. I was always nice to her, but she couldn't feel the passion. That's basically what she said. She put it a lot better."

"Oh, Adam—" Her hand was on his shoulder. It was a caring touch, a touch that transmitted warmth and love so that they penetrated straight to his heart. "I'm so sorry. I don't know what to say. I never thought she would do that to you. I don't know—maybe you could still—"

"No, it's final. And I think she's right. I think... I really liked Rose. She's sweet, she's pretty, she's smart, but... But there wasn't passion between us. I liked her, and that was it. I thought I could fall in love with her, but I didn't. And obviously she didn't fall in love with me either. So I was really hurt when she told me, and then I was really angry, but then..."

He stopped and turned to face her, and she turned to face him. The breeze made quiet music in the maples over their heads, and Adam continued in a softer voice:

"But then I realized that I was never really in love

with her, and I know she was never really in love with me. And I must have known that all the time. I did know it all the time. But all the time there was someone I loved right next to me—someone who cared about me, who kept telling me she cared about me, someone who was perfect for me, and I was so afraid to go further because I loved what I had with her so much that I couldn't bear to lose it —someone who was kind, and funny, and smart, and—and absolutely beautiful,—someone I think I've been in love with since the moment I met her. And it's you."

He looked deep into her eyes and saw the tears welling up, and then there were needles of pain all over his left cheek, and there had been a sharp noise almost like a gunshot that echoed in the hollow. She had slapped him.

"You bastard!" she shouted, tears pouring down her cheeks. "You bastard! God!" She turned away, sobbing.

Adam put his hand on her shoulder. "Hope, I—"

"Shut up!" She whipped around to face him again. "Do you have any idea what you put me through? I gave you my heart—I gave you my soul —and you didn't care. Nothing I did could make you love me. Nothing I said could make you love me. And I loved you so much! I loved you so much I gave you Rose, because I thought if I couldn't be happy at least you could. And every time I thought about you kissing her it was like being stabbed. And when you went on your third date with her—while you were out having fun I was home crying my eyes out all night. And now you think you can just—just —just win my heart with a pretty little speech? God! I don't have a heart, Adam! You ripped it out of me and tore it in pieces and stepped on them! God, I hate you! I hate you! Why? Why?"

That was all she said for a moment, because she was sobbing uncontrollably. She turned away with her hands over her face.

The only sounds in the woods were the leaves moving lightly in the breeze, and a blue jay's raucous cry in the distance, and the quiet sobbing of Adam's best friend in the world.

"I..." Adam began. "I think I'd better—"

"Oh, God, Adam, I hit you!" She turned to face him again, wiping the tears from her eyes with her palms. "Oh, God! I'm so sorry! I hit you! Please tell me I didn't hurt you! Please! I can't live if I hurt you! Please!"

Adam felt the hot stinging in his face, and all sorts of sarcastic replies occurred to him. But she had broken down in sobs again, and all he said was, "I'm not hurt."

She gasped through her sobs. "I loved you so much! I'm going to marry Ralph. I have to go. Don't call me."

She turned and half-ran back along the trail, and Adam watched her go, his eyes telling his brain how beautiful she was as she became smaller and smaller in the distance; and now next to the century-old trees she was really quite insignificant. Then there was a curve in the trail, and the forest swallowed her up completely, and she was gone.

And Adam knew that, in his memory, that would be the final recorded image of her—the Hope he had just seen, Hope with tears streaming down her face, Hope telling him she hated him with a hatred he knew he deserved. And all his anger returned, but there was nothing to throw and nothing to break, and he stood paralyzed and let the anger wash over him like a mudslide. Worst of all, it wouldn't be the last time he saw her—they had to work together, after all. But it was the end. The forest had closed around her with a beautiful and peaceful finality like the closing of a grave.

CHAPTER 33. RETRIBUTION.

IT WAS a long walk back. Adam refused to take the bus; he was afraid that, with his anger simmering the way it was, innocent commuters might get hurt. He had done the right thing at last—he had finally understood everything. And he had been right! That was what hurt so much. He had been right. But he had been right too late.

Now what was left for him? It was a rare day when he had a chance to be rejected by two women within three hours. Normally he kept the rejections down to no more than one a day.

There was Fidessa, of course. Her alternative arrangement, she had said, was still open. And why not? Why the hell not?

He was furious with Fidessa. He held her responsible for—this. Whatever this was, she was responsible for it. Yet she was still his ultimate fantasy. Could they have a relationship fueled by lust and rage on his part and—what?—calculation on hers?

And how long would it last? How long till she decided she was bored with her toy and wanted a new one?

But what was left for him besides Fidessa? If she had been the cause of all his failures, didn't she owe him at least one success? If his lust for her, his greed for her money, all the allurements she had used to trap him in her web—if those things were the causes of his misery, then didn't she owe him some consolation? Physical consolation at least, even if the spirit was irreparable?

He walked and walked and walked, keeping to the back streets as much as possible to protect the innocent pedestrians around him. He began to see that he was facing an internal contradiction. Half of him wanted retribution from Fidessa. The other half was madly in love with her, and had been since his first glimpse of her on Brackenridge Avenue. Hope was right. Love at first sight might be rare, but you don't get over it. You might be older and wiser and calmer, but you never would get over it. He was sure Fidessa would haunt him forever. And forever he would be asking, What if...?

He would be asking that unless he found out what if.

What was this "love," anyway? Was it the same as lust? Surely not. It was something more elevated and more horrible than lust. It involved every fac-

ulty of his mind as well as his body. It was an irrational conviction that Fidessa was worth any sacri-
fice. If she were in danger, he would not hesitate to
die for her. On the whole, he'd still rather not die,
but the simple fact was that he would rather die
than live knowing he could have saved her and
didn't. That was what this love was: an obsession,
certainly, but an obsession that took his very best
qualities and wrapped them around its little finger.

The neighborhoods changed around him. The
broad spaces of the park gave way to the urban bustle of Oakland, which gave way to the serene man-
sion-lined streets of Shadyside, which finally gave
way to the outer reaches of Brackenridge Avenue,
the less fashionable end of the street, where not-
quite dive bars abounded, where—not very much to
his surprise—Adam happened to see Bradley.

Actually, Bradley saw him first. He was just walking down the street, and he saw Adam, and it acti-
vated the gloating circuits in his brain. "Hey!" he
said, with malicious cheer. "It's Adam. How's it going? What's new?"

"Same old crushing futility of modern existence,"
Adam replied. "Same old soul-racking existential
despair." If he gave Bradley no opportunity to make
him more miserable than he already was, perhaps
the man would just continue walking and leave him
alone.

"Look," Bradley said, "I'm sorry about what happened. Well, no I'm not. I mean, I told you I wasn't a nice guy. I gave you fair warning. But there was nothing you could do about it. Best man won. Rose just isn't your kind of woman. Your kind of woman is a lot uglier."

"I'm sure you're right," Adam said. He started walking again, and Bradley insisted on following him. Why couldn't he just enjoy Rose instead of having to enjoy his triumph?

"I mean, she took a chance on a guy like you, and she found out what she was missing."

"Doubtless," Adam agreed, walking faster. He turned into Wallace Street, picking up his pace, but Bradley matched his pace and kept walking beside him.

"I was thinking you couldn't satisfy her in bed, but Rose says you never got her into bed." Bradley was smiling: Adam wasn't looking at him, but he could hear that smile. It sounded like the squeal of a feedback loop.

"I suppose she told you everything. It's her right."

"I made her tell me. I told her I wouldn't do her if she didn't."

" 'Do' her?" Adam stopped and turned suddenly to face Bradley. "I know what it's like to fall in love with someone who's no good for you, so I won't blame Rose for anything. Except for choosing you over me, she has nothing to blame. But you—you grab her by her one weakness and use it to humili - ate her just for the sake of some sick need to be tri - umphant over your competition. Well, that's abom - inable. You're not a gentleman. And you don't care about that, but it makes me feel better to know it."

Bradley was already laughing. " 'Gentleman'! That's funny. You're a gentleman, are you? I don't even know what a gentleman is. I guess it's a word for 'guy who doesn't get laid.' "

The anger was boiling again, which was too bad, because Adam had really hoped this encounter would be as painless as possible—that he could just walk past Bradley and go be miserable by himself. But here he was, in that very rational state of ex - treme rage again, observing with calm interest as his fist headed for Bradley's jaw.

And that didn't work out very well, did it? Bradley easily blocked the punch, and a moment later Adam was doubled over on the sidewalk, his whole abdomen just beginning to register the pain in all its glorious intensity, his breath hardly man - aging to come into his lungs. Bradley was evidently a much more skilled fighter than he was, which was not very surprising, was it?

"Rose loves me," Bradley said. "Rose will do any - thing for me." He was looking down at Adam with a sickening smile; he had really enjoyed punching

Adam in the stomach. "And I'm going to make her do everything."

Then he passed out of Adam's field of vision, having presumably accomplished his heart's desire of triumphing over his enemy.

Strangely, Adam wasn't even angry. In pain, yes. He was having trouble breathing. But the anger had been knocked out of him along with the breath. He had no rage at the moment. It would come back— oh, yes, it would come back often. But right now there was something strangely satisfying about the certain knowledge that Bradley was as bad as he thought he was.

❧

The stiffness would go away sometime, and there were no serious injuries. Just bruises. Adam put ice on the bruises for a while, and then he decided that the ice was more uncomfortable than the bruises were, so he gave up on that. The anger was back; it was like an old friend now.

With slow and painful movements he finished cleaning up the damage in his apartment, putting the variegated ivy in a cup, retrieving the bedding from the various corners of the bedroom, sweeping up the dirt and pot fragments. He tried eating a lit-tle, but he wasn't hungry for the expensive frozen ravioli he had bought, and he ended up putting it in the refrigerator with a plastic bag over the plate.

So what was left? He had lost Rose. He would never really be Hope's best friend again, so he had not only lost his chance at romance with her but also the only friendship he really had.

But he had an appointment with Fidessa tonight, didn't he?

CHAPTER 34. THE PORTRAIT.

THE walk over to her studio was painful. Every step made the bruises ache—not just the bruise in his abdomen, but also the bruises on his knee from falling to the sidewalk in such an undignified manner. And every ache made Adam even angrier.

But there was only one thing left for him. It was Fidessa or nothing. And he would not be left with nothing.

She greeted him at the door of her studio (the pretzel shop downstairs was a pretzel shop again, of course) with a kiss on the cheek, and made no reference at all to his subdued behavior. Not that she didn't notice it: as soon as she started painting, it was clear that she found him a particularly fascinating subject this evening.

She was painting in her usual manner, with long intervals of fine brushwork, and then a considerable pause to examine the subject, and then a few theatrical broad strokes, and then more concentrated fine brushwork. Adam wondered again whether she was still working on the same portrait, or whether she had started a new one each time. It was impossible to tell unless she let him look at the thing, and she still refused to do that.

It was hot in the studio. After about half an hour she slipped off her floppy shirt, leaving her in a tight little men's undershirt that sculpted every detail of her form. The heat was a good excuse, but Adam was sure she had done it for the effect on him. She watched him intently after she tossed the shirt aside, and then came a flurry of painting that seemed to be provoked by whatever change she saw in his face. It was devious and manipulative of her, but deviousness and manipulativeness were part of her attraction. It made him all the more passionately attached to her. His reason registered a formal protest, but then gave in with a shrug and began to cooperate. What did he have left? He had lost two women who could have loved him, who could have made him happy, and all because of his obsessive pursuit of that feeling, that physical thrill of being overcome by passion, lust, whatever you wanted to call it. The thing that made the bottom drop out of his stomach. Now there was nothing left for him but to give in, to admit that he had to have her no matter how dangerous she was to his peace of mind, to his tranquility, to his soul.

"Fidessa," he said. The hoarseness of his own voice surprised him.

"Mm-hmm," she responded. Her silky arms, glowing with light perspiration, moved like a dancer's, the right one making unknowable marks on the canvas, the left one bringing the paints to meet the brush every few strokes, keeping time with some inaudible bass line. Her hair swayed with the rhythm.

"Fidessa," he began again, "I—"

"Don't move." She was concentrating on what seemed to be a series of exceptionally tiny strokes. "Talk, but don't move."

"Fidessa, you must have figured out how I feel about you."

"Mm-hmm." She was still concentrating.

"I sometimes think I'm mad. I sometimes think you are. I sometimes think you know exactly what you're doing. But I can't keep the truth from myself any longer, and so I can't keep it from you. I have to tell you that—I have to tell you that I love you. That I'm in love with you."

"Well, I should hope so." She was painting a few slow, broad strokes now.

"You'd hope so?"

"After all the work I've put into you, I should think you'd be in love with me."

Adam had not imagined, among the dozens of

responses he had imagined, any response like this. He had hoped for joyous delight. He had expected something more like contempt. He had not expected her to keep blithely painting as if they were talking about the weather.

Yet she was still brushing away as she spoke again. "I'm in love with you, too."

A bomb went off in Adam's heart, sending a shock wave of warmth bursting out toward his extremities. She loved him! It didn't matter what he had been through. It didn't matter what strange things were going on with her, what inexplicable folly or wickedness she was involved in. The important thing, the only thing, was that she loved him. He wanted to leap up and take her in his arms, but she said,

"Don't move." He did his best to freeze in place.

She was still painting as she spoke in a neutral and almost cheerfully matter-of-fact voice. "I do love you, but we can't be together just for that reason. I think you know that."

"What?" He felt himself plummeting helplessly. "I don't know that. Why would I know that? I love you. You love me. It's— This is America! Why can't you be with me?"

She was painting furiously now. "I can never be with you, and I can't tell you why. Except to say that pleasure is one thing, but love adds a dangerous variable. Don't you think? I can't tell you any more than that."

"Of course you can tell me. You have to tell me. I mean, if you'd told me you couldn't love me—if you'd told me you didn't care—then I could live with hearing you say you can't tell me any more than that. But you love me. You said you love me. I love you. I have a right to know. I need to know. If something is keeping us apart—if you're in some kind of trouble—you know I'll do anything. I'll move heaven and earth, but—but please! You've got to tell me!"

"Beautiful," she said quietly.

"Tell me!" He was begging, and he didn't like the whine in his own voice. "Tell me, please!"

"You can't know." Still painting furiously. "You never will know."

He could feel tears of impotent rage welling up in his eyes. "Who's doing this to you? Who's keeping you from me? What are you? What's making you do these things to me? Why can't you get out of it?"

"It's something you'll never understand," she insisted blandly. And she was still painting.

Adam was speechless. Someone must have her in his thrall. It would explain everything. It would explain nothing, of course, but it would give a kind of moral shape to his adventures. She must be under the thumb of some horrible Svengali who had been orchestrating all the otherwise inexplicable plots against him. Whoever this manipulator was, Adam would do anything to break his hold. If it was necessary to kill the man, then Adam would be a murderer. It didn't matter. Fidessa loved him. She was worth killing for.

"So perfect," she muttered.

"I can't just sit here anymore," Adam said. "I have to know. If you won't tell me, then I'll find out. I'll kill anyone who tries to stop me from rescuing you. I'll have you no matter what it takes."

"It's finished!" she announced, stepping back with sudden triumph. "One more stroke would destroy it."

Adam stood up. "Now will you tell me?"

"Come see it," she said with the first sign of real emotion she had shown yet this session. "I've made a work of art out of you at last."

He reached her in four quick steps, his arms grasping her, his lips pressed to hers. She didn't resist, but she broke away quickly. "Never mind me," she insisted. "Look at you."

Adam didn't need to see a picture of himself right now, but he glanced at the portrait—and stopped breathing for a moment.

Did he really look like that?

It was the same face she had painted before. The same, but how different! The broad forehead was lightly lined with furrows that converged in the center. The eyebrows, rigidly straight, plunged the upper halves of his grey eyes into shadow—grey eyes that looked tortured, with sagging lower lids and a glow of desperate redness; they glistened with incipient tears of—what? Rage? Despair? The lips were thin and tight, the cheeks hollowed with the unconscious muscular strain of keeping the jaw tightly shut. The chin was foreshortened and thrust forward, the neck showing muscles held taut at the limit of their power. It was a face haunted by vicious desires and terrible passions, and almost trembling with rage even on the canvas. And Adam could see the envy he had felt for all those more fortunate men, the greed that had led him back to Fidessa when he had broken from her at last, the lust that had undone him, the gluttony that Fidessa had so eagerly fed, the idleness that had kept him from meeting his difficulties head-on, and over all the pride that had opened the door for all those other horrors.

Where was the open, cheerful, even bland young man he used to see in the mirror? Oh, if this was what she saw, no wonder Rose went back to Bradley! No wonder Hope had abandoned him!

"Is that really me?" he asked in a whisper.

"I made that," Fidessa said proudly. "I made *you*."

He looked at her. She was smiling, which horrified him even more than the portrait did.

"Oh," she said, "I ought to have had a canvas ready to capture your reaction to the picture! It would be another great work, almost equal to the first!"

And then she laughed.

He had never heard her laugh before. It was a beautiful, musical laugh, like a song, and it crushed the life out of him.

He didn't say a word. He turned and headed for the steps, and as he half ran downstairs her laughter grew louder and louder, as if the woman had stayed upstairs but the laughter was following him. He burst out the door into the cool darkness of Brackenridge Avenue and knew that he could never, must never, see Fidessa again.

And on the whole he was faithful to that vow.

CHAPTER 35. CHECKMATE.

BUT about three years later, on an exceptionally pleasant August day, he did see her again. It was a Saturday afternoon when, for some reason or other, Adam had promised to meet someone at a coffeehouse on Walnut Street. And because he had nothing better to do, he was half an hour early. And there she was at a table along the wall, just standing up and getting ready to go.

He recognized her at once. In fact, he felt the old familiar bottom-dropping-out-of-the-stomach feeling almost before his mind had processed the image. She was very much the same, except that her hair was shorter now, only down to her shoulders. That was the first detail he noticed. She still looked prosperous and happy: she was packing up an expensive laptop, and her black slacks and burgundy blouse looked tasteful and professional and, of course, absolutely perfect on her.

Some cowardly part of him was ready to turn

around and avoid the inevitable, but it was—inevitable. She had seen him, and her face instantly lit up with a bright and sociable smile. "Adam!" she said with the proper amount of delight—the kind of delight one reserves for old acquaintances whose lives have always been peripheral to one's own.

Now that she had packed up and was approaching him, he would have to deal with whatever this encounter meant. If he had told himself he had got over her, he had been lying. Even now, when other attachments had come and gone, when the raw wounds in his battered soul had healed to scars that perhaps gave him a bit of attractive character and distinction, there was something in his mind saying, "It's not too late." But of course it must be too late.

"It's so good to see you!" she said cheerfully, now standing right in front of him. "How've you been? What are you doing these days?"

"Oh, this and that," his mouth said—he had apparently left it on automatic pilot. "How about you?"

"I'm doing well," she replied. "And I have to run, or I'll be late for an appointment with a client. But it's been such a pleasure seeing you." She embraced him with her free hand—the one that wasn't carrying a laptop case—and kissed him lightly on the cheek, that slightly moist brush of the lips he remembered so well. And then she held the embrace for a moment longer and whispered very distinctly into his ear,

"You could have saved me."

She stepped back and fixed her eyes on his with a subtle smile, that old I-know-something smile that was burned into his spirit from his brief time with her. Just for a lingering moment—then she turned and stepped out the door. On the sidewalk outside, she turned once more and gave him a smile and a wave. Then she was gone.

He didn't run after her. He thought about it for a very long time—perhaps as long as fifteen seconds. Then he went to the counter and made a great fuss over ordering exactly the right cup of coffee. There were two college students behind the counter; he discussed the question with both of them, and eventually settled on the Kenyan, because it was "bright," and he craved brightness at the moment. After that, he found a table by the open window—it was one of those garage-door affairs that could be lifted to open the whole front of the establishment in fine weather—and sat down.

She might come back, he thought, but of course she didn't, and he had plenty of time to stare out at the uninterrupted stream of pedestrians—men and women and children and an occasional dog, and all those faces told stories, and how many of those stories were true? For an hour—the man he was supposed to meet never did show up, and he didn't call, and it wasn't worth texting him to find out where he was—Adam sat and stared, and sipped a bit of coffee now and then, and thought about her last whispered words and what they might mean. And after a while he began to think of them as the last move in the game, a game that had not really ended until now, when she had at last, finally and definitively, won.

THE END